# The Union I

## Part 1: The Twilight Exiled

*Lucius Montegrot*

# Table of Contents

Legal notice.................................................................................... VII
Dedication...................................................................................... IX
FOREWORD................................................................................... XI
Chapter 1 – Happy Fucking Birthday................................................ 1
✦ Interlude – The Unseen Hand ✦ ................................................. 23
Chapter 2 – Reluctant steps............................................................. 27
Chapter 3 – Does an elf drink more than a camel?........................... 47
✦ Interlude – The Hollow Monastery ✦ ........................................ 65
Chapter 4 – The town at the edge of the desert............................... 71
Chapter 5 – Kharesh........................................................................ 89
✦ Interlude – Storm and Beauty ✦ ................................................ 115
Chapter 6 – The Shieldmaiden....................................................... 119
✦ Interlude – The Tower of Philosophy ✦ ..................................... 149
Chapter 7 – Khadija's tale............................................................... 163
Chapter 8 – Yousef's Anointing...................................................... 179
Chapter 9 – The Varthian Wall....................................................... 197
✦ Interlude – The Courtesan ✦ ..................................................... 217
Chapter 10 – The Sharif................................................................. 223
Chapter 11 – Sex and Magic........................................................... 239
✦ Interlude –The Voyeur ✦ ........................................................... 259
Chapter 12 – Before the darkness................................................... 265
✦ Interlude – The merciless Emperor ✦ ........................................ 281
Chapter 13 – Into the Sunless Depths............................................ 297
A note from the Author.................................................................. 311
Coming Soon: The Chained Light.................................................. 313

# Legal notice

Copyright © [2025] by [Lucius Montegrot]

All rights reserved.

No part of this publication may be reproduced, distributed, or transmitted in any form or by any means, including photocopying, recording, or other electronic or mechanical methods, without the prior written permission of the publisher, except as permitted by National and International Copyright Law.

For permission requests, contact
luciusmontegrot@gmail.com

The story, all names, characters, and incidents portrayed in this production are fictitious and a fruit of the author's imagination. No identification with actual persons (living or deceased), places, buildings, and products is intended or should be inferred. Any such happenstance is entirely coincidental.

Book Cover by Lucius Montegrot (With AI assistance)

## Dedication

◆

To Marco and Luisa, who have always created stories with me in our adventures and beyond.

◆

To David Dalglish, whose stories kept me entranced, kept me going during the COVID pandemic, and ultimately inspired me to tell my own.

◆

To all those I have played and DM'd with, for the countless hours of stories and adventures we created.

◆

To you, dear reader, in hopes that you will enjoy my story.

◆

x

# FOREWORD

I have written this book with some assistance from artificial intelligence. It is an Alpha version, the first part of the first book, the beginning of a story born of decades of playing and being a dungeon master in role playing games. The entire universe, characters, storyline, and world-building are a blend of my own imagination and the inspiration drawn from the countless days and nights of adventures I have had the pleasure of participating in and narrating. The final prose, its style and cadence, the choice of words are mine, too.

The use of Artificial Intelligence in creative efforts is in its infancy, and is not free from controversy. At the moment, I see it as a tool, yet another evolution of technology that comes to the aid of writers, just as Libreoffice (which I am using to write this foreword) and similar software have taken the place of typewriters, just as those once replaced the pen, the quill, the clay tablet, all the way back to etchings and drawings on stone that our distant ancestors used to tell their stories.

I simply have a story to tell – one I wished to tell for quite some time – and I wished to see how AI could assist me in telling my story. It is very much an experiment of what a human with a love for all things Fantasy and their imagination can do in collaboration with artificial intelligence.

As for the future, I have no doubt that as AI becomes better and better, it will help accomplish (and sometimes even replace) many tasks that humans used to do, as has every technological advance. This will not be the last fantasy book written with the help of artificial intelligence.

To my knowledge, however, it is the first to do so openly and unashamedly.

But ultimately, can AI replace human creativity? I think not. And not just because, in its current state, merely unleashing AI to write something from start to end tends to produce repetitive drivel that lacks the soul of a meaningful story, but rather because human creativity will remain: for one thing has always existed in the human mind and culture, and that is the desire to tell stories. That desire is ancient, personal, and deeply ingrained in our souls.

Before you dismiss this as "just another AI-written piece of trash," give it a read. You've either already paid for it or got it for free somehow, so you might as well. I hope it earns your time.

If this book endures, let it stand as a marker: the moment human imagination and machine learning first truly joined forces in the realm of epic fantasy.

*A note on fonts:* This book uses custom fonts for certain interludes and characters. As you're most likely holding a paper copy of the book, these should have already been printed as intended. But if for whatever reason you're reading a pdf of the paper version, and your e-reader does not support these, it may default to a simpler font. For the full experience, I recommend reading on a device or app that supports embedded fonts.

◆

Lucius Montegrot is a pseudonym.

# Chapter 1 – Happy Fucking Birthday

The night was oppressive, darker, and felt colder than any Aluriel could remember, with clouds shrouding the moons and the forest cloaked in an eerie glow. The towering firs, usually silent witnesses to her failures, now seemed to lean inward almost as if judging her. As the chill bit through her clothing, making her shiver as it began to seep into her bones, the damp air clung to her like a shroud. Every sound startled her: the distant snap of a twig, the rustle of unseen creatures, the clumps of snow falling from tree branches. Each sudden sound jolted her with fear and felt like a constant reminder of how vulnerable she now was.

There were no celebrations for her birthday, like there had been for every other elf stepping across the threshold of adulthood. No drinking elven wine until she fell over, no dancing around fires until dawn, no songs or poetry to fill her ears with joy.

Her previous birthdays had all been celebrations anyway. *Even though it was not me they were celebrating.* Midwinter, they called it. A time of singing and fire, of poetry and promise. A day the elves marked with joy, with wine, with lanterns raised to honour the stars, with bonfires set ablaze to defy the longest night.

This year, no lanterns. No bonfires burned for her. She had been marched out of her mother's home, far enough that she could no longer even hear their songs or revelry.

Instead, on the day she'd turned 40, officially an adult by elven custom, Aluriel sat huddled in the hollow of a fallen tree, her arms wrapped tightly around her knees. *Why couldn't they see me for who I am?* she thought bitterly. *Was it really easier to cast me out than to try and help me?* The questions swirled endlessly in her mind like a whirlwind, one no less a heartache than the next. She squeezed her eyes shut, trying to block out the darkness, trying to ignore the ache of heartbreak and guilt that filled her chest. The bark felt rough against her skin, and the smell of damp earth and rotting wood filled her nostrils with the scent of decay. Her breaths came shallow. They vanished into the cold air like fleeting apparitions. The elders' decree still echoed in her mind, the words cold and firm, closing a door she would never cross again.

Exile.

The word lingered in her thoughts, quiet and inescapable, like the silence after a scream. Final, as the engravings on a tombstone. *Did they even care what this would do to me?* she wondered. *Or was I just another burden to cast aside?* The thought stung, as it had many times before in the days preceding her exile. Deep down, however, she feared she already knew the answer. The council had looked at her with a mixture of fear and disdain, their faces hardened, eager to pass judgment. Some had waited for years to find an excuse to punish her. To them, she was not Aluriel, not the child of their revered Grand Druidess. She was something else entirely, something they could not understand, and so they jumped at the opportunity to rid themselves – and their perfect elven society – of her. She squeezed her eyes shut, trying to block out the memory of their stares, but it was no use. The image was replaced by that of Elenwen's scarred face, the burns forever marring her once flawless skin. The scars that no Druidic magic could fully heal. The scars Aluriel etched on that beautiful face she had leaned in to kiss.

The forest, her home for as long as she could remember, had never welcomed her. But now, it seemed to resent her presence, and it made sure she *felt* it. The familiar songs of the night birds were no longer a comfort to her. An eerie, swirling sense of anxiety seemed to stifle all her other thoughts. She was left alone with her anger, shame, and pain, as her mind replayed the words of the council over and over: the verdict that stabbed through her heart like a cold steel dagger.

"Your magic is out of control. It is a foreign magic, and it is a danger to us all," one elder had said, his voice heavy with authority. "You unleashed it by accident, and this we can believe: you had never managed to cast magic before. Because of this, your punishment will be lessened, and shall be exile in place of death. You will live, but you cannot stay." Aeliana's husband, the Grand Druid Aelavaron, had at least managed to convince the other elders to spare Aluriel's life. "With the power granted to us, we hereby sentence you to exile. You are never to return to the enchanted forest for as long as you live, unless by act of this council you are granted pardon."

Aeliana had pleaded for leniency, begged them to reconsider. But even her mother's status as Grand Druidess had not been enough to sway the council any further. "She's just a child!" Aeliana had cried, as tears welled into her eyes and glistened on her cheeks. The elders remained unmoved, and their decision was final. "She is a child, but next week she will turn 40, and that day marks her adulthood." A pause. "She may remain confined in your home until the midnight before her birthday, but then, she must leave."

Their verdict was final.

Exile.

Aluriel's gaze drifted to the faint glow of the horizon, where the first hints of dawn began to rise through the trees. The light seemed distant. More distant than it ever felt even when she had tried – and always failed – to channel it. It reminded her of the life that had been taken away from her just days before. She rested her forehead against her knees, letting her straight silvery hair fall and cover her face like a curtain.

In the stillness of last night, the whispers had grown louder still. They had begun in dreams, decades earlier. Soft, at first, yet insistent murmurs she couldn't understand. Then, they began creeping from the threshold of her sleep, bleeding into her waking hours, flickering at the edges of her thoughts, baiting her mind with the elusive and tantalising illusion of meaning that was always just beyond her grasp. She had been taught to fear them deeply: to hear such whispers was, in elven teachings, to flirt with madness itself. Their nature did feel maddening, like tendrils of chaos weaving through her thoughts. She clutched her knees tighter, feeling the weight on her chest as she ruminated on the thought. *Am I losing my mind?* "Am I mad?" she whispered back, trembling from a mixture of the cold and her own anxiety. The whispers gave no answer. Not that she expected one. Instead, they simply carried on as relentlessly as before, the same tormenting mystery she had grown accustomed to. She clenched her fists until her nails bit into her palms, as if pain could drown the whispers out.

*Madness.*

That was the word the elders had used to describe mages who heard such whispers. It was said that only mages could hear the Lady of Twilight. It was said that the Lady of Twilight was not a Goddess, that she did not exist, and that hearing her was merely a sign of insanity. Aluriel felt doubly cheated by this. Not only did she have to endure this maddening in secret, but to add insult to injury, she was not a mage. Or at least, she thought she was not. Not before the chain lightning. And yet, despite her fear, a small part of her wished to understand, to uncover the truth behind the voice that called to her in the dark and had done so for decades. Was it related to her latent affinity for lightning? *Is affinity even the right word here?* Where exactly would it lead her, if she surrendered to the whispers? *Who or what is really behind these whispers and now, these visions, anyway?*

The first rays of sunlight filtered through the vegetation, and Aluriel wearily forced herself to her feet. Her legs felt weak, her body heavy with exhaustion, but she knew she couldn't stay there. Her kin would not protect her anymore, and neither would the forest. She adjusted the straps of her backpack, staggering under its burden. *A journey to... where exactly? Where am I even going? I've never even stepped out of the forest!*

With a deep breath, she stepped out from the hollow trunk, her heart pounding as she took her first steps into exile. The clearing where she once trained with Thalion, the home where Aeliana's warmth had once wrapped around her like a shield from the judgment of others... all of it was lost now. She was banished, not just for failing to meet their expectations, but because she had become a danger they could no longer ignore. The memory of that night seared the back of her mind, just like the lightning she'd unleashed. Elenwen's cruel laugh, the others mocking her, the spark of rage that had consumed her, and the searing arc of lightning that had followed. A part of her still loved Elenwen, despite everything. Or was it love?

She wasn't sure anymore. She only knew that the memory of what she'd done to her tore at her heartstrings. Yet, even through her anger and shame, the thought of Elenwen – her lips, her voice, her very presence – lingered in her mind. What wouldn't she give to kiss her, just once more? That longing, as maddening as it was undeniable, twisted her emotions further, making the guilt that much more unbearable.

She hadn't meant to hurt anyone. Or rather, her rational mind hadn't. Not in a million years would she have caused Elenwen, of all people, any harm. *But wasn't there a part of me that wanted to?* she thought. *Wasn't there some dark, angry part of me that wanted them to feel my pain, to feel what I've been through?* The rage inside her had wanted to see them all burn to a crisp. The chain lightning had been wild, uncontrolled, and channelled emotions her will could not contain. She felt anger and guilt in equal measure, and was powerless to untangle them. But the damage was done. Elenwen had been left with burn marks and scars across her chest and face. Not even the most powerful elven healing spells could undo them, to everyone's surprise.

The council had ruled then that Aluriel's magic, and by extension, she herself, bore the markings of a curse. A curse – many had whispered – placed upon her on the night when she was born. Aluriel had overheard much about that night, about how the moons aligned in a strange and unique way. Whenever she asked about it directly, the Elders grew silent. At most, they'd offer vague words, about that night being different, "A night unlike any other," like Aluriel herself.

Only her mother told her more: the night of her birth had not only been the Winter Solstice. All four moons had also risen together, high in the sky, each exactly half-lit. Two waxing. Two waning. A pattern so precise, it was unique rather than rare. The astrologers called it "a harmony of the impossible". A moment not unseen in calculations, but never expected in their lifetimes. Like Aluriel herself, they said, that night was different. Unique.

And yet, she couldn't entirely disagree. She had always known she was... different. Every time she looked at her hands, or looked at herself in a mirror, her physical features reminded her she was not truly one of them. Not fully. Yet, despite her own guilt, part of her seethed at their judgment. After all, they didn't treat the other half-elven children – those born of a union with humans – with such disdain. They could have at least tried. Tried to listen, to begin with. Maybe they could have figured out what her own magic was and guided her on her own path. Instead, they forced her into studying forms of magic she could not grasp. Druidic magic, Nature magic, then Sun magic...

They tried. They failed. She failed to learn even the basics, and not for lack of effort.

Eventually, they gave up, assuming she had no affinity for magic at all, only to blame her later when her own magic, magic she didn't even know she possessed, proved uncontrollable and destructive.

Her failure wasn't hers alone. It was theirs as well.

And the resentment she felt for them burned almost as bright as the rage she aimed towards herself.

Footsteps crunching on the forest floor pulled Aluriel from her thoughts abruptly. Her head snapped up. Instinctively, she reached for her bow and nocked an arrow, prepared to fire at a moment's notice. The vegetation parted, and a figure – one much, much shorter than Aluriel – stepped into the faint light of dawn. *Is this... A dwarf? A gnome?*

He barely reached her waist.

"Aluriel," the man said, his voice loud but steady. His squat frame was weighed down by metallic plate armour and a round shield, both covered in red runes that gleamed even in the dim light. A war hammer, also etched with runes she did not recognise, was strapped to his golden metal belt. On the other side, a hand-axe – runed, too, but relatively plain in comparison – balanced the weight. His bushy ginger beard was damp and frosty from the icy, humid air that surrounded them. He glanced around warily before moving closer. "Dinna shoot! Yer mither sent me."

Aluriel blinked in disbelief. "Sent you? Why? Who are you? *What are you?*" she eased the tension on her bowstring somewhat, though her arrow remained aimed at him.

"Me name is Ian." Aluriel continued to stare at him, poised to fire at the first hint of hostility. Ian approached her slowly, hands raised to let her see he was unarmed, and sat down a couple of metres away from her, placing his shield by his side. If she did fire, and if his armour didn't block it, Aeliana could take care of his wounds.

But he hoped she'd sense the truth: that he really meant no harm.

As he looked her up and down, he couldn't help but notice the striking contrasts that marked her unique appearance.

Her sheer height was the first thing Ian noticed. She was *gigantic*, even for a high elf. Her light turquoise skin, smooth and luminous even in the dim light of dawn, instantly gave away her father's heritage, though it lacked the full depth of his people's dark blue hues. Her violet eyes glowed intensely whenever light struck them. It was a trait typical of her father's kin, and yet unseen in other races, which felt almost alien to the dwarf who rarely saw their kind. *Hers looked tae glow, nae jist shimmer. But hells if I ken if that's normal fer sea elves*, he thought as he strained to remember the last one he'd seen. The straight, silvery white hair cascading over her shoulders stood in stark contrast to the golden locks, common as wheat in summer among High Elves. On her forehead rested a simple silver diadem, its pendant vaguely shaped like a blooming flower, yet wrought from angular lines rather than petals.

Ian's gaze flicked to her hands, where partially webbed fingers held her bow and arrow. Not just a sign, but rather a dead giveaway of her mixed lineage. A head taller than most High Elves, yet just as slender if not more so, she stood before him with a demeanour that blended fragility with the quiet, defiant power seen in the eyes of someone who has nothing left to lose. *At least she's nae shot me yet. That's a guid start,* he thought. Yet, most of all, what had surprised Ian forty years ago – Ian, and everyone else who heard about it – was that a child born of a union between two such as her parents was thought to be impossible. Aluriel knew this all too well, for she'd lost count of the times she'd heard the word "freak" whispered, when others thought she was out of earshot.

"Ian Redhammer," he said, with a voice as soothing as he could conjure. "Priest o' the Tireless Forger, aye. Aeliana thinks ye've a better chance oot there wi' me than left here tae fend for yersel'. Sent me a fire message, she did. Barely a handful o' words: '*Come Forest, urgent, Aeliana.*' I dinnae ken what tae expect, but here I am, lass, and here ye are. The forest's nae kind tae those it casts oot."

A flash of anger crossed Aluriel's face. "She thinks sending me away with a stranger will solve everything?" Her voice rose as her shout mirrored her frustration. *No, not a gnome. I saw visiting gnomes once before. Much shorter than him. Must be a dwarf.*

Ian sighed, reaching into his satchel to pull out a flask. He took a long swig before offering it to her. "It's nae aboot solv–" He paused, his nose wrinkling, and suddenly vomited what he just drank and then some more onto a snow-covered patch of moss. Wiping his face with a rag, he grumbled, "Och, that teleporter still has ma guts churnin'. Bluidy contraptions. Ne'er again. An' mind ye, it was the one yer mither gave me after the battle at Steelforge's gates. She kent I'd need it one day, though I doubt she kent it would be fer this shite." He paused, then added quickly, lest she take it the wrong way: "Shite, I mean, yer bluidy exile. Bleedin' fools, them High Council, aye."

Despite herself, a faint smile tugged at Aluriel's lips, and before she could stop it, a brief chuckle escaped. She took the flask and drank a long swig. It burned her throat and stomach, but it helped. It made her relax slightly, and she felt some of her tension ease. "This is good." She paused to catch her breath and let the fire in her throat dim somewhat. "So, what happens now?"

"This here be Dwarven mead," he said, taking the flask back from Aluriel's hands and placing it into his pack.

"As fer fit we do?" Ian tilted his head upwards to look straight into her eyes.

"We leave. Heid tae Vashlin. Ye might nae ken it yet, but it's a place that's seen its share o' misfits, lass. Folk who dinnae belong anywhere else. Ye'd fit right in."

He hesitated just a moment before finishing: "I ken folk there that can help ye. Teach ye things yer lot here couldnae. An' there's a train atween Vashlin an' Steelforge."

"And if I refuse?"

Ian's eyes hardened slightly, though his tone stayed calm. "Then ye'll be left tae fend fer yersel' in a world that'll chew ye up an' spit ye oot. Ye've got potential, lass. I dinna ken fit kind yet, but I've seen plenty o' misfits turn oot tae be somethin' extraordinary."

Aluriel glanced away and felt her jaw tighten. The weight of his words pressed against her, but so did the sting of her exile. She thought of Elenwen's scorched face. The council's cold decree. The whispers that had trailed her every step since she remembered her first dream. The thought of leaving everything she had ever known filled her with dread, yet staying in defiance seemed an even worse prospect. The uncertainty of what lay ahead felt daunting, but maybe, just maybe, the path into the unknown held more promise than what she'd leave behind. *My life as an outcast... maybe I could leave that behind too.*

"I don't have a choice, do I?"

Ian chuckled dryly. "There's always a choice, lass. Ye can wallow here, waitin' fer the forest an' the snow tae finish what the council started, or ye can get up an' fight fer somethin'."

Silence stretched between them, broken only by the faint whistle of the wind passing through branches and fir needles.

Finally, Aluriel put the arrow back in its quiver, then strapped the bow on her back.

"Fine." She sighed. "But don't expect me to be grateful."

Ian rose, his grin widening. "Wouldnae dream o' it, lass."

They began to walk in silence.

Aeliana was standing on the trail north-east, the great tree that housed her family's dwelling far behind her, waiting to give her daughter one last farewell. She had to endure leading the Midwinter ritual. She had to endure the celebrations. Throughout all that, her mind had been fixed on her daughter alone in the woods. She had spoken the sacred verses, lit the bonfire, led the songs... but none of it had been for her own child. Only when the rites were complete could she slip away to her home and make the final preparations. She forced herself to smile, though her eyes glistened with the effort of holding tears back. Her love for Aluriel had never wavered. Not once, not through the whispers, the judgments, the concerned friends and elders who came again and again to speak to her. It did not waver when her daughter was sentenced to exile. To her, Aluriel was perfect and unique, despite her kin's refusal to see it. Her fingers gracefully held the bracelet she had spent the last week crafting, its delicate elvish runes glowing faintly with protective enchantments. Words engraved in Elvish read, "May you always be protected".

When Ian emerged from the shadows, Aeliana's breath caught. Aluriel trailed behind him. Her daughter's face was pale, and her expression gloomy. Ian approached first, raising his head towards her. "She's comin'. Takes balls, that does. Aye."

Aeliana stepped forward, her gaze locking with Aluriel's. "I..." Her voice faltered. She had so much to say, but the words tangled in her throat and would not come. Instead, she held out the bracelet, her voice soft but steady, barely suppressing her urge to break down in tears. "I love you. No matter where the journey takes you, no matter what path you tread, you will always be my daughter, and I will help in whatever way I can, even from afar." Tears began to well in her eyes. "For your journey," she added, putting it on Aluriel's wrist.

Aluriel hesitated, then adjusted it on her wrist in quiet acceptance. Her fingers brushed against her mother's briefly. "Right. Thank you," she said quietly, though her tone carried no warmth. She turned away quickly, not wanting to linger on the pain in Aeliana's eyes.

Wearing the bracelet made Aluriel's guilt resonate and grow. *What if they take away your seat as Grand Druidess too, Mother?* From her week of confinement in her home, she had sometimes overheard other elves' conversations, and some had hinted at this. *Will you be punished too, just for loving me?*

Ian cleared his throat. "Right, then. Time we were aff."

Aeliana watched as they disappeared into the shadows of the forest. She had always known, deep inside, that one day Aluriel's path would take her far from the forest, but knowing that did nothing to dull the searing pain of this moment. The moment when she had to watch her leave. Not out of her volition, but exiled.

Long after they vanished into the trees, Aeliana spoke aloud, part to herself, and part to the sky: "Your brothers sent word from Varthia. Perhaps your paths will cross again."

Then, in a whisper, "May the Sun guide you, my child."

Only once she was sure they were out of earshot did she finally allow herself to cry.

In the days between the judgment and the exile, she kept herself busy packing supplies for Aluriel and Ian: clothes, food, waterskins, bottles of elven wine, and as many other essentials she thought the two might need.

But more importantly, she had included her own mithril short sword. Light, razor-sharp, and perfectly balanced. She had paired it with an exquisite Elven composite longbow and a quiver full of finely crafted arrows, made by the forest city's finest fletcher. They were made of mithril: Thick enough to pack a punch, yet light enough to fly a great distance. Aluriel's skills with a sword were rudimentary at best, and her archery was just about decent: comparable to a skilled human archer, though far from the level of an Elven sniper. Still, these gifts gave Aeliana a glimmer of hope that she wouldn't be entirely helpless in the journey ahead. As soon as Ian had arrived and she explained the situation, she had handed him a sturdy backpack, almost bursting with provisions. Ian had taken it with a bemused expression, muttering under his breath about having prepared for "a fight, nae a bluidy trek," but he did not refuse it.

As they walked deeper into the forest, Ian kept his steps steady, his warhammer rattling faintly against his armour. Aluriel followed, her gaze fixed ahead whilst her mind spun with a kaleidoscope of emotions. All of them swirled too fast. Far too many. Far too fast to pick one out and focus on it. After what felt like hours, Ian broke the silence. "I dinnae suppose ye ken the way tae Vashlin yersel', do ye?" he asked, half-joking, though his tone held a trace of seriousness.

"I thought you had a plan," Aluriel tilted her chin down to look at him.

"Oh, Ah had a plan," Ian muttered, scratching his beard. "Teleporter wand. One-use, like all o' them. Rare as blue diamonds an' fixed tae one spot. Got me here, right enough. But unless yer druids've somehow learnt tae craft the things an' ye've got two more stuffed in that tunic o' yers, we're hoofin' it."

Aluriel blinked. "You... don't have a way back?"

"Ach, aye, o' course I do. Just nae a quick way. We've three choices, lass." Ian held up three stubby fingers. "Varthia, The Sunless Depths, or the Dragons' Peaks." He paused.

"But before we dive intae the details, lemme explain somethin' aboot Varthia, seein' as it's one o' the routes. Their roads? Mighty fine, marked wi' milestones every ten kilometres, an' maintained like a dwarf's best blade. But those milestones? They come wi' gallows. Aye, gallows, right there by the road. So, route one, we go ower the mountains, the Dragons' peaks, which is certain death from exposure an' dragons, obviously. Unless ye've grown wings and the fur of a yeti an' I missed it."

He grunted, breathing in, and kept walking, "Two, we trek through yer enchanted forest, skirt the edge o' the desert, and cross Varthia. Then we climb No Man's Pass tae reach Vashlin. From there we can catch the train tae Steelforge too, if we want. Long, treacherous, and full o' folk lookin' tae stab us in the dark... An' that's if the Varthian paladins o' the Peacemaker dinnae decide tae hang us first fer nae guid reason. An' their idea o' *justice*? Nae exactly fair."

"And the third?" Aluriel's eyes narrowed. The image of gallows dotting the Varthian roads unsettled her, making that path seem as grim as the other sounded.

Ian sighed heavily, visibly unsettled. "The Sunless Depths. Quicker, aye. But nae *pleasant*, nae by a long shot. Monsters, madness, poison 'shrooms, an' things that cannae thole each other, far less the likes o' outsiders like blue skinned elves an' dwarves who reek o' mead."

*More madness?* Aluriel frowned, the burden of each choice settling uneasily in her mind. None of them sounded appealing, *and yet... What else is there for me? Every path feels like it's designed to test me, to break me.* But perhaps that was the point. Perhaps this was the universe's way of asking her how much she was willing to endure.

The world was not going to make her path easier. It never had.

"We'll decide as we go," Ian said after a moment, his tone softening slightly.

"But either way, ye'd best steel yerself, lass. This... this is where the real journey begins."

Aluriel didn't answer. Instead, she walked in silence, her mind ruminating on the options and the uncertainty of what lay ahead.

Aluriel and Ian walked in silence through the forest. The thick foliage above shrouded most of the sunlight, yet what little did come through would reflect off the blanket of snow on the ground, enough to interfere with her darkvision. She didn't know whether Dwarves had darkvision, too. She thought of simply asking Ian, but she was in no mood to talk. So they walked, hour after hour, and said nothing. The fresh snow crunched softly under their footfalls, and the rustling of fir branches filled the quiet with an almost comforting rhythm. Aluriel led the way with an instinctual ease. No banishment, no exile would take away her knowledge of the forest paths. She avoided poisonous plants and dangerous thickets without hesitation, though her heart ached with every familiar landmark they passed. Each one struck a chord of grief, a silent farewell to a home already lost.

"I've nae seen a forest like this afore." Ian eventually the silence. "Back in Steelforge, a tree's just somethin' that comes already chopped, tae make firewood, a beam, or a barrel."

Aluriel gave a small snort but didn't look back. "It's more than that here." Her tone was laced with a faint edge of jealousy and contempt. "Each tree, every glade, is part of something greater. The druids can commune with the forest. They speak to it, feel its will." She hesitated. Bitterness crept into her voice. "I was never able to do that." The next thought she did not speak, yet it echoed in her mind: *Maybe the forest hates me. Maybe our goddess, the Lady Most Beautiful, resents my existence.*

Ian grunted. "Aye, sacred's one way tae put it. Still feels like it's watchin' me. Like it knows I dinnae belong."

"It does," Aluriel said, the faintest trace of amusement in her tone. "But don't worry. It's not you it hates."

Ian chuckled, the sound rough but warm. "Comfortin'. Aye. Real comfortin', lass."

Their banter broke the weight of the silence, and for a moment, Aluriel allowed herself to relax. Every step forward was a step away from the only home she had ever known, and whilst the forest still felt familiar, it no longer felt like it was hers. She glanced at Ian, his stocky frame trudging along with a resilience she could not help but envy.

"Why did you come?" she asked suddenly.

Ian raised an eyebrow. "Yer mither sent me. Thought we covered that."

"No." Her tone was stern. She shook her head, defiance rising in her voice. "Why did you agree to come? You could have ignored her message. Made up an excuse." Her voice grew louder. "You could have given me a wide berth, as everyone else has done since just about the day I was fucking born."

Her voice grew even louder, booming into a scream. "Why DID you come?"

He paused for a moment, scratching his beard thoughtfully. "Aeliana saved me life once, lass. Back when we fought tae keep

Steelforge from fallin', she did, aye. If she asks, I listen. Simple as that. She asked me to take ye tae Vashlin or Steelforge, an' I will. Even if it costs me life." He chuckled. "Besides," he added with a wry grin, "a forest elf lass wi' lightnin' magic? I *had* tae see it fer mesel'."

Aluriel looked away, visibly deflated. "It's not magic," she muttered. "It's a curse. I... I can't even control it."

Ian stopped in his tracks, forcing her to turn and face him. "Now ye listen tae me," he said, his voice low but firm. "Curse or gift, it's fit ye've got, aye? An' if yer feelin' sorry fer yersel', it's nae goin' tae do either of us any favours. Ye'll learn tae control it. An' when ye do? There'll be nae one who can stop ye."

The conviction in his tone startled her, and for a moment, she didn't know how to respond. She simply gave a small nod and walked on.

As the first signs of twilight made the shadows even longer, Ian pointed ahead. "We'll rest soon. Best find a place tae hunker down afore we're too far oot in the open."

Aluriel gave Ian an amused look. "We're this far south, in the middle of the forest at Midwinter. The sun rises late and dusk comes early. We'll have to travel in the darkness for much of our journey, I'm afraid."

They forged ahead for few more hours. Then, Aluriel nodded, scanning the forest. "There's a small clearing not far from here. It'll do for the night."

The journey ahead loomed like an impossible task, but for now, they had each other, and the quiet shelter of the forest.

As they trudged through the dense snow, Ian broke the silence again. "So, tell me, lass, did ye catch fit I was sayin' aboot them milestones in Varthia?"

"Milestones? With gallows?" She shot him a sidelong scowl. "You said this already. Are you drunk or getting old, that you forget what you said a few hours ago? It's not exactly pleasant to think about."

Ian let out a bark of laughter. "Old an' drunk. Yer nae wrong. Ah, just makin sure ye dinnae forget. Every ten kilometres, ye'll find a gallows standin' proud, a fine monument tae the Peacemaker's *justice*. Paladins an' priests use 'em tae hang folk they reckon deserve it. Sometimes it's bandits. Sometimes a hungry bairn who stole some bread. Sometimes even a beggar they dinnae fancy lookin' at too long."

Aluriel frowned, the image now etched in her mind despite her attempts to banish it. Her voice carried a sharp edge, a mix of disbelief and disgust. "That's barbaric. How could you even *consider* taking us through there?"

"Nae ideal," Ian admitted, scratching his beard. "But the Varthian roads are well-kept." His tone shifted, a touch practical, a touch sardonic. "Smooth paths, aye. Plenty o' rest stops, though meist o' them come wi' sanctimonious lectures free o' charge. Ye'll love it!"

"Sanctimonious lectures I can tolerate," Aluriel said sarcastically. "But hanging for simply existing? That... might be a problem."

Ian's expression darkened. "Aye, but hangin's nae the worst o' it. The ones they really want tae see suffer? They tak them tae Varthia itself, an' I mean the city Varthia, the capital. Impalement's their grand spectacle, reserved fer the folk they think are a proper affront tae their so-called justice." Ian shrugged. "It's nae a picnic, I'll grant ye. But compared tae The Sunless Depths or the Dragons' Peaks,

Varthia's the lesser o' three evils. Long as we keep our heids down an' dinnae draw the wrong kind o' attention, we might just make it through wi' our necks – an' our bums – intact."

Aluriel sighed, her gaze shifting back to the trail ahead. "And the other options? Are they really much worse than that?"

Ian chuckled darkly, but there was an undercurrent of terror in his tone that Aluriel couldn't miss. "The Sunless Depths are quicker, aye, but ye'll nae like the company. Spiders bigger than me beard, things that'll steal yer soul wi' a glance, an' gods help us if we run intae ony Dark Elves or Gaze Tyrants. I'll nae lie tae ye, lass, it's a path I'd sooner nae set foot on, no unless there's nae other way." He shrugged, as if to shake loose the dread that clung to him.

"As fer the Dragons' Peaks, in summer ye might have a chance tae cross, but in winter? Ye'd freeze tae death afore ye even saw the summit. It's suicide tae even try. So that leaves Varthia. But afore Varthia, we've tae cross the desert. Ye'll roast by day, freeze by night, an' maybe take a scimitar in yer ribs fer yer trouble. Worse still, the desert folk dinnae look kindly on magic-users, so ye'd best keep yer lightnin' tricks tae yersel', aye?"

"And yet you don't seem worried why?" Aluriel giggled, raising an eyebrow.

Ian grinned. "Worryin' does nae solve problems, lass. Planning does. We'll make it. One way or another."

A small, genuine smile tugged at Aluriel's lips. "You're an optimist, Ian."

"Nae." His grin widened. "I'm a realist who drinks enough tae make optimism look like a plan."

Aluriel pursed her lips and offered no comment in return, her mind suddenly distracted by a whisper.

A whisper of madness. Or maybe of a Goddess. Or, for all she knew, maybe a Demon. *Happy fucking birthday, Aluriel,* she thought.

# ✦ Interlude – The Unseen Hand ✦

The chamber lay buried in darkness, deep underground. So deep that not even the bravest archaeologists had ever heard of its existence. Its only source of light was the faint green glow of soulfire trapped within crystalline prisms. Shadows moved unnaturally across the walls, as if stirred by unseen hands. At the centre sat a throne, fashioned of bleached bone. Femurs and ribs intertwined, spinal cords twisted like vines. Upon it rested a figure that did not breathe, whose hollow eyes glowed cold and unblinking.

An Arch-Lich.

He sat silent and unmoving, save for the rhythmic tapping of one polished fingertip upon the skull-shaped armrest.

A skeletal servant approached, joints creaking, bearing a goblet filled with blood drawn moments before, for it was still warm. The Lich waved him away. Sustenance was of no interest to him. "Go feed it to our vampire guest." The skeleton bowed and skittered away.

"Friend."

Silence stretched, and then his voice returned. It was little more than a whisper, and yet it echoed through the chamber with unnatural force. "Come forward."

From the gloom emerged a tall dark elf, his vibrant ginger hair neatly trimmed into a buzz cut. He carried a necromancer's staff crowned with a tiger's skull. He bowed low, his black cloak sweeping the floor.

"My lord."

"The preparations for the dwarf city."

"Proceeding as planned." The necromancer's voice was calm. "According to schedule."

The Lich said nothing.

The necromancer hesitated, then added, "But... the morningstar still resists. Despite all our blood rituals, all our attempts to defile it, it refuses to yield. Even to *Demon sacrifices*."

A long silence. The Lich leaned back. One hand rose to steeple bony fingers beneath his chin.

"Perhaps," he whispered, "it requires the blood of its creator. Or at least, his offspring. But don't forget to focus on the rest, too."

The necromancer's eyes widened slightly. He nodded once, understanding without needing more. "It shall be done."

The necromancer said nothing of the morningstar's true complication.

It was no longer in his possession.

That omission was deliberate.

The Lich's wrath was not something one tempted lightly.

Without another word, he turned and vanished into the shadows.

The Lich sat motionless, surrounded by bone and silence. Behind him, dozens of undead figures toiled ceaselessly, preparing more rituals, more death, more defilements.

He tapped his finger once more against the skull-shaped armrest. A soft clack echoed.

Then stillness.

And the faint whisper of something old and cruel, drifting in the air like a forgotten curse.

# Chapter 2 – Reluctant steps

Aluriel led the way to a clearing as the moons were already high in the sky, their dim light bathing the blanket of snow around them. The air was cool, filled with the scent of fir and damp earth. The whispers had grown stronger, as they always would at twilight and in the hours of darkness, and Aluriel busied herself with setting up the tent and preparing their bedrolls. Ian grunted as he gathered stones into a circle. Axe in hand, chopped down saplings, small trees, and hacked at whatever branches of larger ones he could reach, piling the wood in preparation for a campfire.

"This'll do," Ian said to himself. He tapped his hammer on the wood, and in a flash of magic, the kindling was set ablaze. Even though the wood was sopping wet – some branches still covered in snow – within moments, the campfire crackled warmly, bathing them in a flickering orange glow.

Aluriel tilted her head, curiosity flickering in her eyes, which now glowed fiercely violet, stoked by firelight and magic. "How did you manage to light wet wood?"

Ian winked at her, grinning coyly as he chuckled. "Priest o' fire, lass. Fit did ye expect?"

Aluriel decided not to question Ian further, even as her own thoughts nagged at her. *At least one of us has useful magic...* she thought as she sat cross-legged, her silvery hair reflecting the orange glow of the firelight, her face pensive. She had been quiet most of the day, and the evening was no different. Her thoughts were clearly elsewhere. *How did it come to this?* she wondered, just as she had ruminated countless times before. *Cast out, humiliated... everything I thought I could be, turned to ash. I didn't even want to BE anything special.*

*I just wanted to... exist. To love. To be loved.* She wrapped her cloak tighter around her shoulders. *They couldn't be bothered to tell me where to go. Just wanted me gone. Forgotten.* Her gaze lingered on the flames, as if she were seeking answers in their flickering dance that licked the wooden logs they had engulfed. *Can I truly start over? Or am I just running until there's nowhere left to go? Oh, here we go again. The same memories, the same thoughts, looping over and over. Why can I not stop them?*

As if sensing her mood darkening further, Ian rummaged through his pack until he found a flask. "More mead?" he asked as he pulled it out, holding it up with a grin. "It's nae elven wine, but it'll keep yer belly warm. An' ye seemed to like it earlier. This one? Apple flavoured. A tad stronger too."

Aluriel hesitated, then took the flask. This time, she started with a small sip. The sweetness hit her tongue first, followed by the sting of the alcohol, and then the warmth spreading down her throat as she swallowed it. She took a few more cautious sips, then handed it back. "It's... strong."

"Aye, lass. Strong's the way tae go. An' if ye think this is strong?" Ian cackled, then took a swig himself before sitting down beside her. "Wait until ye try Gnomish firewater."

Sitting beside her, he watched her brood in silence for a while before saying – without warning – "Now, tell me somethin'. This Elenwen lass... fit did ye see in her?"

Aluriel froze, caught off guard by the sudden question. She looked at Ian, and felt her mouth open... and then close again. No words came out. Instead, she grabbed the flask and gulped as much as she could before her throat begged her for mercy and she doubled over, coughing into her sleeve. Ian watched her quietly, with a hint of compassion, as she punished herself with his mead.

He waited until Aluriel stopped coughing and caught her breath again. "Nae aboot fit happened," Ian clarified, his voice softer now. "I mean 'afore. Fit did ye feel for her? Fit does she mean tae ye, even now?"

For a moment, Aluriel stared into the fire. Her violet eyes caught the glow and returned it, refracted and emboldened, the orange of the campfire transformed into a violet blaze. To buy more time, and perhaps courage, she reached for a flask from her own pack. It was full of Elven wine, and she took several gulps as the memories came rushing back. *Easier on the throat than Ian's mead.* Elenwen's laughter, the way her golden hair caught the sunlight, the quick wit that had always left Aluriel both frustrated and enchanted. *Why can't I forget her?* she wondered bitterly. *The memories should fade, turn grey and lifeless like ashes*, she hoped. Instead, they remained vivid, searing, and kept tearing at her heart. *Was it love, or just the idea of being loved by someone like her?* Aluriel swallowed hard, gripping the flask so firmly it made her knuckles pale. *Even after everything, part of me still hopes she'll come back, that she'll say it was all a misunderstanding...*

"She was everything," Aluriel said finally, her voice barely a whisper. "She was kind to me when no one else was. For a time, I thought she might understand me, see me for... well, for... Not... Not just a freak. She struggled with Druidic magic too. That brought us close at first."

Ian nodded, calm as ever. "An' after?"

The question brought back painful memories. Aluriel's hands trembled, and she clenched them into fists to steady herself. *It's none of his business... but...* her tone turned sour and bitter. "After Thalion taught her sun magic? Suddenly, she belonged. Suddenly, she had a future: that of a Sun channeller. Suddenly, she was everybody's new best friend. Slowly, she grew more distant. Until at some point I became... I became... something to be ashamed of." She paused. "And when she humiliated me? I hated her. I hated her so much it burned. But even then..." Her voice faltered, and tears began to glisten in her eyes. Quickly, she pushed her head forward, letting her hair fall to shield her face from Ian's gaze just in time. Tears began to drip, and she started sobbing. "Even then, I still wanted her. I still want her. I still... love her," she croaked between sobs, her tears now streaming down her face and neck. *Even now*, she thought, *I still wear the diadem she made for me when we were friends.*

Ian shifted closer, placing a hand on her shoulder. "Och, lass, it's nae easy, is it? Wantin' fit ye cannae have."

Aluriel had nothing to say. The whirlwind of feeling was so intense, she could not think of words. All she could do was let out more choked sobs, her shoulders shaking as the pain she had held back for so long poured out. Ian pulled her into a firm embrace, letting her cry against his shoulder. He didn't speak, didn't try to offer meaningless platitudes. He simply held her, as if to share the burden of her darkness. The burden of her pain.

When her sobs subsided, Ian handed her the wine flask again. "Here. Drink more. It'll help."

Aluriel took several more gulps, and the familiar taste of sweet Elven wine took the edge off her sorrow, if just for a moment. She wiped her face, her voice hoarse when she spoke. "Ian... do dwarves ever... I mean, do they..." *Why is this hard to say? she thought, her stomach twisting in knots. Will he judge me? Laugh at me? No... Ian wouldn't do that. But what if he doesn't understand? What if Dwarves aren't free, like elves, to love who they wish? What if he, too, decides to judge me?* She'd heard of other races being less than understanding. The weight of her hesitation felt more palpable with every instant, and her heart fluttered as she waited for his response to her unspoken question.

"Love someone o' the same sex?" Ian finished for her, his tone neutral, matter-of-fact. "Aye, it happens. It's nae somethin' we encourage, but we dinna punish it, either. Worst that'll happen to a gay dwarf'd be some gossip an' maybe some banter. Gnomes are the same, only less... formal about it. They dinna encourage it – nae shoutin' from the rooftops – but really, they truly dinna care fit ye do or who ye're doin' it wi', so long as it doesnae disrupt their work. An' they sure dinnae care enough tae gossip, much less banter. Ye ken," he added, "a fair few dwarves live in the Gnomish half o' Steelforge. Some gay, some nae. The gnomes dinnae care either way."

Aluriel managed a small, bitter laugh. "And Varthians?"

Ian's face darkened. "Different story entirely. They see it as a sin, an affront tae their precious bloody Peacemaker. Ye'd best keep yer feelins tae yersel' while we're crossin' their land. Those paladins wouldnae think twice about stringin' ye up. Or worse." He continued, slowing his words, "A pretty lass like ye... Varthians would lock ye up and try tae *convert* ye. Forcibly."

Aluriel shuddered, her fingers tightening around the flask. *Hanged, or raped by Varthians. Fucking lovely.* She decided not to dwell on which prospect was worse. "It'll be exhausting, hiding who I like. I've never had to..." *Until they fucking exiled me. Thanks, council of dickheads.*

"Aye," Ian said quietly. "But it's survival. An' ye've got more tae fight fer than most, lass. Ye've got a fire burnin' inside ye, stronger than any o' them'll ever understand. Just dinna let naebody put it oot."

Aluriel allowed herself a small smile. "Thank you, Ian."

"Och, think nothin' of it," he said, leaning back and staring into the fire. "Now we should eat and get some rest. We've a long way tae go, an' ye'll nae want tae face it hungover."

"It's a bit too late for that!" Aluriel burst into laughter, suddenly realising how much the alcohol had gotten to her head.

Ian stood, dusting off his hands and reaching for a heap of thin branches he had piled next to the tent. He took seven of them, and began planting them evenly around the clearing. Aluriel watched in silence, forcing her weary eyes to follow Ian's every move as carefully as she could, despite the drink.

"What are you doing?" she finally asked.

Ian did not answer immediately. With his pocket knife, he roughly shaved the bark off, then began carving runes into the surface of each one. When he was done with the first, he moved to the next. Then the next. Meticulously, he carved all seven.

He finished with the last one and glanced at her. "Protection. Nae idea fit lurks in these woods, but I'll nae be caught unawares."

Aluriel tilted her head, her curiosity now definitely piqued. She could sense the faintest hum of magic emanating from the carved runes, though she didn't recognise their origin. "Are those... dwarven runes?"

"Aye," Ian replied. "They'll keep meist nasties oot... unless they're cleverer than me." He gave her a brief smile before hammering the staves into the ground. Once all seven were planted, Ian stepped back, and his face turned serious. He closed his eyes and began to chant in a deep, resonant voice. The words were in a language Aluriel didn't recognise, and the cadence was both calming and ominous, like a lullaby laced with warning. The runes on the staves began to glow faintly, a warm orange light that pulsed in synchrony with Ian's chant. A thin orange mist swirled up from the campfire and reached the staves, forming a shimmering heptagram that encircled their tent like a dome. Even the snow was repelled, as the warding magic softly displaced it to the edges.

Aluriel's breath stopped for a moment as she watched the display in sheer awe, wondering exactly what kind of magic she was witnessing. *How does he do this so effortlessly?* she thought, feeling a pang of envy. Magic had always been a battle to her. A battle she had always lost, unable to conjure even the most basic spells they'd tried to teach her. But this? This was control, precision, and purpose. She longed to ask Ian about it, to understand the runes and the power they held. But she hesitated, unsure of how to voice her curiosity without sounding foolish. So she just sat in contemplation, letting the magic wash over her like a gentle hum in the air around her, a soothing yet powerful presence that left her both amazed and drawn to it.

"That... that's incredible," she whispered, her violet eyes flaring brightly whenever they fixed on a glowing rune, as she moved closer to inspect them one by one. "I've never felt magic like this before!"

Ian leaned back and smirked. "Told ye I'm nae just a hammer-swingin' brute. There's more tae dwarves than axes an' booze, ye ken."

Aluriel snort-laughed. "I didn't doubt you. Not really."

Ian chuckled, reaching into the pack again and pulling out a wrapped bundle. He opened it to reveal a loaf of Lembas.

The sight of food jogged her memory. She rummaged through her pack and pulled out a small sack. She fumbled trying to open it, until two fish – whose scales still glistened in the moonlight – fell onto the ground. She handed them to Ian. "They smell fresh still." He sniffed them, setting them on a flat stone by the fire. "Ye any good at guttin' fish, lass?"

Aluriel tilted her head, laughing and slurring her words. "Hah! I caught them, actually! I caught them myself! Hahaha! In the river, a bit before we met. It's been so cold, they just stayed fresh in my bag!"

Ian raised an eyebrow, impressed. "With yer bare hands, eh?"

"Something like that!" Aluriel didn't mention the brief burst of electricity she had used to shock the water, stunning the fish just long enough to scoop them out. It was a trick she had discovered by accident that night. Since the chain lightning, this was the only thing close to magic that she had ever managed. Soon after she left her mother's home and her exile began, she felt the urge to take one last swim in the river. Her mind, eluding her control as usual, fed her the same familiar feelings: rage and despair. And then, the tiniest current of electricity flowed between her hands. It was fleeting. It was wild. It was out of her control. But it caught her dinner.

Aluriel staggered to her feet, took a knife, and began to work on the fish. But Ian quickly realised she was far too drunk for the task. "Och, gimme those, afore ye gut yer own hand." He grunted as he took the knife from her.

"Me? Gut my own? Hahahahah!" Aluriel suddenly burst into laughter again.

"Yer too pished, lass!" Ian retorted. Having taken the lot from her hands, he worked deftly to prepare the fish. Aluriel sat back, still giggling, watching him drunkenly. "You sure you're a priest of fire and not a fishmonger?"

"Aye, well..." Ian replied, his tone casual. "Dwarves dinnae get far without learnin' tae fend for themselves. Ye'd be surprised how useful a campfire meal can be in diplomacy."

Aluriel arched an eyebrow as she kept laughing. "Diplomacy? Over fish?"

"Fish, ale, cheese... fitiver gets folk talkin'." Ian grinned. "Ye can tell a lot aboot a person by how they eat."

When the fish were cooked, their skin crisp and the meat flaky, Ian passed Aluriel a portion. She bowed her head slightly, drunkenly reciting a druidic blessing over the meal, a habit ingrained from years among the forest elves.

The words felt hollow and meaningless, like the trappings of a ritual performed by one who no longer believed. *Did these words ever mean anything to me?* she thought, even as they left her lips. As she finished, a stronger whisper pierced her mind. It was louder than the rest. It had the cadence of words, however incomprehensible. It sent a pleasant shiver down her spine. It vanished as quickly as it came. She froze, her breath catching. Only her usual, quiet whispers remained in the background.

Ian noticed her hesitation. "Ye alright, lass?"

Aluriel forced a smile, taking a bite of the fish. "Just tired, I suppose. And drunk!"

They ate in silence before the softly crackling campfire. Ian broke the lembas in two and handed one half to Aluriel. "This'll keep us goin' till mornin'." When their meal was finished, Ian leaned back, patting his stomach. "Nothin' like a good meal tae end the day."

Aluriel nodded, though her mind was still on the whisper, its elusive nature gnawing at her. She pushed the thought aside, focusing on the warmth of the fire and the feeling of camaraderie between them, no doubt fuelled by alcohol. For now, it was enough.

"We should get some rest," Ian said, standing and stretching. "Long trek ahead."

Aluriel agreed, crawling into the tent they would share. As she settled into her bedroll, the faint hum of Ian's protective magic surrounded them. The forest had never been a danger to Aluriel, but the extra protection felt reassuring. Yet, even with the magic's protection, her thoughts lingered on the whispers.

Their meaning was, as always, out of reach.

The fire outside crackled softly, and its glow filtered through the tent's thin walls. Ian's rhythmic snoring soon filled the tent, drowning out the crackling of the fire and the calls of night birds. Sleep, however, did not come easily for Aluriel. She lay awake, her mind swirling.

When it finally overtook her, her dreams were vivid and strange. Yet, as they progressed, they began to feel familiar, just like countless times before. As always, the whispers reached her first. In her dreams, they felt much more intense than when she was awake. Initially they were faint, a mere caress on the edge of her consciousness. Then, they grew louder, though never fully clear. The tone carried urgency. A call to action, or perhaps a warning. They made her shiver. She felt all the more powerless, unable to understand. Try as she might to make sense of the sounds, they remained a tantalising riddle just beyond her comprehension.

Then came the swarm of butterflies appearing before her, their wings iridescent, colours shifting in patterns no one could dare to follow. A swirl of impossible hues. Some colours no eye was meant to glimpse. It felt like watching thought through a spinning kaleidoscope. They flitted all around her, dancing around in chaos, utterly without order. Slowly, as always, the butterflies began to converge, forming a perfect circle before her, only to dissolve moments later as the whispers faded. The scene darkened, leaving Aluriel alone in an empty void, her heart pounding.

As she woke with a gasp, she sat up, her thoughts already racing. *Was that a warning?* she wondered, her breathing uneven. *A memory? Or something trying to reach me?* She was no stranger to this dream, but every time, its vividness unsettled her, clinging to her consciousness. Every time, the same thoughts looped obsessively in her mind. Despite the lingering unease, she resolved to make sense of it. *If the Lady of Twilight truly exists... If she really is a goddess and she speaks to me, then why, why me? What does she want from me? It's been years she sends me whispers and butterflies. And now, the butterflies show me a **circle**. Why?*

Her violet eyes darted around the dim interior as she continued her endless rumination, and her hands clutched her bedroll tightly, to ground herself in reality. The protective hum of Ian's wards was still there, but it did little to calm the pounding of her heart. Ian stirred beside her, mumbling something incoherent before turning over and resuming his snoring. Aluriel wiped a handkerchief across her forehead, which was damp with sweat despite the cold air, and lay back down. She closed her eyes, but sleep did not return easily. The whispers resonated faintly in her mind, like the echo of a melody.

A melody she could not quite recall.

It was not the first time and – Aluriel was certain – it would not be the last.

Eventually, exhaustion took over again.

Ian's gruff voice shattered what little dreamless slumber she had managed. "Lass, it's morning, even if the sun's nae risen yet. Time tae be up. We've a long trek ahead."

Aluriel groaned, her eyes fluttering open to see Ian's stout frame silhouetted against the soft light of the campfire he had already reignited. She sat up, stretching the stiffness from her limbs, and reached for a piece of lembas that Ian had set beside her. The elven bread was sweet and filling, and yet carried the bitter aftertaste of a home Aluriel would likely not return to. She knew how to bake it. Aeliana had taught her elven cooking, precisely and patiently. Yet, Aluriel knew hers would not taste the same as the very bread they now consumed. This one was baked by her mother. This one was made with love and magic.

Aluriel, for now, felt entirely devoid of either.

They ate in relative silence, the birdsong providing a pleasant soundtrack to the morning, a distraction from the bitter chill in the air. After breakfast, Aluriel picked up her bow and quiver, deciding to try her luck at hunting. She moved silently through the snow-covered underbrush.

*Elves, always so... graceful,* Ian thought.

Aluriel's decades of wandering the forest and training with Rhovan made it look easy, at least to Ian. Spotting a hare nibbling at something, she nocked an arrow, pulled the string, and fired. The arrow struck it. It was not the clean hit in the eye that Rhovan used to perform every time they hunted together. It was a messy kill. The arrow penetrated the hare's abdomen and dug into the ground, leaving the animal pinned, flailing in pain and panic. Aluriel cut its throat with her short sword, swiftly and cleanly, to end its suffering. She held it by its hind legs to bleed it dry, and returned to Ian with a twinge of pride on her face.

What she did not say, however, was the Druidic hunter's prayer.

The ritual words to thank the animal for its sacrifice, and the forest for its sustenance.

"Ye're nae bad wi' that bow, lass," Ian nodded in approval, taking the hare. "We'll feast tonight." He gutted it and left the unwanted entrails for whatever animal would be lucky enough to find them first.

The two finished packing up their camp and resumed their journey. Aluriel led the way, her knowledge of the forest paths keeping them on track. The silence between them was peaceful, broken occasionally by Ian's muttered complaints about the snow, or Aluriel's observations of the terrain.

It was late afternoon when they entered a patch where the forest had begun to thin. Not quite a clearing, but the trees stood wider apart here, as if most had chosen to retreat, though some lingered. It felt like the sort of place where something might watch from above.

It was then that the attack came.

The eaglebear dived from the sky with a deafening screech, and Ian only just managed to step back in time to avoid being crushed. It landed in front of them, wings unfurled, making the ground shake slightly as it absorbed the full force of its weight.

Its massive, feathered bulk towered over them menacingly. Having failed to snatch Ian, it folded its wings and readied itself to fight on the ground. Its whole body was covered in hardened feathers that gleamed like armoured scales, shimmering with movement. The creature was bear-sized, and yet unmistakeably unique. It sported four limbs: its forelegs ended in hooked talons like an eagle's; its hind legs were thick and clawed like a bear's. Its jagged beak snapped several times.

*Does it mean to threaten us? Or is it simply savouring its next meal?* Its talons and claws gleamed like polished daggers. Aluriel froze for a heartbeat, momentarily overwhelmed by the eaglebear's sheer size and the surprise of the attack. This beast was taller than her, and the only living things she was used to looking up to were trees!

Ian reacted first.

"Get back, lass!" he bellowed, stepping forward with his warhammer raised. His runed armour caught the fading sunlight as its enchantments flickered, making the runes glow fiercely red as he prepared to engage the eaglebear. Aluriel nimbly stepped back, and reached quickly for her bow. She nocked an arrow and loosed it, grazing the eaglebear's flank. It screeched in anger but did not falter, its attention locked on Ian.

The dwarf swung his hammer in a wide arc. With a crushing thud, the warhammer mauled the eaglebear's side. The beast staggered but retaliated immediately with its talons, raking across Ian's chest. The runes on his armour flared brightly, absorbing some of the impact, but Ian grunted in pain as the claws slashed through the breastplate, tearing flesh beneath. Aluriel loosed another arrow. This one struck deep, embedding itself in the creature's shoulder. Drops of its blood peppered the otherwise pristine white of the snow-covered terrain. The eaglebear roared and turned its gaze towards her, its birdlike eyes filled with fury. Panic surged through her, but she forced herself to stay calm, fumbling a little as she drew another arrow from her quiver. Before she could nock and fire, the eaglebear charged, closing the distance faster than she had anticipated.

Ian threw himself between them, smashing his hammer onto the eaglebear's face, halting the beast's advance, if only for a moment. "Keep shootin'!" he yelled, as blood began to drip from the wound he'd just taken. "I'll haud it aff ye!" Aluriel obeyed, her arrows whizzing one after another. One grazed its chest. Another skittered uselessly against its hardened feathers. But the next found its mark and skewered its hindleg. Ian pressed the attack, movements fluid despite his plate. *Well,* Aluriel thought as she loosed another arrow, *never seen anyone fight in full plate.* She fired another. The beast parried it with its wing.

Ian dodged a swipe from the eaglebear's talons, countering with a blow to its leg, which made it stumble for a moment. But the beast was relentless, and it continued to assault Ian. A swipe from its right talon, blocked by Ian's shield. Then he countered with a swing that smashed hard against its chest. The beast, screeching in pain, exacted its revenge, and raked Ian's forehead with its beak. Aluriel's arrow made it leap backwards just in time, and Ian could steady his stance again. He swung his hammer sideways, aiming at its foreleg. The eaglebear screeched in pain from the blow, and immediately raked Ian's left shoulder with its right talon. Ian's pauldron runes flared brightly, but the armour tore free. The talons raked his arm. Despite the searing pain, Ian attempted to hit the beast once more, but it managed to swipe its talons at his chest again with a furious screech.

This time, the hit sent Ian sprawling to the ground.

Aluriel's heart raced as she watched the eaglebear rear up, its talons and beak poised to strike the killing blow. With no time to pause and think, she nocked another arrow and aimed it. Her breath hitched as she released it. The arrow impaled the beast's left eye. A jolt of savage thrill coursed through her as the eaglebear shrieked in pain, staggering back. *Wish Rhovan could've seen this shot!*

It wasn't enough to stop it, but it bought Ian some crucial seconds. As determined as he was bloodied, Ian pulled himself up, gritting his teeth, planted his feet, and raised his hammer high. He bellowed an enchantment in Dwarvish. Flames danced along the hammer's head as he raised it for a final strike. The moment it struck, the flames erupted, engulfing the beast in a fiery blaze. The eaglebear shrilled with fury, its feathers igniting. More than the blow itself, the surprise of being on fire made it stagger aimlessly. Before it could recover, it was too late: the fire consumed it quickly, leaving behind the acrid smell of burnt feathers and flesh as it fell, rasping weakly, before it closed its uninjured eye for the last time.

Ian collapsed right after.

The forest had fallen silent. Whatever animals lingered nearby had long since fled. The snow around Ian was quickly blooming crimson.

The runes on Ian's armour glowed weakly, the armour itself streaked with blood from his wounds. Aluriel did not know whether the armour was doing something to protect him still, so she rushed to him, but hesitated to remove it, looking at Ian as if to ask for guidance. Beneath the metal, Ian's tunic was slashed, and Aluriel could see that even more blood was oozing from his arms. The deeper cuts were from slashes across his chest, where the eaglebear's claws had sunk deep into Ian's flesh, and were bleeding profusely with each strained movement he tried to make. Ian clutched his side as he tried to get back on his feet, his breath laboured, only to collapse back onto the ground. Pain twisted his features into a panicked grimace. His hand, covered by a hard gauntlet, normally steady as stone, trembled as it pressed against his ribs, where the talons had gouged deep through the protective enchantments. A trickle of blood ran down his brow, matting his beard and mixing with sweat as it dripped onto the snow. His left pauldron hung askew, its strap severed, and the plates bore dents from the eaglebear's relentless strikes. Despite his injuries, Ian managed to raise his head, his eyes meeting Aluriel's with a flicker of defiant determination. "Och, dinna fash yerself, lass," Ian said, his voice weak but kind. "I've taken worse hits an' still managed tae crawl home." His tone, despite the pain, was calm and gentle; he was trying to shield her from the true extent of his wounds. *Taken much worse, aye, but then yer mither saved me...*

Aluriel had not seen much real battle. In fact, she had seen *none* at all. But not all of her druidic training had been useless: as druids and priests of the Lady Most Beautiful were believed to be the most skilled healers, part of their early training focused on triage. Learning how to determine how seriously injured someone was. Recognising who needed healing at once – and who could wait – meant saving more lives when every second mattered.

That much, at least, Aluriel had learned, even though she could cast no healing magic herself. Knowing this, Aeliana had packed a few healing potions for her. Elven healing potions, the most potent of all. Realising Ian would not survive without one, she rummaged through her backpack frantically and pulled out a vial of the ruby red liquid. She uncorked it, and pressed it to Ian's lips. "Drink this," she said, her voice almost commanding. Ian drank it without argument, and the potion's magic surged through him, knitting torn flesh and sealing open wounds. He breathed with relief, felt his strength return, and pushed himself to stand. "That was a close one," he muttered, wiping sweat from his brow and blood from his armour. Aluriel sat back, and as the adrenaline of the fight began to fade, it left behind a crushing sense of inadequacy. "If you hadn't been here..." she began, her voice barely above a whisper. "I... I would've been killed."

Ian looked at her, his expression softening. "Aye, lass, but ye were nae useless. Yer arrows helped. Yer potion saved me. It's fit a team does, ken?"

She shook her head slowly and muttered under her breath, "I can't fight like you. I can't hold my own. What real use am I?" *Useless. A failure. A mistake. That's all I am.*

Ian placed a hand on her shoulder, his grip firm but comforting. "Listen tae me, Aluriel," Ian said, leaning slightly closer. "Naebody starts as a master warrior, ken? These things tak time. Ye did well, better than ye think. Without yer shot in its eye, without yer potion, it's me who'd be dead. An' remember, ye're nae alone in this." *Wish she'd stop broodin' an' see she's nae useless.*

They sat in silence for a moment before Ian broke it. "We'd best harvest fit we can. Its beak an' talons'll fetch a fine price. Its gallstones too. Its feathers coulda been sold, had they nae gone up in ash. The meat, though? It tastes so foul even a starving orc'd think twice afore touchin' it. Sae vile, even dragons dinnae eat 'em."

Aluriel nodded, wiping her tears and forcing herself to her feet. Together, they worked to remove the eaglebear's valuable parts. The practical act grounded her in the present by giving her a task to focus on. By the time they finished harvesting what they could from the carcass, Aluriel felt thoroughly drained. She forced herself to lead them to the closest clearing, a couple more hours away, where they set up camp again. The bright glow of the fire illuminated their weary faces, and Ian planted his protective wards, muttering something about "bluidy eaglebears" once he'd finished. As before, the staves linked to the central campfire, and the wards hummed with a soft, low buzz. As they roasted the hare, Ian regaled her with tales of his past adventures. His humour lightened the mood and even managed to coax another small smile from her. "I'll tell ye somethin', lass," Ian said. "First time I faced a cave troll, I froze up affa bad I crapped meself! Thought I'd be its supper. It's only natural tae feel fear. 'Tis what keeps ye alive. But it's fit ye do wi' that fear that matters."

The hare tasted delicious, and paired well with lembas wafers and some dried figs that Aeliana had packed along with the rest of the provisions. And as her hunger eased, Aluriel began to relax a little. She survived. They survived. The road ahead was long and dangerous, but she was not walking it alone.

# Chapter 3 – Does an elf drink more than a camel?

The night passed uneventfully, the crackle of the campfire fading into soft embers as the hours stretched on. Ian's snores offered a steady rhythm to the night, almost a counterpoint to the distant call of owls. Aluriel lay awake far longer than she would have liked. The whispers – louder, as always, after twilight – gnawed at the edges of her consciousness. They came and went, flitting like distant echoes, weaving through her mind with their usual, maddening lack of clarity. A message that was, as always, just beyond her grasp. When sleep finally claimed her, it was shallow and restless. The usual nightmare came. At first, the darkness. Then, the butterflies flitting chaotically. Then, they settled into a circle before vanishing. She woke slick with sweat, pulse racing, as she always did. *Ever since the chain lightning, she's started to show me a **circle of butterflies**. Before, it was just butterflies flitting around randomly... I feel as if she's trying to show me something important. But what?* Aluriel's thoughts kept spiralling obsessively, looping cyclically. Her ruminations reclaimed their space as her constant, unwelcome background noise. Eventually, exhaustion took her again, and sleep returned. Brittle. Uneasy. And never quite enough.

When Aluriel was awakened, the camp was bathed in a soft golden glow. "Lass," Ian called, glancing up as he packed their supplies. "I tried tae let ye sleep a wee bit longer, but dawn's come, which means it's already far too late. Time tae move." Aluriel stirred, her body heavy with fatigue, though her face betrayed little of it. Ian must have been awake for a while, for his preparations were nearly complete. She pushed herself upright, stretching her sore limbs. She cast one last glance at the dying embers of the fire, then to the path ahead. It was time to shoulder their burdens and march once again.

The forest stretched endlessly before them, its ancient firs standing tall and resolute, their branches whispering in the soft rustle of wind. For four weeks, Ian and Aluriel marched north-eastward. The whispers and ruminations tormented her each day; the visions came each night. Aluriel grew more tired with each passing day. *Maybe I'm getting madder and madder.* Their path was marked by the days growing slightly longer, and subtle shifts in the vegetation. After the first three weeks, the snow became patchy, then disappeared entirely, giving way to damp earth thick with moss. Slowly, firs and pines gave way to chestnuts and oaks as they descended towards warmer latitudes. Occasional rivulets carved their way downslope, meandering north-eastward.

Aluriel realised she had never been this far from home, not even on her longest expeditions with Rhovan. The air was humid, and the underbrush glistened with the dampness of morning dew. She carried herself with quiet determination, her thoughts often wandering as they moved. *How did I end up here?* she thought. *Not just the forest... this life, this exile, this aimless march... Why did it happen to me?* She tightened her jaw, relieved that Ian couldn't notice her brooding as she slowed down and let him walk a few paces ahead, his gait steady despite the armour he bore and the weight of his pack. He hummed to himself occasionally, snippets of dwarven songs that brought a sense of rhythm to their otherwise silent march.

Aluriel had caught a few rabbits one morning, her shots accurate enough despite her ever-present self-doubts. Ian had nodded approvingly, but she could sense he held back words. Whatever he wished to say, she wasn't in the mood to hear it.

"Weel, ye've got a fine eye for game," Ian eventually remarked as they later sat for a rest and he skinned one of the rabbits. His hands moved deftly, making it all look easy, though his tone carried a touch of something more. *Perhaps an attempt to lighten the mood?*

"Thank you," Aluriel replied softly, though her voice lacked conviction. Her gaze drifted towards the sun, which was now high in the sky. "I wonder if the desert holds anything to hunt at all."

Ian chuckled with deep rumbling sound that broke the quiet. "Och, lass, ye'll nae find rabbits hoppin' through the sand, that's fer sure. But there'll be something. Always is, aye." Aluriel's mind was already spinning with dread. *The desert.* The word alone carried a weight that made her stomach twist. *What if I can't handle it? What if Ian's wrong and there's nothing to eat? How about water? Will he regret coming to rescue me?* She swallowed hard, pushing the thought aside. There was no room for turning back. *The desert.* A place she had never seen but heard of in tales. Endless dunes of sand, scorching heat, a scarcity of life and, most troubling, water.

Even though she had retrieved the arrows, cleaned them, and sharpened their mithril points, she reached into her quiver to count them yet again. *Twenty-four arrows. Twelve arrows twice. If there's less than twelve, that means trouble.* She had been obsessing over this ever since she started carrying a quiver, from the early days of her training with Rhovan.

The day passed in a quiet blur of steady movement. They stopped briefly at some point in the afternoon, as the sound of running water greeted them from a brook that cut through the forest, its surface glinting in the warm, waning sunlight filtering through the trees.

Aluriel's face lit up, and did not even try to hide the enthusiasm that broke through her weary expression. Ian set his pack down on the mossy ground and stretched his shoulders with a groan. "We'll fill the waterskins here an' take a break. We've been marchin' fer weeks, an' my feet are feelin' it."

Aluriel nodded absently, her steps already heading towards the water. She glanced back over her shoulder and said, matter-of-factly, "I'm going to bathe." As if it were beyond obvious, clearly the most natural thing to do when one saw a brook large and clear enough.

Ian blinked. "Bathe? Here? Lass, it's nae a bathhouse."

She shrugged, pulling her cloak from her shoulders. "I need to. The dirt itches, and the water…" She trailed off, as though the rest deserved no further explanation.

Before Ian could offer any further protest, Aluriel unlaced her boots and slipped them off, removed her outer garments, and finally her underwear, then stepped nude into the brook. As her webbed toes sank into the cool, silty bed, she felt immediate relief. The cold water lapped at her ankles, then her calves as she waded in deeper.

Ian turned away, muttering, "Bluidy hell. A warnin' woulda been nice." He busied himself with refilling the flasks, but curiosity got the better of him, and he stole a glance.

Aluriel swam with a grace that bordered on the magical. The water seemed to embrace her as though she belonged to it. She ducked beneath the surface, emerging with her wet hair plastered to her back, her skin glistening in the cool sunlight. Then, she did something that made Ian gape: she drank directly from the brook, her hands cupped to her lips, drinking a stream of water with deep, greedy gulps. Almost as though she meant to drink the whole brook dry.

"Ye'd think ye've nae seen water 'afore!" Ian was unable to keep the astonishment from colouring his tone.

Aluriel looked at him, droplets clinging to her lashes. "I told you. My body needs it." She dove again, her limbs cutting through the water in graceful, effortless motions, with the ease of a creature born to live in it.

Ian watched in silence, his earlier annoyance fading into something closer to awe. "Yer nae just part sea elf," he muttered, "Yer bloody near mermaid."

But Aluriel could not hear the last sentence as she'd allowed herself to sink beneath the surface. The waters of the brook were cold, even as sunlight filtered through the forest, but this did not bother her. The muffled world above was suddenly overwhelmed by the brook's rushing embrace. Her silvery hair fanned out like threads of moonlight. Her body felt weightless as she gently sank. For a moment, she felt at peace, until the memories came crashing in. Her mind, traitorous as ever, drifted back to the one memory she could never outrun.

The memory that returned to her again and again. Unwanted and unwelcome. The memory she could not block out, no more than she could the whispers, or her obsessive thoughts. The memory searing with guilt and rage, the one that hurt her most.

It had been on a bright, moonlit night, the clearing illuminated in a way that now seemed mocking in its beauty. Aluriel remembered the folded letter she had clutched tightly in her hands, her heart pounding as if it sought to break free of her chest. *Did I really believe this could work? That a letter could change everything?* She had asked herself that a thousand times. She had spent days crafting that letter, every word infused with her unguarded soul, her trembling hope. Elenwen – her childhood friend, her first innocent childhood love, her once-beloved confidante – had been the centre of her universe for as long as she could remember. They had been inseparable once, when they were children, innocent and untouched by the prejudices of their kind. Back then, Elenwen had cheered Aluriel on during their games, laughed with her beneath the sunlit treetops, and whispered shared dreams of the future beneath the starlit skies.

But time had changed things. Aluriel and Elenwen had both struggled with their studies under the druids, and then the priests. This brought them closer as the others began to view them more and more as outcasts. In time, Aluriel and Elenwen were told that neither the path of the druid nor priesthood was for them, and were placed under Thalion's mentorship to see whether they could learn Sun magic. Aluriel was unable to grasp even the simplest of spells. Elenwen, however, proved to have a natural gift for it, and quickly grasped its intricacies. Thalion, though patient and understanding towards Aluriel, began to focus more on Elenwen as her talent started to shine brighter, as bright as the Sun she was learning to channel. Suddenly, Elenwen became popular. Her future changed. Her trajectory as a future Sun channeller became clear to everyone. This earned her admiration from peers and elders alike, the very same who once dismissed her, just as they had Aluriel.

At first, Elenwen had tried to bridge the gap, remaining close to Aluriel, offering words of encouragement and support. Yet, as the years passed – the whispers and glances from their peers, the discussions with elders, and her own realisation of Aluriel's lack of talent – it had all become too much. Peer pressure, and her newfound popularity, drew her away from Aluriel. She let their bond slowly fade into a memory, and left Aluriel more isolated than ever. *Even Elenwen, with her radiant smile and boundless confidence, turned away from me.* She had started avoiding Aluriel. Her once warm greetings grew colder and more distant, slowly but relentlessly. Their long conversations became shorter and shorter, and then finally... almost ceased.

But hope lingered. Aluriel had poured her heart into that letter, a plea for one last chance. She had asked Elenwen to meet her in the clearing, to give her the chance to finally confess everything she had kept hidden for so long. And to her surprise, Elenwen had agreed. Her reply had been brief but clear: "I will be there."

In the clearing that night, Aluriel had stood beneath a fir, the moons' light casting shadows that danced with every gentle sway of the leaves. Her voice had trembled as she spoke, baring her soul in a torrent of feeling. *Every word felt like a drop of my essence spilling away, never to be reclaimed.* She had confessed her love, her admiration, and her deepest fears. Her words had spilled out unguarded and unfiltered. And then, emboldened by the blaze of her own feelings, she had stepped closer, reaching for Elenwen as if to seal her confession with the kiss she had yearned for.

The slap had been swift, the sting sharper than any wound she had ever known. Aluriel recoiled, and her eyes turned wide in disbelief when Elenwen began to laugh. Stunned, Aluriel stood silent until Elenwen spoke in a cruel, mocking voice that echoed in the clearing.

"Did you really think someone like me could ever love a lunatic like you?" Elenwen's voice was sharp, cutting through the night like a blade. "You're a half-breed. A mistake. How could someone like you ever hope to love a pureblood... A Sun channeller?"

The words struck harder than the slap. Aluriel staggered, her chest heaving as though the very air had been stolen from her lungs. She tried to speak, without knowing what to say, but her voice failed her.

A rustling sound broke through the haze of her shock. Figures emerged from the shadows, their faces grinning with cruel amusement, eyes glinting in the moonlight. They had been hiding, listening, waiting. Many more elven youth, their peers, came out and laughed at her. They pierced the night with mocking voices that felt like daggers piercing her heart.

"Look at her," one sneered. "Pathetic."

"She really thought she had a chance," another chimed in, her voice dripping with disdain. She spat at Aluriel.

Others emerged, joining the jeers, but Aluriel's mind had already gone blank.

Aluriel felt her knees about to buckle. Her heart, just moments before filled with hope and trepidation, now felt completely shattered. And, amidst the rising choke of humiliation and despair, a new emotion stirred. It quickly kindled into a blaze, fierce and unrelenting, uncontrollable as it surged within her chest.

Rage.

Her hands trembled. She found herself screaming at the top of her lungs. Not in fear, but in pure, blinding fury. She raised her fist to punch Elenwen, and the air around her crackled with energy. *"They hate me... no, they FEAR me. And I hate THEM,"* she could have thought, but she had no words to think with. All she had was rage. All she could do was scream. And at the peak of that scream, a thunderbolt shattered the night. The laughter around her stopped. Gasps erupted, then cries of pain and horror. Elenwen's taunting smirk disappeared. Her expression went blank with shock. She staggered backwards and fell to the ground. Curls of smoke circled up from her.

By then, it was too late. Whatever unknown power had slept within Aluriel had already surged forth. It had taken the form of a blinding arc of lightning, white and merciless, and had torn through the clearing. It had struck Elenwen first, then arced as it leapt to the next. And the next. Until none were spared. The brilliant flash burned the terrified faces of those who had just mocked her. It was over in a flash, quicker than the blink of an eye. Trees were set ablaze. The acrid scent of ozone and burned flesh filled the air. A cacophony of screams followed. Elenwen, sprawled on her back, struggled to breathe, and Aluriel stood alone in the scorched clearing, her hands still crackling with static and residual magic.

The silence that followed was deafening. Whatever animals hadn't been hit outright fled quickly. A few squirrels, a hedgehog, and a couple of owls were among the casualties. The groans of the fallen were the only sounds to fill the air. She had stared at her trembling hands, horror and disbelief washing over her in waves. Elenwen lay among the injured, her face and chest bearing burns so severe that, despite the combined healing efforts of the druids and priests of the Lady Most Beautiful, the scars would remain. Her beauty, once so flawless, was forever marred by the rage Aluriel had unleashed.

The adults arrived. Druids and priests began to heal the injured. The Rangers were quick to restrain her as she stood stunned in the clearing. *Did I really just do this? Is Elenwen going to be okay? Please be okay!* She silently prayed.

Suddenly, the memory dissolved like ripples in the brook, shattered by the sudden sound of a splash that yanked her from her reminiscence and flung her back into the present. She opened her eyes beneath the surface, only to see Ian floundering in the brook, still in his full plate armour. She surfaced abruptly, her lungs suddenly dragging cool air. The shock of it made her gasp, but she managed to shout, "Ian! What in the world are you doing?" And then she let out an explosion of laughter she just could not hold back.

Ian, sinking like a rock, managed to plant his feet firmly on the shallow, silty bed. "Fit does it bluidy look like, lass? I thought ye were drownin'! Ye've been under fer ages!"

Aluriel wiped the water from her face, her expression shifting from shock to exasperation. "I'm not drowning, Ian. I was just... thinking." She pointed to her neck, where faint slits marked her underdeveloped gills. "I can breathe underwater for a fairly long time. Not indefinitely, but long enough. Eventually, I have to surface for air." She paused, a glint of mischief flashing through her eyes. "You, on the other hand? I don't know if you can swim, but sure as yer beard is red, ye canna swim wearin' plate armour!" She laughed, attempting to mimic his accent with affectionate mockery, before plunging into the water again.

Ian grumbled, boots squelching in the silt, beard soaked and dripping as he clumsily waded back to the bank. "Coulda fooled me. Dinna scare an old dwarf like that again." He muttered, quietly ashamed to admit – even to himself – that he had been terrified, and had jumped in without thinking to shed his armour first.

When she finally climbed out, dripping and radiant, Ian handed her a dry cloth from his pack. In the meantime, he had lit another campfire to dry himself and his gear, muttering grumpily to himself about "bluidy fish elves". She took the cloth with a nod of thanks, wrapped it around her shoulders, and settled on a nearby rock. The campfire's warmth was welcome after the swim in the freezing brook. Her skin seemed to glow faintly, the turquoise hue more brilliant and vivid after her time in the water. Still, her expression betrayed her dark mood and darker thoughts. She had not exactly been cheerful for the whole journey. But even Ian could sense she was more troubled than usual.

"Fit's wrong, lass?" Ian asked, his voice gruff but tinged with concern.

Aluriel hesitated, fingertips interlacing. The weight of the memory pressed heavily on her chest. "I was thinking about the night that led to my exile," she said softly, her voice barely rising above the rushing sound of the brook. "About Elenwen and what she did to me. What I did to her."

"Aye, that'd be enough to haunt anyone."

Aluriel nodded, her gaze distant as she stared at the rippling water. *How can I redeem myself?* "It's not just what she did. It's what I did after. I lost control... I became everything they accused me of."

Ian placed a heavy hand on her shoulder, his grip firm but reassuring. "Yer more than that, Aluriel. Yer nae defined by yer worst moment. Nae unless ye wish tae be."

She met his gaze, her eyes searching his for something. Forgiveness, perhaps? No, she did not deserve forgiveness. Understanding was the most she could hope for. His steady presence was a small comfort against the storm that still raged within her. "I wish I could believe that," she whispered.

Ian's lips curled into a faint, wry smile. "Ye will, lass. In time, ye will."

"It must be somethin'." Ian's voice was quieter than usual as he changed the subject. "Tae feel that connected tae somethin'. Water, I mean..."

Aluriel glanced at him, measuring her words. "It's a part of me I can't deny. But it's also a part that reminds me how different I am. From everyone."

Ian snorted. "Different's nae a bad thing, lass. We've all got our quirks. Hells, gnomes are half the size o' anyone else, or a tenth of *yer* size, that is, an' ye don't hear them complainin'."

She chuckled softly, but did not reply. Her gaze drifted back to the brook, to the water rushing past. Silently, she wished it could carry her thoughts and her guilt away with it. The moment of peace was fleeting, but she clung to it all the same. They would reach the desert soon enough. There, the reality of survival would be harsher. But for now, in the heart of the forest, she had let herself feel the water's embrace one more time.

As night descended, they made camp in another small clearing nearby. As the starlight bled gently into the darkening sky, the whispers grew louder as always. Ian built another fire with his usual magical efficiency, and the flames engulfed the wood, casting flickering shadows on the trees around them. The scent of roasted rabbits filled the air as they ate, Aluriel kept mostly silent, whilst Ian regaled her with stories of dwarven feasts, his words tinged with nostalgia. Aluriel listened, yet her thoughts were distant. Even now, the memory burned like an open wound, the diadem on her forehead constantly carrying the weight of a reminder. A reminder of why she could trust no one with her heart again.

As the fire crackled softly in the clearing, Ian leaned back against a tree trunk, watching Aluriel sip from her waterskin for what felt like the hundredth time that day.

"Ye ken ye drink like a camel, lass," he said, half in jest, and half in genuine wonder. "I've seen folk thirsty afore, aye, but ye've been suckin' that waterskin dry every hour. An' the brook..."

Aluriel glanced at him, her turquoise skin now gleaming radiantly in the firelight. She hesitated, her fingers tightening around the waterskin, before sighing softly. *How much do I tell him? How much does he need to know?* The weight of her secrets swirled in her mind. *He already knows more than most. But if he knew everything? Would he still call me a friend? Is he even my friend, or is he doing this just because he's grateful to my mother? Am I just a favour he's returning?* "It's not just thirst. It's... well, it's... it's part of who I am."

Ian tilted his head, as if nudging her to say more. "Aye? Ye mean tae say it's somethin' more than the trek?"

She nodded. Her silvery hair caught the flickering orange glow. Her eyes reflected it with an intense glow of their own. "My father's a sea elf," she admitted quietly. "I've inherited... traits. My body craves water more than yours would. If I go too long without drinking or bathing, I can feel it. My skin dries, my muscles ache."

Ian leaned forward, his arms resting on his knees. "Sea elf, aye? That explains a bit. Yer skin... yer fingers." He gestured with his hand, miming the webbing he'd noticed before. "Though I've kent it since the day ye were born, lass. Yer heritage is no surprise tae me, as much as ye might think otherwise."

Aluriel extended her hand, palm up, showing him the webbing between her fingers clearly, which only reached about two thirds of the length. "They're not fully developed," she said, with an edge of apology in her voice. "And my gills... they're underdeveloped too, as I was saying before."

*Not enough of a high elf to cast their magics... not enough of a sea elf to live with them beneath the waves... Is there somewhere for me to go?*

Ian nodded, his gaze lingering on her features. "Must feel like hell thinkin' o' the desert ahead."

Her lips pressed into a thin line, and she glanced down at the waterskin in her lap. "Yep. It does. The thought terrifies me, honestly. I don't know how I'll manage. I was hoping the Sunless Depths might be an alternative, but..."

Ian's face darkened, betraying the same dread that he had not concealed when he spoke of them before, and he shook his head, firm and solemn. "The Sunless Depths arenae salvation, lass. Water there's as scarce as it is foul. An' fit ye do find'll likely poison ye quicker than it'll quench ye." He sighed, then shrugged again, as if to shake the thought off him. "Stick tae the desert. At least there, the sun'll light yer path, the moons'll guide our nights, an' the barbarians... well now, they're better than the dark elves, that's fer sure. Ruthless warriors, aye, but honour-bound. An' their laws, strange as those may be, they do respect them. Meistly."

She exhaled heavily, her shoulders slumping. "The desert it is, then," she murmured. Her voice carried a note of resignation.

Ian studied her for a moment longer before his usual gruff humour resurfaced. "Well, if ye cannae handle the desert, ye'll fit right in wi' the gnomes at Steelforge. They're wee water drinkers too, y'ken. Always takin' baths tae keep their wee gadgets clean."

Aluriel could not help but chuckle. "You think I'd fit in with the gnomes?" she asked, giggling. "And surely you jest about the water?"

"Firewater, lass. Still water. Fit's left o' it after they distil it, anyhoo," Ian said, grinning. "Yer half elf, half fish. Ye'll dae just fine wi' the half-men. An' fit I said aboot them bathin', that's nae jest, ye ken? Their doctors, the necromancers, insist on sanitation and hygiene. At least they smell a sight better than dwarves."

She rolled her eyes but couldn't help her giggles turning into a full laugh. For a moment, the heaviness in her chest lightened, as she muttered something about needing a whole gnomish swimming pool just to stretch her legs. They both erupted in laughter.

Later, as the fire burned low, Aluriel lay on her bedroll, wrapped in her cloak, gazing through the tent's window, fixed on the star-speckled night sky. She drifted to sleep slowly, her mind heavy with questions she dared not voice.

And then the whispers in her dreams began yet again.

Faint at first, like the rustle of leaves, then growing louder, more insistent, until they formed a pattern, a rhythm that made her breath hitch. The voice felt familiar yet foreign, like a part of her she'd forgotten... or something waiting to claim her. The butterflies came next, their wings iridescent and ghostly, swirling in the darkness of her dream. They moved in an intricate dance, converging into the same shimmering circle she saw every night, pulsating with an otherworldly light. The whispers continued, as haunting and melodic as they had ever been, the words incomprehensible yet friendly, laden with a weight that pressed against her very soul. She felt it, deep in her core, a pull she could not deny, a call she could not understand.

And then, within the circle of butterflies, something appeared. She could not make sense of what it was. It looked like a myriad of lines, drawn in pencil, with no apparent pattern, nothing familiar that she could discern.

She woke drenched in sweat with the usual panic, her heart pounding, her breath coming in short gasps. The fire had burned down to embers, casting a dim glow. Fearing that it would die, and with it so could the wards, Aluriel added more wet wood to it. To her surprise, Ian's magic lingered, and the wet logs caught fire as if they were bone dry. Aluriel sat for a moment next to the fire, hugging her knees, her mind racing.

*The whispers. The butterflies. The voice. Then, the circle. And now, she's... showing me something... Is it madness?* she thought bitterly. All the old tales of mages succumbing to it, of whispers that lured them into ruin, echoed in a relentless assault from within her own mind. She clenched her fists so hard her nails bit into her palms, hoping the pain would ground her against the fear that threatened to consume her. "I'm not mad," she whispered, though the words rang hollow.

*You're getting there,* her mind replied silently. She glanced towards the tent, where Ian was still sound asleep, snoring loudly and steadily. She could never tell him of the whispers. She knew she couldn't. He would pity her, or worse, he would look at her the way the others had: as if she were broken, cursed. She went back to the tent and lay back down, forcing her eyes shut, but sleep would not come. The whispers lingered, faint but persistent, their meaning just out of reach. Aluriel pressed her hands to her ears, desperate to block them out, but they slipped through as if her hands were nothing. *Perhaps they are like phantoms? Or maybe they are just in my mind?*

Either way, the whispers were something she could not banish, nor ignore. *The arrows will keep me safe. Two times twelve. Twenty-four in the quiver.* She counted them again, and then again. Eventually, exhaustion took over once more, and she fell asleep.

When morning broke and Ian eventually roused her, she rose with heavy eyes and a heavier heart, the rays of sunlight gave her a small reprieve from the chaos of her dreams. Whatever madness gripped her, she would face it alone. There was no other way.

# ✦ Interlude – The Hollow Monastery
✦

The table reeked of mould and spoiled beer. The kind brewed by monks long dead and long forgotten.

The dark elf necromancer with ginger hair and a buzz cut sat alone in the vaulted cellar of an abandoned monastery, elbows resting lightly on a granite table mottled with brown stains. He'd lit a single candle, a courtesy to his guest, a human who lacked the perfect darkvision of his kin. A coin pouch sat beside the flame. His staff, topped by the skull of a tiger, leaned against the table's edge.

The walls glimmered faintly with damp moss and decay. Far above, the moonlight struggled down through the trees and the small cracks in the stonework, spreading pale dots across the floor in a scattered, eerie mosaic.

Footsteps echoed. Measured, deliberate. Velvet-soft.

Darghul stepped into the gloomy cellar with the exaggerated grace of a Vashlin-trained mage. His robes, all silvers and deep violets, shimmered with protective enchantments. Embroidered runes spiralled across the hems. A small gold pin at his collar bore the sigil of the Vashlin Arcane Academy: the school of arcane magic within the Tower of Philosophy.

Or – at least – a flawless forgery of it.

He had similar forgeries, complete with matching outfits, of the Varthian Mages' Guild, Zahira's Guild of Alchemists, and other more obscure magical societies. He even had two more that mimicked extinct sects, which he kept for flair alone.

In the low light, though, none of that mattered. He let the mask slip. His smile was just a touch too sharp.

"You sent for me." His tone was clipped and urbane. "I had to cancel a healing rite in the next village. Poor dears are overrun with the pox."

The necromancer shrugged. "The pox can wait. You can go tomorrow and heal even more. Besides, that *pox* was your doing anyway."

Darghul chuckled. "If it were the real pox, I'd give them a wide berth and leave it to a priest."

The necromancer nodded. "But Illusionary pox? That, you can indeed cure." He tapped the table once. "Let's get to business, shall we?"

"Let's."

The necromancer rose. His ginger hair caught a flicker of moonlight. His robes were black, fashioned from fine embroidered spider silk. A thin cord of vertebrae looped at his waist like a rosary. Six golden skulls, delicately stitched, adorned each cuff.

"The morningstar is trapped," he said. "Not hidden. Not broken. *Trapped*. Inside the altar of that ruin they once called holy."

"The Cathedral?"

He nodded.

"The wards are ancient, the altar itself has been defiled, but the morningstar is trapped within..."

He sighed, slowly and wearily.

"And it *resists*."

"We sacrificed innocents. Even summoned demons to defile it. But it resists. Our master has a new plan."

He stepped closer, almost reverently, and tapped the table once. "Beneath those wards, it waits. It *sings*, Darghul."

"I've heard things sing when you're involved." Darghul folded his arms. "Usually, right before they scream."

"This is different." The necromancer leaned in, his voice betraying frustration. "It sings like a choir of angels, trapped in steel. If one of us tried to wield it, it would blast us. But it *wants* to be used. Aches to be wielded. But it won't yield. Not until we give it a reason."

"And the unseen hand approves?" Darghul suddenly tensed. "You told me we'd wait."

The necromancer gave a slow nod. "I spoke with him not long ago. He agrees. The relic must be defiled now. It cannot be used yet. Not until it's been defiled. We must offer it hope, and take it."

He opened a pouch and withdrew a potion. Its glass container, thick and heavy, was shaped like a child's skull. The lid was sealed with black wax.

Darghul's nose wrinkled, but he did not step back.

"You want me to bring them, then? The children of its creator?"

"Yes." the necromancer carefully set the potion on the table, beside the coin "The half-elf twins. You know who I mean."

"They may be foolhardy, but they are not stupid," Darghul muttered. "If they saw what the cathedral has become..."

"Then... *entice* them. Use the potion. Why do you think I brought it? For a master of illusion, slipping a drop in their drink should be child's play. So, feed them a tale. Something that'll make them bite the hook. You still frequent Berenovus's tavern, do you not?"

"I play the wise old mage most Thursdays." Darghul smirked. "A silver for fortunes. Two for blessings. A kiss on the ring, if they want it to *really* work."

"Then next time they pass through, sell them a quest," the necromancer said, voice low. "Make it local. Make it personal. Say villagers are vanishing, or a spirit sobbing beneath stone. Tell them your apprentice has gone to investigate and never returned. Whatever it takes to lure them to the cathedral. Let them walk right through its cursed doors of their own accord."

Darghul stroked his beard. "And if they don't bite?"

"Then we try again later." The necromancer took a breath, then raised one finger as a warning. "But not too often. We mustn't seem too eager. Curiosity will do the rest."

He stepped back into the deeper shadow.

"And Darghul... when they least expect it... capture them, and send word. I will perform the ritual sacrifice when the moons' alignment is right."

At the stairwell, he paused, just long enough to add: "The three bells must toll before the blood is spilled." Then he vanished into the night. The door closed behind him.

Darghul stood alone in the darkness for a while longer, eyeing the potion and the coin pouch the necromancer had left on the table before pocketing them. He flexed his fingers once, then climbed up towards the moonlight, smiling.

As long as the coin flowed plentiful, Darghul would serve *anyone*.

# Chapter 4 – The town at the edge of the desert

The transition from the lush forest to the desert was softened by an expanse of fertile grassland, a verdant patch between the two extremes. Aluriel and Ian stood at the edge, where the cool green of the forest faded into rolling plains of grass, dotted with grazing cattle and fields of hardy crops. Beyond that, the arid desert stretched endlessly, its dunes still too far to see, yet close enough to be felt.

In the distance, nestled against the vegetation of the desert's border, they could see a settlement. As they marched towards it, it came more and more into focus. Elven merchants came here to trade with the tribes fairly regularly. Aluriel had heard their tales and stories. Strange spices, stranger customs. But seeing it with her own eyes was different, in a way no mere tale could ever capture. Roughly constructed huts of wood and hardened clay stood clustered together, encircled by a sturdy palisade of sharpened stakes. Smoke curled from hearths and braziers, mingling with the scent of dry air, distant spices, and cool earth. Not yet scorched – far from it – but readying itself for the season to come.

"Och, that'll be their place, Al-Hadiqa, they call it." Ian pointed towards the settlement. "These folk dinnae take kindly tae most strangers oot there in the sands," he added, waving at the vast expanse looming ahead.

"But in their towns? If ye're civil, they'll be the same. Mostly."

Aluriel adjusted the strap of her pack, scanning the settlement with cautious curiosity. *Will they see me as a threat... or just another traveller?* She wondered. "They'll have supplies we need. And perhaps some answers."

They approached at a measured pace, so as to avoid alarming the guards stationed by the settlement's gates. The two men eyed them warily, their faces painted with streaks of ochre and charcoal, but they allowed Aluriel and Ian to pass with only a grunt and a gesture towards the village centre.

The settlement bustled with activity. Children darted between huts, laughing and screaming, whilst adults worked on tasks ranging from tanning hides to sharpening weapons. They were all rather short, even for human standards, but Ian had mentioned that about Barbarians at some point during the trek. In the heart of the village stood a hut larger than the rest, its entrance marked by bright, chaotic patterns painted onto stretched canvas. Smoke curled lazily from within, carrying a sweet, herbal scent that was the giveaway of alchemy.

"That'll be the alchemist." Ian pointed towards the tent, nodding. "They're the mages of the desert tribes. An' their priests, too. If it's potions or magics ye're after, they'll have 'em."

Aluriel turned to Ian as they neared the heart of the village. "We'll cover more ground if we split up." She gestured towards the market. "You'll see to the food and water?"

Ian nodded, adjusting his pack. "Aye, I'll see tae it. Ye deal wi' the alchemist, an' I'll see tae getting me armour fixed, too. Meet back here when ye're done."

With a parting nod, Aluriel headed for the alchemist's hut whilst Ian veered towards the bustling market. Her steps quickened with purpose as she parted the heavy curtain across the threshold. The hut's interior was dim, illuminated by the glow of dozens of bubbling vials and glass jars filled with strange, swirling substances. The air was thick with the tang of brewing concoctions. Each one was distinct, yet the blend of mingling fumes formed an overwhelming medley.

Behind a makeshift wooden counter cluttered with potions and powders, stood an elderly man. He greeted her in Common Tongue, in a warm and welcoming tone. "Ah, traveller, I am Hafez. What is your good name?" He was a man in his seventies with dark brown skin, his bald head gleaming faintly in the light of the bubbling vials around him. His white moustache and short, curly beard gave him an air of quiet wisdom. Despite his calm demeanour, a slight limp betrayed an old injury as he shifted his weight carefully, protecting his left leg. Yet there was a strange energy to him, an edge that came through in his darting eyes and the way his hands hovered over the vials as if one might blink, and they could start moving of their own accord.

"Aluriel. Of the Enchanted Forest."

"Ah, an elf. And yet, you do not look like a high elf. Not completely. Like in my dreams…" he trailed off, muttering the last sentence. "Ah, er, yes, but where were we?" he snapped abruptly. "I am Hafez, of the Guild of Alchemists."

He turned and stared at one of his concoctions before turning back towards Aluriel. "What brings you to Al-Hadiqa, the garden on the edge of the sands?"

Aluriel inclined her head politely. "I need healing potions." She hesitated. "And…" her voice lowered. "And something to aid with sleep." *Elven healing potions are the best, but the Guild of Alchemists' are a close second,* she thought. *Better stock up, if he has some for sale.*

Hafez's brows rose slightly at her mention of sleep, but he began rummaging through several vials from the shelves behind him. Eventually, he selected two small bottles, which he placed onto the counter. They were filled with red liquid. Almost ruby-red, yet with a faint orange tinge. They looked almost exactly like the potions Aeliana had packed for her, save for the warmer hue. "These will mend wounds quickly and efficiently." He handed them to her, even as his eyes were twitching and darting across the hut.

"As for sleep..."

His eyes darted to the entrance, then to Aluriel, then back to the entrance, then onto Aluriel again. Then he paused, staring at her intensely.

"Tell me, young one. Do you seek rest because of whispers?"

Aluriel stiffened, too afraid to speak. A long moment of silence passed. Then, Hafez's expression softened with understanding. He nodded slowly.

"Ah." he nodded to himself. "I see. They've unravelled me before, these whispers..." He paused, turned around to look behind his back, then turned towards Aluriel again.

"But they also stitched me back together. I wonder what they'll make of you..." he trailed off, taking a few limping steps around his hut that seemed aimless, before turning to a shelf and retrieving five vials of a shimmering blue liquid. Setting them gently before her, he leaned forward, his voice dropping to a near whisper. "These will silence the whispers and relieve the madness for a time, several hours, a day at most. Use them sparingly, for they are potent, and addictive. And do not fear the whispers: they are not your enemy. Not entirely. They are only... fragments. Yes, fragments of something greater. They unravel the mind, yes... but they also weave it anew." His eyes darted all over the room again before locking onto Aluriel's. "You'll see. And *see,* you will."

Aluriel's gaze remained locked onto the vials. "What do you mean?" *He's mad*, she thought, but she couldn't deny the truth in his words. The whispers had begun unravelling her too.

Hafez straightened, his sharp eyes narrowing slightly. "Not here, not now," he murmured. "The sands have ears, as does the market. But... do they listen? Do they know what we've done, what's yet to come?" He blinked rapidly, his gaze darting haphazardly before refocusing on Aluriel. Then, with a sudden clarity, he pushed the five blue potions towards her. "Ah, never mind. Where were we? Oh yes. Take these! They are freely given. One day, should I call upon you, I hope you will show me the same kindness."

Aluriel reached into her satchel, retrieving a few gold coins for the healing potions. She placed them on the counter, her fingers brushing one of the blue vials. "Why gift these to me? You don't even know me..." Her voice was barely audible.

Hafez smiled enigmatically. "Because I *know*. Because you will need them," he said simply. "And because I trust you will remember."

Aluriel offered a small, respectful bow to Hafez. "Thank you. "I won't forget this."

Hafez inclined his head. "Safe travels, Aluriel. The desert holds both trials and treasures. May you find your way through them."

He paused and remained silent whilst Aluriel said her goodbyes, but he did not seem to acknowledge them. Then, as she was about to cross the threshold, Hafez snapped out of his trance. "Oh, and one more thing: seek me out just after midnight, in my home. There are matters we should discuss." He gave Aluriel a description of his hut and directions to find it.

Meanwhile, Ian navigated the lively marketplace, his expression amiable despite the occasional puzzled look he received. The vendors, clad in loose robes and headscarves, called out their wares in a mix of Lughat al-Barbar and heavily accented Common Tongue. Stalls overflowed with baskets of dates, oranges, and other exotic fruits. Others offered fragrant spices, another stall dried meats. One sold large earthenware jugs filled with water; alongside lay empty waterskins ready to be filled.

Ian stopped by the vendor selling water, a burly man with a thick beard and a sun-weathered face. The man's sharp eyes flicked up and down the dwarf, assessing him with curiosity, as if trying to decipher whether the stout creature was a customer or some peculiar being who wandered through the desert. "Och, I'll need three of yer biggest jugs." Ian's dwarven accent was light.

The vendor squinted, tilting his head. "Three…?" he asked, glancing at the jugs, and dragging the word out with a slow, cautious curiosity that suggested he wasn't entirely sure Ian knew what he wanted.

"Aye, jugs! Water!" Ian pointed to the jugs, miming drinking.

"Ah! You want drink!" the vendor said, grinning. "Not three, one drink?"

Ian chuckled, shaking his head. "Naw, naw! Three jugs! Big jugs! Big as yer thick heid!" He gestured wildly with his hands, his frustration mounting as the vendor's expression remained blank. Nearby, a couple of younger men leaned against a cart, chuckling quietly as they watched the exchange.

The vendor frowned, glancing at a younger man nearby who muttered something in Lughat al-Barbar. After a pause, the merchant finally nodded, and brought out two jugs.

Ian groaned as the vendor handed him only two jugs, shrugging helplessly as if to say, 'This is what you get.' "Close 'nuff," Ian muttered under his breath, filling the waterskins and stashing them into his pack with an exaggerated care, his grumbling just audible enough to draw quiet laughs from the younger men nearby. *This'll be a lang day.* "How much?"

The vendor held up three fingers, and Ian sighed in relief, handing over the coins. At the next stall, a young woman with piercing dark eyes and a kind smile sold dried meats. Ian attempted to buy strips of goat jerky but quickly found himself wound up in the familiar pantomime of gestures. The woman laughed warmly, eventually understanding, and handed him a generous portion.

As Ian paid, she said something in Lughat al-Barbar that Ian did not catch. He grinned anyway and replied, "Aye, an' tae ye as well... fitiver ye just said!"

The woman laughed harder, and several nearby vendors joined in, the light-hearted mood spreading through the market. Ian chuckled as he walked on, rubbing the back of his neck. "Friendly folk," he muttered. "Even if they've nae idea fit I'm sayin'."

After leaving Hafez's hut, Aluriel wandered through the cattle market, scanning the pens of livestock. *A mount would make this journey bearable. Maybe even manageable,* she thought, her gaze settling on two giant goats, the kind bred for the desert and its surrounding lands. She had heard of them before, but never seen one up close. Their sturdy frames were somewhat smaller than a pony's, yet they were built for speed, their muscles honed for distance. Their thick, coarse coats gleamed in the winter light, and their sharp, fearless eyes followed her movements as she drew near, unflinching.

The merchant, a wiry man with a sun-weathered face and a bright green turban, stepped forward, greeting her in heavily accented Common Tongue. "Fine beast, strong and swift." Then, in Elvish, "Very good for travel. Very fast."

Aluriel inclined her head politely, answering in Elvish. "Do you speak this tongue?"

His response came swiftly in fluid Elvish. "Ah, yes. I speak it. Better than the Common Tongue. I have traded with elves for many years. My name is Qais. What is your good name?"

Aluriel felt relieved and smiled at him. "I'm Aluriel. A pleasure to meet you. These goats... how much for the pair, with saddles and saddlebags?"

Qais rubbed his chin, his expression calculating. "For you, traveller Elf, I offer a fair price. Fifty gold pieces for both, saddled and ready."

Aluriel smiled, her tone turning shrewd. She knew Barbarians haggled, from the Elven merchants' stories. "Fifty? These beasts are fine, but not worth that much." She gestured towards the other pens. "I see others of equal strength being sold for far less."

Qais chuckled, a glint of admiration in his eyes. "Ah, but those are not desert-bred, Al-Hadiqa goats. These here are resilient, used to the harsh sands. They can carry you far without tiring. Forty-five, then."

"Alright. Forty-five it is then."

Qais clasped her hand firmly, a wide smile breaking across his face. "You bargain well, traveller. I'll have them saddled and ready at once."

*Elves... They don't know how to haggle. I would've sold them for thirty,* Qais thought to himself, even as his lips sang praises of Aluriel's haggling skills.

Qais's helpers readied the goats, and Aluriel inspected the saddles and bags, admiring their quality. *Faster than horses, and smarter too, he'd said.* She ran her hand over one's thick coat, wondering if it was true, or merely a clever nudge to coax her into buying them. Their demeanour was calm yet alert, and they tracked her every movement with their piercing eyes. Giant goats were notoriously fearless. "You'll do well," she murmured. *Perhaps better than I will.*

Meanwhile, Ian made his way to the forge. The blacksmith's hut stood at the edge of the settlement, a high-roofed building with thick walls of baked clay and a chimney, tall enough to be seen from anywhere else in the village, if a dwarf looked high enough.

The rhythmic clang of hammer on metal met him as he approached. The blacksmith was a broad-shouldered man with weathered skin and a mane of black hair drawn back into a ponytail. He glanced up from his work as Ian entered. His dark eyes lingered first on the damaged pauldron Ian carried, then on the dented breastplate strapped across his torso.

Ian removed his breastplate and placed it with the pauldron on the counter. "Took a fair beatin', this," he said, tapping the metal. "D'ye reckon ye can fix it?"

The blacksmith frowned, concentrating on examining the armour. He picked up the pauldron, then the breastplate, turning them over in his hands, tracing each deep gash. When he finally spoke, it was brief, and in Lughat al-Barbar, the language every other villager here spoke. Ian did not understand a word.

"Och, nae much fer words, eh?" Ian muttered, then gestured to the armour. "Fix? Hammer? Aye?"

The blacksmith squinted at Ian, then nodded slowly. He pointed to his forge and gestured for Ian to follow. Together, they entered the heat of the smithy. The fire roared and tools hung from just about every surface. The blacksmith started to work, striking the armour with his hammer. But as he worked, Ian could see the man's frustration growing. The metal refused to cooperate. Ian had not expected a Barbarian smith to manage dwarven plate, much less enchanted plate as his was, but thought to let him try regardless, if only out of respect. That, and to allow the smith to think the inevitable segue was his own idea.

After several minutes, the blacksmith threw down his hammer with a curse. He turned to Ian, gesturing to the forge and shaking his head. Ian sighed, understanding the unspoken message he had waited for all along.

"Aye, alright. Let me have a go," Ian said, stepping forward. He glanced around the smithy, noting the tools and the glowing embers of the forge. He flexed his hands. The faint hum of fire magic stirred, ready to respond. He could not risk being discovered, not here. Carefully, he picked up the pauldron and a hammer, feigning the motions of a seasoned smith.

With his back to the blacksmith, Ian focused on the damaged metal. As he hammered, he let a small, controlled burst of fire magic flow into the forge, heating the metal just enough to make it pliable, far hotter than a Barbarian's forge could ever muster. He disguised the flickers of flame as stray sparks from the anvil, with precise and deliberate control of his motions and his magic.

The blacksmith watched in silence, observing carefully as Ian worked. Slowly but surely, the gashes in the pauldron began to smooth out, and the metal regained its shape. Ian kept his breathing steady and his focus unwavering as he finished the repairs. When he was done, he held up the pauldron, inspecting his work.

"There," Ian said, placing it on a table nearby to let the metal cool. "Good as new," he muttered to himself. He then turned to his breastplate and began to work on it in much the same fashion.

Once Ian was finished, the blacksmith studied the pieces, and his expression shifted to one of grudging admiration. He nodded, then patted Ian on the shoulder. His stern features broke into a smile as he said something in an admiring tone that Ian did not understand. Ian chuckled, rubbing the back of his neck. "Aye, dinnae thank me too much. Was yer forge an' hammer did the trick."

The blacksmith replied something in his own tongue, in a respectful tone. He gestured to a small rack of freshly forged blades, inviting the dwarf to choose. Ian picked a short, sturdy dagger, its hilt wrapped in leather. *This might come in handy fer Aluriel,* he thought. The blacksmith nodded approvingly.

"Much obliged," Ian said, tucking the dagger into his belt and paying some coins to the blacksmith, after another round of wordless haggling. As he left the smithy, he could not help but grin. *Friendly enough, even if we dinnae share words. A good day's work, I'd say.*

As the sun sank behind the western treetops, Aluriel watched what she knew would be her final glimpse of the sunset over the Enchanted Forest as the sky bathed it all in a beautiful, golden-pink glow. Eventually, after the sun had fully set and the stars glimmered brightly in the sky, the market began to quiet. Aluriel and Ian made their way to a large communal fire pit and joined a group of villagers.

They drank imported elven wine and locally brewed beer from rough-hewn wooden cups. The warmth of the flames and the friendliness of the barbarians made the long journey feel momentarily lighter.

"Good people," Ian said with a grin, raising his cup to a cheer from the group. His attempts at mimicking their Lughat al-Barbar greetings had drawn laughter and warm smiles from the villagers, despite his thick Dwarven accent muddling the words.

Aluriel chuckled softly, watching Ian's animated exchanges with the barbarians. She sipped her beer, savouring its salty, smoky flavour. For the first time since the swim in the brook, she allowed herself to relax, even if only for a moment. Watching the forest for the last time carried a note of sadness. But she had left it already, and now the only path was forward.

As the villagers began to retire to their huts for the night, Aluriel and Ian returned to their rented quarters, a simple but sturdy hut with a thatched roof and a hearth that provided a welcome reprieve from the chill of the desert evening. Ian stretched out on the straw mattress with a contented sigh, and began to snore almost immediately. Aluriel, however, remained restless. The whispers at the edges of her mind felt louder in the twilight, and the deepening silence of the night only fuelled her ruminations. She looked at the stars now and then, waiting for midnight, and her thoughts were pulled back to Hafez's cryptic words. Once the time was right, she steeled herself, took a deep breath and slipped out of the hut, inhaling the cool night air.

Hafez's home was easy to find, a faint light still aglow within. She pushed aside the canvas flap and stepped inside. The alchemist was seated at a low table, and his sharp eyes lifted to meet hers. Several shelves – cluttered yet functional – lined the hut, stacked with vials that glowed faintly and herbs that hung in fragrant clusters. It felt like a sanctuary teetering between order and chaos, much like the man himself.

"You came," he said softly, motioning for her to sit. "Good." He appeared much more collected than when they met earlier, if still somewhat odd. *Maybe he self-medicated with some of his potions...*

Aluriel hesitated before lowering herself onto a cushion opposite him. "You said there was more to discuss."

Hafez nodded, his expression growing thoughtful. "Our meeting was not by chance." He stood abruptly, peered outside his hut, then returned to his seat. "No one followed you. Good. I saw you in a dream, long before today. The Lady of Twilight... She speaks to me as well, though her whispers are faint and fleeting." He lifted his gaze and stared at the ceiling, tapping his fingers before continuing. "In that dream, she showed me your face and said only this: *'Help her.'*"

*Why me?* Aluriel thought, her pulse quickening. *Of all people, why would She choose someone like me?* The idea unnerved her... and yet it stirred something else. Her ever-flickering doubts mingled with the faintest stirrings of purpose.

"You hear Her too?" she asked quietly.

"Not as often as you, I suspect," Hafez replied. "But yes. Her voice has grown clearer with time. You should not fear her, though I understand why you might. She is not your enemy. Not entirely..." His gaze sharpened slightly. "You wield magic, don't you?"

Aluriel shook her head. "Not really. I've not been able to... except once. It was unintentional. I was so angry, and then... lightning struck. White-hot, searing lightning." *I've never understood it,* she admitted silently. *Was it truly my magic? Or just some freak occurrence?* The memory of that moment still burned vividly in her mind, terrifying as ever. But now, sitting in Hafez's hut, it also felt liberating. Exhilarating, almost.

Hafez leaned back, his eyes narrowing thoughtfully. "Interesting. May I?" He extended a hand, faint wisps of mist trailing from his fingertips.

After a moment's hesitation, Aluriel nodded. Hafez's magic brushed against her gently, warm and searching. He blinked several times as he withdrew, as if digesting something unexpected.

"Fascinating," he murmured. "Wait here." Hafez rose and moved to a nearby cabinet, retrieving a deck of intricately engraved cards. He returned to his seat, shuffling them quickly. He handed them to Aluriel. "Shuffle them," he said. "Before you leave Al-Hadiqa, I would like to read your Tarot. Dreams and whispers only reveal so much. The cards may offer more clarity. If there is such a thing as clarity. But yes, clarity can come in a bottle, if the whispers are clear enough. Let's see what the cards have to say."

He moved with a calm precision that hadn't been there earlier. She noticed a half-empty vial on his table, identical to those he had gifted her earlier. *So I was right, I guess. He's been self medicating.* As if reading her thoughts, Hafez took the vial to his lips and drank the rest of the liquid, muttering, "Enough to dampen the storm, but not to silence it."

Aluriel hesitated, her curiosity piqued. "Tarot? Cards? What will they tell me?"

Hafez smiled enigmatically. "The cards do not lie, but their truths are layered. They reveal paths, choices, and warnings. Shall we?"

Aluriel nodded, curiosity nudging hesitation aside. "Go on."

Aluriel shuffled the cards, then passed the deck back to Hafez, who shuffled it again with fluid movements and asked Aluriel to cut it. He then laid out three cards in a neat line on the low table, each one illustrated with vivid, intricate designs. *What could they show, really?* Aluriel wondered, her eyes fixed on his movements. *Answers? Or just more questions?* His eyes lingered on each card as he turned them over. His expression grew more intrigued with every reveal.

"The first card," he said, pointing to a figure engulfed in flames, "represents your current state. The Burning Soul. It speaks of suppressed power, turmoil, and an untapped well of potential." He then began tapping the table with one finger, rhythmically. Tap, tap, pause, tap. Tap, tap, pause, tap. Then he muttered to himself, "I don't often draw the Burning Soul at night. Makes one wonder…"

He turned to the second card, a towering mountain illuminated by lightning. "The Storm's Ascent," he murmured. "This is your path: a journey of hardship and discovery, but also one of growth. You will be tested, yet you have the strength to endure. To climb, despite adversity."

At last, he revealed the third card, a phoenix rising from ash. "The Rebirth," Hafez said, his voice now frankly reverent. Aluriel's breath caught. Her eyes locked on the fiery bird. *The phoenix… is this truly my destiny? To rise above everything that's tried to destroy me?* Doubt clawed at her thoughts, the weight of her failures pressing against the fragile hope the card ignited. *I've been cast out, shunned, humiliated. How could someone like me rise? And yet… if I don't try, then what am I left with?* The image on the card seemed to glow faintly in her mind, its fiery wings promising a challenge she wasn't sure she could accept. Yet there, beneath the uncertainty, a flicker of defiance sparked. *Maybe*, she thought, *maybe I can.*

As if sensing her inner storm of thoughts, Hafez took Aluriel's hand, to ground her in the moment. Then, he spoke. "This is your destiny. You are meant to transform, to rise far above the limitations that bind you. Your potential is vast. Enormous, even. But only if you embrace what lies ahead."

The cards laid bare her fears and her hopes, but it was the phoenix that struck her deepest chord. Was she truly capable of rising from the ashes of her mistakes, of her failures? Aluriel stared at the cards, her breath shallow. "And if I fail?"

Hafez's gaze softened. "The cards do not predict failure, only possibilities. The path is yours to walk, the choices yours to make. But know this: you are capable of more than you believe. Your potential is *vast*," he repeated, his voice tinged with awe and wonder. "But something holds it dormant. Unlocking it will take time and effort. And *blood*." He stood abruptly and wandered to an empty spot in his hut, staring at the wall as though expecting it to speak. His voice dropped to a near whisper, too faint for Aluriel to make out, "Blood and Mist... Why did She show me..."

Then, as if nothing had happened, he regained his composure and turned to address her once more. "I suggest you seek the gnomes for training. They are skilled in lightning magic, and their methods may help you channel your power."

He then reached behind him and produced a rather large flask of a swirling purple-black potion, placing it gently in front of her. "This is for you. I will not say what it will do, only that when the time comes, you will know to use it."

Aluriel stared at the vial, her mind racing. "Why give me this?"

Hafez handed her the flask, his lips twitching in what might have been a smile... or a grimace. "Because this will be... necessary. Yes, necessary. But only when the time is right. Do not let the wrong hands touch it. Do not ever do that. They might..." he muttered, his gaze distant before snapping back to Aluriel with a sharp smile. "Ah, but I trust you'll keep it safe. I trust you will use it wisely. And because, like I said before, one day I may ask for your kindness in return."

She nodded, carefully tucking the vial into her satchel. "Thank you."

"Go now. Rest. The journey ahead will test you, in ways you cannot yet imagine."

As she stepped back into the cool night air, the weight of the potion in her satchel felt heavier than it should have. "When the time comes," Hafez had said. But would she be ready when it did? His words struck a chord she could not ignore. *Was it madness that gave him such clarity? Or was it something else entirely?*

She did not hear Hafez mutter to himself, almost inaudibly, "The wrong hands... they might... they might unravel everything... They might *unravel **you**...*"

# Chapter 5 – Kharesh

The morning sun rose over the barbarian settlement of Al-Hadiqa, its golden rays casting long shadows across the fertile grasslands. The village was alive with the sounds of a new day. Roosters crowed, goats bleated, and early risers had begun chattering at the market stalls since well before dawn. The scent of baking bread and roasting coffee mingled with the earthy aroma of damp soil, creating an atmosphere, even in the early hours, as bustling as it was serene. Smoke curled lazily from the communal fire pits, whilst goats, chickens, and even a few shaggy desert horses moved about, tended by children and elders alike. Ian was already on his feet, but chose to let Aluriel rest as she was fast asleep. She'd cried out during her dreams again, waking him briefly with a scream. He pretended not to notice, but concern lingered in his mind. He felt protective of her, wanted to offer comfort, but knew instinctively that any questions would only push her away. Aeliana had told him, her voice quivering with worry, about her daughter's nightmares and whispers, and Ian knew what those whispers meant: the beginning of a slow, devouring madness. Though the whispers were most often heard among elven ones, some mages of other races claimed to hear this would-be goddess as well. Unlike elves, who were somewhat resilient and could withstand the whispers for centuries before eventually succumbing to the madness, others would slip into madness in a matter of decades, or even years. *I hope this lass is as sturdy as her mither,* Ian thought as he left their rented quarters and set out to explore the settlement. His belly rumbled, aching for breakfast.

Aluriel slept through until the late morning. Unsettled by the encounters with Hafez, she had tried to get to sleep and, as usual, the whispers and the butterflies returned. This time, in the midst of the circle, a vision of the potion Hafez had given her briefly appeared, and with it came words that felt both soothing and unsettling at the same time, yet, as always, beyond comprehension. Waking up, drenched in sweat as always, she checked her pack to see if the potion was still there. It was. Its purple swirls were dancing within the black liquid, and she briefly wondered whether to drink it. She uncorked it, pressed it to her lips, and tried to sip. But no liquid flowed. The purple-black substance continued to swirl within, oblivious to gravity, even as Aluriel attempted to pour it in her mouth, tilting the flask. She recorked it and put it back in her pack. *Hafez said that when the time came to use it, I would know for sure. So best to avoid more experiments and save it for now,* she concluded, and lay down to sleep again. This time, as though the whispers had done their job for the night, they left her in peace, and Aluriel fell into a deep, dreamless slumber.

The palisade of sharpened stakes that encircled the settlement was as much a defence against invaders as a deterrent to wandering predatory beasts. Beyond it, small fields of hardy crops stretched outward, watered by a clever irrigation system fed from an underground spring. Ian marvelled at the ingenuity, lingering on its simple yet efficient design, which reminded him somewhat of the wonders of gnomish engineering. For all their rough appearance, they were clearly adept at surviving in these lands.

After exploring a short while, Ian managed to find a stall selling sweet breakfast fare. With gestures, nods, and a bit of coin, he exchanged mutually unintelligible words, and procured several freshly baked, still-warm honeyed flatbreads, wrapping them carefully before heading back to their hut. When he arrived, Aluriel was still fast asleep. He hesitated at the door, almost feeling guilty at the thought of waking her, but the day ahead demanded it. Kneeling beside her, he gently shook her shoulder. "Lass," he said softly, "rise an' shine. I hate tae wake ye, but we've got tae get movin'."

Aluriel woke with a groan, brushing her silvery white hair out of her face as her eyes adjusted to the morning light. Despite her initial reluctance, she realised she felt more refreshed than she had been on any morning since the exile. "What time is it?" she mumbled groggily.

"Late 'nuff," Ian replied with a small grin, holding out the honeyed flatbreads. "Figured ye might be hungry."

She took them gratefully and began eating the sweet, sticky bread. "This is good," she said between bites. "Quite a treat. Thanks!"

Once she had finished, Aluriel quickly packed her things. Together, they made their way to the stables, where their giant goats waited. As they began loading the saddlebags, Ian handed her a waterskin. "Dinnae forget tae drink, lass. Ye've been emptyin' these faster than I've seen a party o' dwarves drain a keg o'ale."

Aluriel took the waterskin with a small nod. "It's this... dry air," she replied, her voice dry, as she drained half the contents in one go. "We need to ration carefully, or I'll be drinking the desert dry."

Despite her attempt at humour, a knot of unease settled in her chest. She couldn't shake the thought of running out of water in the unforgiving desert ahead. *What if there isn't enough? What if I can't keep going?* The questions spiralled in her mind, but she forced herself to focus on the task at hand. They had prepared well, hadn't they? The goats were strong, the saddlebags full of waterskins. Still, doubt clung like a shadow at the edge of her thoughts. After a few final purchases and some good-natured bargaining in the market, with waterskins filled and enough food to last them until the next settlement, the pair mounted their goats and set off. The villagers waved them off warmly, in a final reminder of the unexpected kindness they'd found in this strange town.

The first day of travel passed uneventfully. The goats strode fast, far faster than a horse, and Aluriel wondered just how fast they could go on Varthia's paved roads. The terrain transitioned from grasslands to rockier foothills and then to sand as they moved closer to the desert's heart. The ride gave them ample time for conversation, and Ian, as always, filled the silence with his humour.

"Ye ken, these goats," Ian muttered, giving his mount a fond slap on the flank, "smarter than some dwarves I've served wi'. Though I'll grant ye, that's nae a steep hill tae climb, mind."

Aluriel arched a brow. "Smarter than their rider, you mean?"

"Oof!" Ian clutched his chest in mock pain. "Right in the pride. Ye wound me, lass."

She let out a small laugh as the desert wind ruffled her hair. "You'll live. The goat might be carrying the brains, but you've still got the beard."

"An' the charm," Ian added, straightening up proudly. "Let's nae forget that. Handsome devil, me. Smarter than most, prettier than some, and blessed wi' a goat that listens better than half the council back home."

Aluriel snorted. "You do realise I'm part high elf, part sea elf? One hundred percent freak. Makes me everyone's favourite mistake. Hard to beat that in a beauty contest!" She erupted in a laugh.

"Aye, but you're the exception tae a lot o' things," Ian said, more softly now, his gaze drifting forward. "Rules were made for folk like ye tae break."

She did not answer right away. The horizon ahead shimmered. The sands surrounded them in every direction. Her laughter slipped away, replaced once more by the weight of the journey they would endure.

"Ian," she began hesitantly, her tone more serious, "what more do you know about Varthia? About what we'll face there?"

Ian's smile faded slightly, though his tone remained steady. "Varthia's a harsh place, lass. Rigid an' unyieldin', much like its rulers an' the army. The laws there are as unkind as the desert. Ye ken already aboot them gallows. As fer their priests... well, let's just say they dinnae ken mercy, either.

But nae all Varthians are the same. Many o' the common folk – the folk who were there 'afore the Varthians invaded and took the lands from 'em – follow the Merry Gentleman, the god o' wine, mischief, and fun, an' they are tryin' tae survive under the Empire's iron grip. There's even pockets o' resistance growin', fit with the Varthian army bein' busy, stretched thin fightin' the Eastern empire... Ye ken, the place where Varthians first came from? So aye, the resistance is risin', though they've got tae tread carefully."

Aluriel shivered. "And Vashlin? Is it better?"

"Better? Aye. Better than Varthia, fer sure. Better than other places... Depends on fit ye value, really. Vashlin's a place o' scholars an' seekers. Its libraries an' arcane workshops are second tae none, an' it's friendly tae outsiders, seein' as most folk there came from somewhere else. Ye'll find all sorts of races, an' they manage tae coexist. Even the faeries an' the pixies share a patch o' woodland. A fair sight mair welcomin' than Varthia, that's fer sure. If it's lightnin' magic yer after, their mages are among the best. Aside from the gnomes o' Steelforge, maybe."

Aluriel nodded, digesting his words. "Do you think..." Her gaze drifted to the horizon. "Do you think I can do it?"

"I think ye've got more strength in ye than ye realise, Aluriel. Ye just need tae trust yersel'." Aluriel wished she could believe that she could trust herself, but a glimmer of possibility had begun to float within her. *What if Hafez was right, and this journey is meant to make me stronger?*

She looked away, her chest tightening with a mix of gratitude and doubt. *Trust myself*, she thought. *Easier said than done.*

The goats proved resilient and obedient mounts, and easily carried them across the endless sands. By the time the sun dipped below the horizon, painting the sky in hues of red and orange, they rode some more, then found a sheltered spot to pitch their tent. With the saddlebags stuffed with as much water as they could hold, there was no room for firewood. This meant no campfire, and no protective wards.

They decided to sleep in shifts. Ian would keep watch first. Aluriel lay awake in her tent, her thoughts restless as always. The desert air was cool, and the whispers of the Lady of Twilight seemed louder in the stillness. *They're always louder at night. Maybe She's more awake? Maybe there's less distraction? Does night and day even matter to a Goddess?* She closed her eyes and tried to focus on the rhythmic breathing of the goats. Yet, her mind kept returning to the waterskin at her side. She had already drunk more than her share that day, and guilt gnawed at her. *What if it's not enough?* she wondered. *Will Ian resent me if I keep drinking more than my share?*

The next three days passed in relative calm. By day, they rode north-east. The sands stretched in every direction as far as the eye could see. Ian kept the mood light with stories from Steelforge, and Aluriel listened more than she spoke, letting his voice distract her from the whispers that haunted her day and night. As always, the usual nightmare came whenever she slept, and she could not shake her growing worry about how much water she was drinking. The goats proved as sturdy as promised, forging ahead without complaint. They made good progress, even if each night brought little rest. Yet even that routine felt like thin, cold comfort.

On the fourth night, having pitched their tent again under the stars, deep in the Desert's heart, Ian took first watch. Surprisingly quickly, she managed to fall asleep. No sooner had she drifted into a fitful sleep – not even long enough for her usual nightmare – than the attack began. Battle cries split the air. Shadows loomed over the tent. Aluriel barely registered the sounds before a net was thrown over her, pinning her arms to her sides, and three strong pairs of hands began to tie her up.

Outside, Ian's furious shouting filled the air. The clash of steel and heavy grunts pierced the silence of the night. For a moment, hope flickered in Aluriel's chest: Ian was fighting back.

But it was brief. His roars of defiance turned to sharp cries of pain, and then silence. Heavy footsteps and murmurs in a harsh, guttural tongue drew closer. Aluriel's heart sank as she realised Ian, too, had been overpowered. The attackers took their goats and their packs. They quickly dismantled their tent and took it with the rest.

Soon enough, Aluriel found herself bound, arms locked onto her chest, and gagged, slumped uncomfortably across the back of a camel. Ian had been knocked unconscious, bound and gagged on the back of another camel. A frustrated-looking raider paid just enough attention to keep him from falling. Their kidnappers had tied them securely, and even as Aluriel struggled against her bindings to try and fall off the camel, she could not manage to do so. For quite some time – maybe an hour, maybe three – they jolted along the sands, the desert stretching endlessly around them, until the flickering glow of an encampment came into view. The camp, nestled among jagged rocks, was a chaotic sprawl of tents and campfires. The chieftain, towering for his people's measure, with scarred skin and a braided beard, introduced himself as Kharesh once they were roughly hauled from the camels and thrown to the ground. His voice was harsh, his words cruel as he addressed his captives.

"Who are you?" Kharesh barked, his gaze flicking between them. "Merchants? Soldiers? Speak!"

Aluriel glared at him and rose onto her feet. Though Kharesh was imposing by barbarian standards, she stood much taller still, a fact she clearly knew. A fact that made her hold his gaze unflinchingly, defiantly, even as her bindings bit into her wrists. Ian remained unconscious, just beginning to stir, mumbling incomprehensible sounds.

One of the pillagers gestured towards Ian's armour and hammer. "This one's gear is worth a fortune," he said in Lughat al-Barbar. "Maybe a knight or a lord. Could fetch a hefty ransom."

Kharesh's gaze lingered on Ian. He crouched beside him, narrowing his eyes as he studied the runes etched into the metal. "A knight or a lord, perhaps..." he muttered in a calculating tone. He leaned closer, and his sneer thinned into a glint of recognition. "No... a priest of Fire."

He straightened and barked orders to his men. "Gag him well. Bind his hands with adamantine cuffs. He'll not be casting spells with those on. His gear is worth a fortune, but the man himself... he might fetch even more, if we play this right. As for you, pretty girl..." He turned towards Aluriel. "What are you doing, travelling through the desert with that dwarf?"

Aluriel tried to speak again, then pointed at her gag. One of the raiders removed it. "I am Aluriel, daughter of Aeliana, the Grand Druidess!" she snapped, her tone feigning authority, projecting an air of *lèse-majesté*. "Release us immediately! If you do not, there will be consequences. My kin, the forest Elves, will not ignore this!"

The barbarians paused, exchanging sceptical looks. Their fear was palpable despite their mocking words that followed.

One of them laughed nervously, pointing at her. "This? A Grand Druidess' daughter? She's a sea elf, nothin' more, probably a servant. If she had elven magic, she would've used it by now."

Yet, their sidelong glances betrayed their unease. Elemental mages were rare and deeply feared, and none of them dared to approach too closely, as though mere proximity to Aluriel might spell their doom, should she invoke a deadly outburst of power.

Kharesh approached her, looking up to meet her gaze. "A sea elf servant, perhaps," he mused, his tone dripping with disdain. "What is your business with that dwarf, girl? His slave, are you?"

Aluriel's blood boiled at his words, but her further protests were ignored. Kharesh stood and barked orders to his men. "Take the dwarf to the cages, keep him bound and gagged. We'll deal with him later. As for this one..."

Kharesh strode forward and shoved her to the ground, flat onto her back. He then crouched to her level, and softened his tone. "Now, young sea elf, you must understand... fate has brought you here," he began, his voice slick with feigned charm. "You see, I am Kharesh, victor of the Bloodsands, conqueror of six tribes, Khan of the southwestern sands. Perhaps you've heard of me?"

Aluriel spat on the ground and glared at him. "Your name means nothing to me."

Kharesh's smile tightened, but he pressed on, his voice even more honeyed. "You're spirited; I like that. It will make your surrender all the more rewarding. But why must we quarrel? You're beautiful. Clever even. Together, we could rule the sands."

Aluriel's jaw clenched as she forced herself to stay composed. "You flatter yourself," she said coldly. "I'd sooner see you rot in the desert than share anything with you."

The barbarians murmured among themselves, some stifling laughter at their chieftain's obvious irritation. Kharesh's face darkened as the last of his charm gave way to frustration. "Perhaps you misunderstand your position. Do you think you have the luxury of refusal? Look around, little elf. You are alone, powerless. It would be wise to accept the kindness I'm still willing to offer."

"Kindness?" Aluriel scoffed, her defiance unwavering despite the fear that rippled through her like a whisper, sharp and cold. "You don't know the meaning of the word."

Kharesh's face darkened further, his pride clearly wounded by her words. Without a further word towards Aluriel, he barked orders at his men. Moments later, Aluriel found herself hauled to her feet and dragged to a sturdy wooden post at the centre of the tent. The raiders made her kneel. Tied her tightly. The rough ropes bit into her wrists at every struggle. Her heart pounded as she watched Kharesh pick up a whip. Its leather strands looked heavy and menacing.

"You think your words can wound me?" he growled, circling her slowly, caressing the whip in his hands.

"Let me teach you..."

He kept circling.

"The consequences of insolence."

The first strike lashed across her back. Pain bloomed like fire on her skin. Her spine arched from the force. Aluriel clenched her teeth, refusing to cry out. Each lash landed harder than the last. Her body seared in agony, yet she kept defiantly silent. She glared at anyone who met her gaze with burning hatred. *I won't give him the satisfaction.*

Kharesh sneered between blows. All traces of his previous feigned charm had vanished. His tone dripped venom with each word. "You will learn obedience, little sea elf. You'll beg for my mercy before long."

Kharesh's sneer vanished entirely, his wounded pride now palpable. He lashed Aluriel with increasing fury, but her silence and defiance only seemed to stoke his frustration. Finally, his anger boiled over. He stood towering over her, but only because she had been forced to kneel. Barking at his men, he snarled, "Gag her again!"

The pillagers hurried to obey, forcing the gag back into Aluriel's mouth, despite her attempts to twist and buck away. Kharesh waited, his gaze cold and calculating as the tent quieted. Once the gag was secure, he turned to his men. "Leave us," he commanded. "Except for you two." He pointed at two of his most trusted warriors. "Hold her down, and make sure the gag doesn't fall off. She kept silent through the whipping? I'll deny her the screams she'll soon beg for."

The pillagers hesitated for a moment, exchanging glances, but none dared to question him. Without another word, they scurried from the tent, leaving Kharesh alone with his captive, save for the two who were holding her down. A cruel smile spread across his face as he began to disrobe, his movements slow, deliberate, and dripping with arrogance.

Aluriel saw his manhood swell. His arousal was as plain as it was sickening. He clearly savoured the anticipation of what he was about to do. He stepped towards Aluriel, reaching down to grasp the neckline of her tunic, and tore the fabric quickly, ripping it clean down the front with his bare hands.

"You'll learn to submit," he murmured threateningly. "One way or another." He slowly placed himself on top of her and pried her legs open, his manhood poised to violate her. She squeezed her eyes shut, memories of past humiliations flooding back. The whispers in her mind now roared like a storm. *I can't... I won't let him... I won't...* Her heart pounding, she felt something raw and powerful coil in her chest, a crackling tingle of rage coursing all over her...

Suddenly, it was too late.

Aluriel's terror, stoked by his arrogance.

The searing pain of the whipping still burning across her back.

The sheer panic of Kharesh about to rape her.

It all boiled over, and with it came the searing heat of her untamed power. Her fear twisted into fury, a white-hot rage that surged through her blood like a coiled lightning.

The whispers in her mind turned louder.

They were now deafening screams.

And then the world exploded with thunder.

A crackling bolt of lightning erupted from her and struck Kharesh squarely in the chest. The sheer force of it flung him outside the tent. Before the two barbarians who were holding her down could even scream, the lightning struck them both and they collapsed. Smoke curled from their lifeless, charred bodies. The lightning did not stop there: quicker than the blink of an eye it arched outward, leaping to the guards stationed outside the tent. One by one, they were struck down in the same instant, their cries of shock and pain silenced almost instantly as the searing energy coursed through them and turned their bodies into burning, lifeless husks.

The force of the lightning set the tent ablaze, flames licking through the fabric and casting eerie, flickering shadows over the chaos. The lightning seared through her bindings, incinerating the ropes that were holding her wrists. Aluriel swayed on her feet, electricity still arcing along her arms. Smoke clung to her hair and the taste of burned flesh filled her mouth. She walked outside and blinked, trying to see through the swirling dust. Many bodies littered the ground, charred and motionless.

*What have I done...?*

She forced the thought aside. *I had no choice,* she told herself silently, though her stomach churned at the sight. Only then did she tug her gag free, as though just now remembering it was still there. Her chest heaved as she surveyed the destruction she had unleashed. *Did I really just do this again? And this time... killed them? What if I'd killed Elenwen...* For an instant, she imagined it. But this was not the time to think too long. Not the time to spiral.

The camp had fallen silent. The remaining dozens of pillagers stared at her in stunned terror. Aluriel, still unsteady on her feet, arcs of lightning dancing along her arms, towered over the stunned raiders. Ozone, burnt flesh, and smouldering canvas filled the air with acrid fumes.

To the raiders, the scene before them was a nightmare realised. They had just kidnapped... **an Elemental Mage!** Legends spoke of their ability to summon storms and raze entire camps to ash. Their superstitions painted them as avatars of wrath, wielding powers beyond mortal comprehension. Though her legs trembled, she stood unfazed, unashamed of her own nudity.

Aluriel lowered her chin and fixed the group with a piercing glare, fully aware of their terror.

"Would anyone else like to test me?" she snarled. Her voice was cold. Commanding. *I can't do that again,* she thought. Her heart was beating like a thunderstorm in her chest, but the terror in their faces gave her the energy to continue. "To rape me, perhaps? Like that pig you called your chieftain tried?" The arcs of electricity dancing around her fingertips were proof enough to them, and whilst she knew it was unintentional, they did not. *They don't need to know I can't control it.* The moment that thought struck her, Aluriel straightened further, forcing herself to appear unyielding, to steady her voice and make it as menacing as possible despite her inner turmoil. *If they fear me now, then I'll give them cause to fear me even more. I will make sure that fear stays with them forever.*

"All of you vermin, come at me! Make my day easier: charge together! Let the Gods witness how I'll fry you all at once, and spare me the trouble of hunting you down one by one!" she shouted, taunting them further.

The pillagers exchanged nervous glances. Some understood her words, and quickly translated for the rest. None dared to accept her challenge. They fell back in a scramble, their faces pale, weapons falling on the sand from trembling hands. "She is a Storm Bringer!" one whispered in Lughat al-Barbar. She did not understand the words, but the terror in his eyes was unmistakeable.

She stepped forward, her voice unwavering despite her legs barely keeping her upright.

"Release my companion. Return our belongings," she commanded.

"As reparation," she continued, "I'll be taking your chieftain's riding goat, your water, your gold, and all your camels with their provisions. If you hesitate..." she raised one hand, mimicking a complex spell – in truth, the gestures of an elaborate Druidic blessing – "I'll fry every last one of you where you stand."

One of the raiders, visibly shaking, moved to comply and brought a barely conscious Ian to her. Another fetched supplies and placed them before her. A third led the chieftain's prized giant goat to her. Others followed with waterskins, coin pouches, and gold. They stacked it all in a neat pile beside her. Then, they started leading camels to her.

Freed, Ian rubbed at his wrists and gave her a wide-eyed look. "Ye've got a talent for makin' an impression, lass," he muttered weakly, with equal parts admiration and disbelief.

He glanced over at their foes' smouldering corpse, then back at Aluriel. His head was still ringing. His thoughts were a hazy blur. *By the Forger... again? That's twice... nae just sparks. That were real lightnin', that. From her. Like before. Nae a fluke, then...? Somethin' in her. Somethin' wild. Raw. Nae right, nae safe... but, Forger save me, she burned them doon like kindlin'!*

Ian rubbed his beard thoughtfully as his thoughts cleared, his eyes narrowing as he considered her potential. *The gnomish wizards o' Steelforge... mibbe they could help her make sense o' it. They're affa quick, those wee bastards. Born wi' a spark in their veins, ken how tae twist lightnin' tae their will near as soon as they pull on a wizard's robe,* he thought, recalling how easily gnomes mastered lightning magic. *But the Vashlin mages... aye, they're the ones wi' the sense tae handle power like that. They've worked wi' wild stuff, dangerous as hellfire.* Worked with folk scarier than her, I'd wager. *If anyone kens how tae channel uncontrollable power like hers, it's them. Mibbe they'd ken how tae help her wield it safe-like.* He sighed inwardly, glancing at Aluriel. *Steelforge or Vashlin... affa long road tae either. Plenty o' time tae decide.* For now, he resolved to keep a watchful eye on her, knowing well the danger – and the promise – of such raw magic.

"What was I saying earlier? One hundred percent freak. Maybe..." she chuckled, "maybe that works in my favour sometimes." As she spoke, Aluriel walked purposefully towards Kharesh's charred body to claim a prize, a token of her victory. The pillagers watched in stunned silence as she bent down, pried the scimitar from his blackened corpse, still in its scabbard. Strapping the weapon across her back, she stood tall, sparks still crackling faintly around her fingers. *If I look like I know what I'm doing, they'll believe it,* she thought, her confidence growing with every passing minute of their submission.

After securing the scimitar, her gaze swept over the camp, assessing the damage. In the flickering firelight, she noticed a smaller tent nearby, its flap loosely tied open, with four women standing at the threshold. Ignoring the pillagers' terrified stares, she strode towards it. Three of the women retreated back inside. The fourth remained before the entrance. The closer she got, the clearer the muffled sounds from within became. Peering inside, she saw that their wrists and ankles were bound with heavy chains. Whilst they were given a fairly long leash, their bindings were secured to a heavy log. Worse still, the wind had carried flames towards the tent. It was just about to catch fire.

Aluriel's heart twisted at the sight, fury rising anew. She stepped inside, and the women recoiled slightly, their fear evident. She gasped as she saw them. They were exhausted, bruised, beaten, and broken in ways she couldn't fathom. She thought of Kharesh's hands on her, of the rage and terror she had felt. *How many nights had they endured his cruelty... and that of his brutes? How many times had they tried to resist, before giving up hope?* The thought made her blood boil. The one who had stood by the opening slipped back inside the tent. Her eyes never left Aluriel.

Compassion welled up in Aluriel's heart. "I'm here to help," she said softly, though her words were met with blank stares. *They've heard a lot of lies before, and probably speak no Common Tongue*, she realised, but her resolve did not waver. They might not speak her languages, but tone and actions would have to suffice.

Looking closer, Aluriel noticed that the chains on their wrists and ankles were bound with heavy locks. She pointed at one of the locks, glancing between them as she asked, "Where are the keys?" First, in Common Tongue. Then, in Elvish. But their confused expressions confirmed they did not understand her.

Thinking quickly, Aluriel mimicked turning a key in a lock, her fingers twisting in an exaggerated motion. One of the women hesitated, then murmured a single word: "Kharesh."

Aluriel's stomach twisted at the name, but she wasted no time. She turned on her heel and sprinted towards Kharesh's burning tent. The heat from the flames licked at her skin as she ducked inside, coughing against the acrid smoke. Her eyes scanned the remnants of the tent, and amid the scattered debris – including her own cloak, which was smouldering to ash – she spotted a bronze key ring glinting faintly in the firelight. Snatching it up with Kharesh's scimitar, she turned and hurried back to the women. The tent had caught on fire, and it would not be long before they all burned alive. She poured what was left inside her waterskin onto the red-hot iron keys, hoping to cool them just enough so they would not warp in the locks. A hiss of vapour rose as they cooled somewhat, but not enough. They still burned her palms, searing her flesh as she took them in hand. Grimacing through the searing pain, Aluriel dropped to her knees and quickly tried each key in turn until, with a satisfying click, the first lock sprang open. One by one, she freed the women, her anger burning hotter with each released shackle. The women exchanged wide-eyed glances, spoke hushedly in Lughat al-Barbar. Their disbelief slowly seemed to give way to tentative hope.

A flicker of doubt crept into Aluriel's mind as she worked. *What will this cost me?* she thought, her mind drifting to the waterskins in her goats' saddlebags, the precious liquid she had already rationed so tightly. Bringing them along meant sharing. *I can't take them through the desert without supplies.* The thought lingered for a moment before she forced it aside. She looked at their bruises, their haunted eyes. It tugged at her heart. *What these women suffered for Gods know how long... Only moments ago, Kharesh had tried to do the same to me. I certainly couldn't have let them burn. But now, I can't leave them alone, either.*

The memory fuelled her resolve, flaring hot inside her chest. "You're free now," she whispered, voice unsteady. *The raiders will pay for that. Every last drop of water they have will be ours.*

Once outside, the women hesitated, glancing at each other and then at Aluriel. She gestured towards the camels outside and then to herself and Ian, hoping they understood the invitation. "Come with us," she said firmly, even if she knew they couldn't grasp her words. The women exchanged murmurs in Lughat al-Barbar before nodding hesitantly and following her into the night.

When Aluriel returned to Ian's side with the women in tow, he whistled in surprise. The one who had stood outside paused along the way, stooping to pick up a few scimitars dropped by the dead guards. She tested its weight briefly, then spotted a cluster of daggers scattered nearby. Without hesitation, she picked up several, tucking one into her belt and handing the rest to the remaining three. Their fingers closed around the weapons, hesitant but firm, and they exchanged brief words in Lughat al-Barbar. "Quite the saviour tonight, aren't ye?" Ian remarked. Aluriel could not tell whether his tone meant admiration, sarcasm, or simply exasperation.

"They're coming with us," Aluriel replied curtly. Her voice left no room for argument or doubt. "We'll take them to the next settlement. Somewhere safer."

With the women freed, they wasted no time preparing to leave. The six of them scoured the camp for every waterskin and any other supplies they could find, loading the camels with as much as their saddles could carry. The task felt endless. And yet, when they finally glanced back towards the camp's perimeter, they saw the raiders had fled. All of them, down to the last, were gone. *Good*, Aluriel thought. *Let them run. Let them fear. They'll think twice before attacking us again.*

At some point, Aluriel realised she was still nude. She found a padded white robe in a tent that had been spared by the fire. It likely belonged to a raider who had fallen or fled. The robe was far too short on her. It barely reached her knees, but it would have to do. For good measure, they torched whatever else they could not carry.

Ian nodded. "Aye, lass. Ye've done right by them. Let's get movin'." As the group moved away from the pillagers' camp, Aluriel and Ian tried to communicate with the women. Their features were striking: olive-skinned with deep, expressive eyes and the angular beauty common to the region. Each carried herself with a mix of fear and quiet resilience. Their chains were gone, but trust did not come easily. Not after their previous treatment. Not towards outsiders like Aluriel and Ian, even though she had just saved them.

Aluriel pointed at herself and said, "Aluriel." They looked at her quizzically, so she repeated, "My name. Aluriel."

One of the women stepped forward tentatively, her voice soft as she introduced herself. "Layla," she said, pressing a hand to her chest. She was tall and slender, her long black hair braided neatly down her back. Her brown eyes held a quiet dignity despite all she had endured.

The others followed her example. "Zahara," said the woman who had stood outside the tent. *The one who'd picked up the scimitars and handed out the daggers to the others,* Aluriel noted in her mind. She was the oldest of the group, with a pretty, round face framed by dark curls. *I'm not really good at estimating the age of humans. I've seen so few...*

*She looks old enough to have been an adult for some time, yet young enough to bear a child.* Zahara was shorter than most barbarian women Aluriel had seen. Sturdily built and muscular, her hands were calloused – perhaps from hard labour, perhaps from training – and her gaze was sharp, with an undercurrent of defiance. She wore countless scars across her face and arms, and many more revealed themselves along her body when she moved, glimpsed through the rips in her tattered tunic. *Was she a warrior? Or was she tortured that much? Or both?*

The third mumbled some words in Lughat al-Barbar, then after a brief pause said clearly, "Nadiya," offering a handshake which Aluriel accepted. Her tone was friendly, yet her dark brown, expressive eyes remained wary, flicking between Aluriel and Ian. Her skin was slightly darker than the others'. She wore a tattered tunic that she had tried to keep in as good a condition as she could, and her cautious movements suggested she was assessing the situation as much as she was introducing herself. A rose was tattooed on her left ankle.

The last, visibly younger and even more malnourished than the others, hesitated before whispering, "Farah." She was petite, with wide, expressive eyes that darted nervously around the camp. Her black hair was loose and unkempt, and she clutched her arms around herself as if trying to make herself smaller. Farah's voice was barely audible. But when Aluriel smiled at her reassuringly, her expression softened.

Aluriel nodded, pointing to herself again. "Aluriel," she said simply. Then, she gestured towards Ian, who gave them a slight bow. "Ian," he said, smiling.

Though their words were sparse and fragmented, they managed to communicate enough through gestures. Aluriel gestured to the night sky, tracing constellations to communicate direction. Layla's eyes lit with recognition. She pointed north-east and spoke quickly in Lughat al-Barbar, whilst miming the act of drinking from a well.

"An oasis," Aluriel said, catching on. "There's a settlement there?" She pointed in the same direction.

Zahara nodded enthusiastically, repeating the gestures and saying, "Oasis." The others repeated, "Oasis!" too. *So that word is the same in Common. In Elvish too. Probably a loanword from Lughat al-Barbar,* Aluriel mused. Ian rubbed his beard thoughtfully. "If they're pointin' us tae water an' a town, it's as good a place as any tae aim for."

Aluriel pointed in the same direction as Layla, and the women nodded, clearly relieved. Though their communication was far from perfect, it was enough to spark a fragile alliance. Aluriel pointed towards the camels. Zahara rode a giant goat, and the rest each picked a camel and sat astride it.

As they rode away from the camp, the surrendered gold jingling in their saddlebags, their camels in tow, loaded with waterskins and whatever else they could salvage, the burning pillagers' tents shrank into the distance. Ian let out a hearty laugh. "Chief Aluriel, eh? Remind me never tae get on yer bad side."

Aluriel allowed herself another brief smile. "I think I like 'Chief Aluriel.' It has a nice ring to it." Ian noticed and grinned, "See, nae all lightnin's a bad thing. Yer smilin' more, too."

Aluriel chuckled, but no sooner had she done so than the intrusive rumination returned.

*So my lightning can kill.*

*What if I killed Elenwen?*
*Why am I such a failure?*
*This lightning... what is it?*
*Am I cursed?*
*What if Kharesh had...*
*No.*
*Don't think it.*
*What if Kharesh managed to rape me?*
*Damn it. I said don't think it.*
*Am I becoming mad?*
*Who or what is the Lady of Twilight?*
*Why me?*

Her spiralling returned, looping tighter, louder, and made even more turbulent by the recent ordeal.

The night stretched on, the desert vast and silent around them, but – save for Aluriel's fractured mind – the group's resolve burned brighter than ever.

Kharesh's prized goat must have been enchanted, as it was far faster and stronger than the other two, and left the lumbering camels behind without effort. If she hadn't held it back, Aluriel would have easily outpaced the others. So, whilst waiting for them to catch up, she turned her attention to the scimitar. The curved blade shimmered faintly under the moonlight, and intricate etchings in an unknown tongue ran along its length. As her fingertips brushed the blade, a faint chill pulsed through them. *This is no ordinary weapon,* she thought, though the nature of its enchantment she could not begin to guess.

"Ian," she called, riding over and handing him the scimitar. "What do you make of this?"

Ian took the scimitar, tracing his fingers along the surface as he examined the craftsmanship. He repeated the motion, this time summoning a wisp of fire that swirled around his fingertips. "It's enchanted," he murmured, his Dwarven accent thick with concentration. "Keek at these runes. They glow affa' chilly when ye provoke 'em wi' magic." He sparked another faint ember of fire magic in his palm to show Aluriel, and again, the etchings on the blade lit up with a sharp, blue-green glow. "Nae dwarven runes, nae gnomish. Bit o' old desert craft, maybe. Wouldnae call it friendly, but I've seen fiercer runes on kitchen knives back home in Steelforge."

As Ian worked, sparks danced briefly in the air. The four freed women exchanged worried glances, their murmurs in Lughat al-Barbar hushed but tense. Aluriel caught a few snippets of their conversation, though the words meant nothing to her. Their anxious glances said enough: fear was written plainly on their faces.

Layla, the tallest of the group, gestured towards the glowing blade and Ian's magic, whispering urgently to the others beside her. Aluriel didn't need to hear the words to know what they feared. *They think they've escaped one nightmare only to fall into another.* She sighed, stepping closer to the women and raising her hands in what she hoped looked like reassurance.

"We won't harm you," she said gently, though she knew they couldn't understand. She pointed to herself again. "Aluriel," she repeated, then gestured to Ian. "Ian. Friends. Not masters." She mimed unlocking chains, then held her hands up to show them they were free. Her tone softened further. "Safe."

The women hesitated but seemed to relax slightly, their expressions softening as Aluriel's meaning began to register. Nadiya murmured something to Layla, who gave a hesitant nod. Though their fear didn't vanish entirely, it ebbed enough for them to follow more willingly.

By dawn, the horizon began to shift, and a faint glimmer caught Aluriel's eye. She squinted against the growing light of dawn, her body aching from the unrelenting ride. "Look," she called softly, her voice hoarse. "An oasis."

Ian followed her gaze. "Aye, it's there. Seems the lasses kent fit they were speakin' aboot." He turned to the women, giving a small nod, though they were too weary to react.

# ◆ *Interlude — Storm and Beauty* ◆

The beach was silver tonight.

Moonlight rippled across the waves like broken glass. No mortal wind stirred the trees behind. In fact, no mortal soul had ever set foot onto this plane of existence. And yet, the sea churned, restless.

Two figures stood where water kissed sand.

One was tall and graceful, adorned in flowing robes that shimmered with every colour of the rainbow and then some more no mortal eyes were meant to see. Her skin was flawless, her golden hair braided like strands of divine silk. She did not walk. She glided. The Lady Most Beautiful, serene and untouchable, the Goddess of beauty, music, nature, and perfection. The Goddess forest elves worshipped.

The other had emerged from the ocean itself. She looked wild. Barefoot, and in fact wearing no clothes over her skin, her violet irises were spinning like deep whirlpools. Long strands of seaweed clung to her bare shoulders like jewellery. This was the Lady of the Abyss, Goddess of storms, waters, and secrets. The goddess of Sea Elves, worshipped by human sailors, pirates, and some thieves, too. Though she would not turn down worship from anyone else who wished to offer it. Her laugh, when it came, was the sound of thunder heard from beneath the waves.

"You've been watching her again, sister," said the Lady Most Beautiful. Her voice was soft, yet heavy with reproach. They did not speak each other's true names. Not even here, in this secret place beyond time. Not even among kin. To speak a God's true name was to tempt fate itself.

"Every now and then," the Lady of the Abyss replied, grinning with the sharp teeth of a shark. "She *amuses* me."

"She was *never* meant to be born."

The Lady of the Abyss tilted her head. "Oh, come now. You're starting to sound like the Peacemaker."

"Because, as much as it curdles me to say it, the Peacemaker... Just this once, is right. The child defies the natural order, The natural cycle. Her *lineage* defies reason."

"Reason," repeated the Lady of the Abyss, amused. "We are goddesses, sister. Since when have we ever been slaves to reason? Was it Reason that made you turn your back on her before she even drew her first breath?"

"You gave her lightning."

"I did."

"Why?"

The waves rolled in, touched the Lady of the Abyss's legs like a blanket of loyal kittens, then receded.

"Because you denied her your gifts. I, at least, gave her mine. Lightning, and Water. Though she has yet to master either."

The Lady Most Beautiful turned away, chin raised and eyes gleaming. "It was not cruelty. It was restraint. That girl... if the prophecy is true..."

"Then she may be the only one who can fix the mess we've made," the Lady of the Abyss interjected, no longer smiling. She raised her hands high and swept a wide circle around her. "The mess we ALL made." At that word, her voice boomed, wrapped in rolling thunder. The waters resonated with a roar.

"By being the catalyst of an even bigger mess?" the Lady Most Beautiful replied.

A long silence passed between them. Only the sea dared make a noise.

"You meddle too much," She said at last.

"And you," replied the Lady of the Abyss, "are too afraid to meddle until it's too late."

She turned towards the sea. "Mark my words. This time it will be different."

The waves surged forward, and when they fell back, the Lady of the Abyss was gone.

The Lady Most Beautiful remained a while longer, watching the horizon, feeling the sting of her sister's words resonate within her in a pang of guilt.

Even a Goddess could feel regret.

*Then, with a sigh as soft as falling petals, She too vanished, leaving only moonlight and waves behind.*

# Chapter 6 – The Shieldmaiden

The sight of the oasis in the distance was a spark of hope that nudged them from the edge of their exhaustion. Aluriel felt a second wind take hold, and though her body protested with every jolt, at least it was Kharesh's goat plodding in her stead. The camels trudged forward, their overstuffed saddlebags swaying as the group pressed on into the golden chill of early morning.

A couple of hours later, the oasis lay before them, ringed by a strong palisade, its heart a cluster of palm trees around a large, shimmering pool of water. The air smelled faintly of greenery and wet earth, a sharp contrast to the arid desert. Beyond the pool stood another settlement, much larger than Al-Hadiqa, bustling with the labours of early morning. Clay huts and tents made of woven fabric formed a loose circle. Their colours were bright, standing in defiance of the muted tones of the sand. The palisade stretched farther than their eyes could see, likely enclosing it all.

As they entered, the freed women spoke quickly to the guards, who waved them through. The locals began to cluster around them. Their voices were animated despite their exhaustion. Aluriel dismounted, her legs stiff, and watched the interactions. Layla seemed to take the lead, gesturing emphatically as she recounted their ordeal. In the torrent of unfamiliar words, all Aluriel could catch was her own name and Kharesh's, but Layla's tone held both relief and awe.

A man stepped forward from the group, his long robes trailing softly as he approached. An embroidered symbol marked the robe at the centre of his chest: a triangular flask encircled by a ring, with six five-pointed stars arched above it. His skin was olive, and his neatly trimmed, greying beard gave him an air of wisdom that he wore like a badge. He carried himself with the calm authority of one accustomed to having the final say.

"I am Khalid," he said in clear, if accented Common Tongue. "Vice Sharif of the Guild of Alchemists, and this place is Lulu'at Qalb al-Sahra. I speak some of your language and a little Elvish. These women tell me you rescued them from Kharesh." His gaze swept over Aluriel and Ian, lingering on the scimitar strapped across her back.

Aluriel nodded, brushing a damp strand of hair from her face. "Yes. Kharesh is dead. Many of his men are ash. The ones who didn't flee, that is."

Khalid raised an eyebrow sceptically. "And you defeated him? You, a single elf, against Kharesh and dozens of his raiders?"

Ian hesitated, just a breath. *Magic's nae small thing under the Tribal Laws.* But there were too many witnesses. Too many eyes. And Aluriel had just admitted to it herself. Silence was no longer an option. "Aye, she fried him wi' lightnin'. Like he was naught but kindlin', ken?" Khalid did not appear convinced, and he turned his attention to the freed women. One by one, he questioned them. His tone was stern. Each question was clipped and precise. To Aluriel's ears, it was made harsher still by the cadence and grit of Lughat al-Barbar.

"Zahara," he began, fixing her eyes with an unblinking gaze. "Speak the truth, and the whole truth. Did these two truly defeat Kharesh, or is there more to this story? Be warned: to lie or mislead this tribe is to invoke punishment."

Zahara straightened, her voice steady but laced with emotion. "It is true. The elf struck him down with lightning, and his guards too. She freed us and brought us home when we asked her to."

Khalid gave a slow nod, turning to Layla. "And you? What do you say? The same warning applies to you: to lie or mislead this tribe is to invoke punishment."

Layla lifted her chin, choosing each word with care. "They are elemental mages, both of them. But they saved us. When we asked for their help, they gave it and brought us back safely." Her eyes flicked briefly to Aluriel and Ian before returning to Khalid's stern face. "Without them, we would still be his slaves."

Khalid nodded gravely, and he continued his questioning, now addressing Farah, the youngest of the four. He gave her the same ritual warning, though his words were softened by her youth, "Young lady, tell us what happened. I must warn you, as I did the others: to lie or mislead this tribe is to invoke punishment. But simply speak the truth, and nothing bad will happen to you." He let his stern expression soften with a smile to reassure her.

She hesitated, her wide eyes welling with tears. She darted forward and wrapped her arms around Aluriel, just above her waist, sobbing into her chest.

"She saved us. Even though it hurt her."

Farah choked out the words between sobs, her voice muffled against Aluriel's chest. "She killed him, and brought us here. Please don't punish her."

Aluriel knelt and hugged her, pulling her close as she continued to sob into her shoulder. Khalid nodded, taking a quiet note of the stranger's kindness. Finally, he turned to Nadiya, whose face remained unreadable. "And you? Do you confirm their story? I warn you as I did the others: to lie or mislead this tribe is to invoke punishment."

Nadiya gave a single nod, her voice quiet and firm. "Yes, they are mages. But they never harmed us. They fought for us." Her gaze turned pointed as she added, "Look at the dwarf's wounds. Look at the elf's... ill-fitting tunic. She wears it only because Kharesh ripped *hers*. Look at her freezing skin: she left her cloak in Kharesh's burning tent when she chose to save us instead. Look at her whip marks if you doubt our words. Look at her burned hands, the same hands that clutched Kharesh's searing-hot keys to free us, while the tent burned around us. Let this stand as proof of what they endured to protect us from a greater evil."

The murmurs among the townsfolk grew louder, disbelief turning to awe as they heard their own women confirm, whilst Khalid translated a summary of what had been said for Ian and Aluriel's benefit. Soon, the atmosphere shifted entirely. Men and women came forward, offering thanks, some bowing their heads in respect. Khalid raised a hand to quiet them before speaking again, his tone formal and measured.

Khalid then turned to Aluriel. "Young elf, listen well. Your actions require me to weigh them against the Law and pass judgment. But I cannot do so without hearing your side of the story. I warn you, as I did all the others: to lie or mislead this tribe is to invoke punishment. Now, tell me the truth of what happened to you, and what you did. And start with your name, so I may know it."

Aluriel shivered under Khalid's unflinching gaze. Then, with nowhere left to turn, she began recounting her tale. "My name is Aluriel. I grew up in the Enchanted Forest. We were crossing the desert to reach Vashlin via Varthia. I had just fallen asleep, while Ian was keeping guard, when Kharesh's men attacked. I could not see the fight, for I was bound first with a net, then with tight ropes. Ian, the Dwarf beside me, fought back, but he was bested, knocked unconscious. We were carried to Kharesh's camp. He first tried to seduce me. He whipped me. He had his men hold me down and then he tried to rape me. And that's when chain lightning burst out of me. It killed him. It killed many of the men around me. The rest fled. I freed these women from a burning tent. They abandoned them still chained in there. There, in the burning tent. We took what they left behind... and came here."

Khalid nodded gravely. Then he turned to Ian. "Priest, tell me your side of the story. You have heard this warning already, but I must repeat it: to lie or mislead this tribe is to invoke punishment."

Ian wasted no time replying. "Aye, just like she said. I was standin' guard beside the tent, when a dozen or more o'them raiders came doon swoopin'. Tried tae fight as much as I could. They were tryin' tae kill me. Burned doon one or two o' them bastards tae ash, but they were too many. Knock me oot, they did, aye, an' caged me in their encampment. Ah didnae see whit Aluriel did, but at some point, they brought me back and freed me, and they all fled. Aye. That's the full truth."

Khalid once again raised his hand to quiet the crowd's growing murmurs, then began to speak in a solemn, ceremonial tone.

"As Vice Sharif of the Guild of Alchemists of Lulu'at Qalb al-Sahra, I am tasked with upholding the Laws that govern the use of magic in the tribes," Khalid proclaimed, his sharp gaze sweeping over the crowd and landing on Aluriel and Ian. "Magic users are tolerated among us only when their actions serve the people against an evil greater than themselves. We accept ourselves as a necessary danger, tolerated for the sake of the greater good. We are afforded respect so long as we follow our laws and protect our kin. Foreign elemental mages, such as these two, are allowed to cross our lands, and may even be granted safe passage if requested by the Guild, provided they uphold our laws."

He paused, letting the murmurs die down before continuing.

"In this case, I am ready to pass judgment. They were attacked – not inside a settlement, not by an oasis – but on neutral ground. They were taken by force and kidnapped. This is permitted under our Laws. However, it is also permitted grounds for retaliation. Therefore, when they killed in self-defence, they did so lawfully. They wielded elemental magic to harm, yes, but the dwarf did so only in the extreme defence of their lives, and the elf when she was about to be violated. This, too, is permitted in Law, though it carries weight, and must be examined carefully, as I have now done. Kharesh's raiders surrendered. They threw down their weapons. By our customs and tribal traditions, it is the victor's right, and the victor's alone, to set the terms of negotiation when one side surrenders. This is a custom older than any written code, and later written judgments have only confirmed it. By this custom, they did no wrong in taking whatever spoils they wished.

Therefore, the judgment is clear. The judgment is lawful. The judgment is final: these two broke no Law.

Moreover, in this particular case – and I say this again so that all may hear – these two furthermore acted with restraint and honour. And they acted with mercy. They returned our women unharmed. They spared those who fled. They did not pursue. They did not slaughter. They showed restraint where they would have had the right, and the power to kill. And that, too, is a mark of honour.

Therefore – and let all bear witness – with the full binding authority of the Guild, and as an act of gratitude from the tribe, I grant them Safe Passage through the Great Desert under the protection of the Guild. Let it be known. Let it be remembered. So shall it be."

The crowd murmured in astonishment, though a ripple of tension passed through it as a young man stepped forward. His olive-toned skin glistened with sweat under the desert sun. His muscular frame, honed from years of combat and survival, spoke of strength, agility, and unwavering discipline in training. His dark eyes burned with determination, and his angular features and height gave him an imposing presence. Clad in hardened leather armour reinforced with metal studs, he carried himself with the confidence of one accustomed to leadership. In his hand, he brandished a gleaming scimitar, its edge sharp and well-maintained. "With Kharesh dead," the man declared, lifting his scimitar high in the air, as custom demanded, "I claim the title of Khan. My name is Yousef, and I will lead this tribe, and the tribes of the southwestern sands."

Khalid turned to him, unsurprised, as though he had been expecting it all along. After a moment, he spoke, his voice ringing out clearly. "A claim has been issued. As is tradition, if any here would challenge Yousef for leadership, let them step forward now. A duel will be held. The loser shall be given the chance to surrender and, if they wish, leave in peace, either to join another tribe or form a new one, as is our custom."

The air grew tense as the crowd exchanged glances, but no one dared step forward. Yousef stood tall, his presence commanding as he surveyed those gathered. Beneath his composure, however, his thoughts roiled. He was merely twenty years of age. And yet, he had waited his entire life for this moment. His father's defeat at Kharesh's hands when Yousef was just a child had stripped the tribe of their stability and plunged them into years of fear and brutality. Now, with Kharesh dead, the weight of leadership was his to claim again.

*I am ready,* he told himself, though a sliver of doubt gnawed at the edges of his resolve. *I have to be. My kin need me to be.* The thought of failure terrified him, but he couldn't let his uncertainties show. He squared his shoulders and forced himself to project the calm authority they needed.

Yousef scanned the crowd. His heart fluttered in his chest. He saw relief in older men's eyes, a spark of hope in the younger. Some, including the newly widowed mothers, looked to him with raw desperation, as if he were the only shield between them and the vast, uncertain desert beyond. *I must not fail them,* he thought. *Not after all we've lost.*

His gaze shifted briefly to Aluriel, and for a moment, a flicker of gratitude warmed his otherwise steeled expression. Without her intervention, this moment might never have come. She had returned something to his people. Something they hadn't dared even hope for. For that, he owed this stranger more than he could ever repay.

Khalid nodded solemnly and continued, "Then it is decided. Tonight, Yousef will formalise his claim through the ancient ritual. In one full turn of the first moon from tonight, if he defeats all challengers, he will be anointed as Khan in a feast to honour his ascension, and our freedom."

The announcement settled over the crowd like the first warm wind after a freezing night, and though most seemed content, a few faces tightened in resentment. Three men stepped forward, offering Yousef their blessings before quietly leaving the settlement to seek their fortunes elsewhere. A fourth man stood briefly, muttered a curse, and stormed off without another word. Yousef raised a hand, calling after him. "Peace be upon you, brother. May your path lead you to prosperity." The tension broke as the townsfolk began to cheer, their spirits lifted by the promise of new leadership and, perhaps, a brighter future.

Standing next to Aluriel, Zahara let out a cry, her hands flying to her mouth as an older woman, tears streaming down her face, stepped forward. "Mama!" Zahara exclaimed, rushing into the woman's arms. The reunion overflowed with sobs and words Aluriel and Ian couldn't understand, but the raw emotion needed no translation.

Zahara's mother turned to Aluriel and Ian, bowing deeply. When she rose, she clasped Aluriel's hands, her gratitude shining in her tear-filled eyes. Though she knew no Common Tongue, she began speaking rapidly in Lughat al-Barbar, her voice trembling with gratitude. Khalid, stepping closer, translated her words.

"She says you saved her daughter and brought her home when hope seemed lost," Khalid explained, his tone reverent. "She offers her blessings and says you are the moons' light in the desert night."

Aluriel stepped forward. Her expression was clouded. Yet, her voice was calm. "Zahara... I had lost all hope too. When they captured me in my sleep, I thought I was doomed. The raiders had me bound and humiliated. I heard Ian fighting, but even he was overwhelmed. We were dragged to their camp like trophies."

Khalid translated her words into Lughat al-Barbar, his tone steady as Zahara listened intently. Aluriel kept looking straight into her eyes. "When Kharesh whipped me, tried to break me, tried to rape me, something inside me refused to yield. Rage, desperation... whatever it was, it erupted as lightning. It struck him dead, and his guards with him. Their weapons, their threats... none of it mattered then."

Zahara's eyes widened as Khalid translated, her expression shifting to one of awe. "And then," Aluriel added, with a tired little laugh, "I stood amidst the chaos and challenged the entire camp, all the survivors, to fight me, all at once if they dared. It was a bluff, of course. I could barely stand, let alone summon another lightning like that. I don't actually know how to summon magic at will, you see? But they didn't know that, and it worked."

Khalid's voice was steady as he relayed her words, but now it was the expression on *his* face that began to shift to awe and reverence. Zahara, too, gasped, and she took a half-step back. "She... she challenged them all? That's what that whole speech she gave there was about?" She glanced at Khalid for confirmation. When he nodded, they both turned back to Aluriel, silent for a moment as if the words had shaken them deep into their core. Khalid was the first to speak. "Do you know what that means?"

Aluriel answered casually. "It means I wasn't going to let them win." She let out a tired, nervous giggle. "Whatever else it means, you'll have to tell me."

Khalid translated her words faithfully, and the murmurs of the gathered townsfolk grew louder. Zahara's mother's eyes widened, and when they found Aluriel's, reverence joined her gratitude.

Khalid then turned to Aluriel, his expression grave. "These are sacred words, Aluriel. Did you truly challenge Kharesh's surviving tribe – all of them – to an all-against-one fight? Did they all flee after you did?"

Aluriel nodded, meeting his gaze evenly, slightly piqued at being asked to repeat herself. "I did. It was a bluff." She let out an annoyed sigh. *As if I wanted to repeat how much of a failure I am at controlling lightning...* "I literally just said this moments ago. I could barely stand, let alone summon another strike of lightning. But they didn't know that, and so I made them believe I could fry them all. Dared them to come at me, all together, to save me the trouble of chasing them down and frying them one by one. And it worked! They all ran off!" She erupted into a giggle as she finished the sentence, the absurdity of the situation striking her all over again. The tension in the crowd seemed to ease at the sound, though Khalid's expression remained stern and did not waver.

"The fact that it was, as you describe it, a *bluff* does not matter," Khalid said firmly. "What matters is that the challenge was issued. The words were spoken. By our laws, they are binding, and they bind you as a Shieldmaiden. However," he added, turning to Zahara, "a woman must formally step forward to declare the rise of a Shieldmaiden before the tribe, for the whole process to commence. Zahara, I suggest you do so now."

No sooner than Khalid had spoken, Zahara stepped onto a podium in the centre of the crowd, raising her arms high. Her voice rang out, clear and strong, invoking the stars above and the gathered people. "Hear me! I call upon the Stars Above and all of you who stand here today to bear witness to my words. This elf, Aluriel, is no ordinary woman."

The townsfolk fell silent, their attention fixed entirely on Zahara. She turned back towards her mother, her words taking fire with conviction. "When the lightning stopped, she stood amidst the destruction and challenged the entire camp – Kharesh's surviving men, all of them – to fight her if they dared. Not one moved to raise a weapon. Not one dared to challenge her. I repeat: she is no ordinary woman. She is no mere traveller. She is a Shieldmaiden."

Khalid hesitated, glancing at Aluriel before turning back to Zahara. "Do you mean these words in truth? These are sacred words, and to declare one a Shieldmaiden is no light matter."

Zahara turned to Khalid, lifting her chin. "I mean this. My words are truth."

Khalid nodded gravely before addressing Zahara's mother. "Do you question your daughter's truth?"

The older woman shook her head, tears spilling down her cheeks as she clasped Aluriel's hands again, whispering blessings in her own tongue. Though Aluriel couldn't understand the words, the emotion behind them needed no translation. She felt a deep warmth bloom in her chest: a mixture of pride, gratitude, and the uncertainty of responsibility settling over her.

Khalid turned to the gathered townsfolk and spoke loudly. "Before such a title is bestowed, there must be affirmation. I ask for testimony both in favour and in rebuttal. Let all those who witnessed the events speak truthfully."

One by one, the rescued women stepped forward.

It was Layla who came forth first. Her voice was unwavering. "I saw it. When she struck down Kharesh, the lightning consumed him and the guards around him. Then, she spoke to them in words I could not understand, but the threat was clear. The challenge was evident when she waved her hands wrapped in lightning, beckoning them forward: she was daring them to fight. One of Kharesh's men translated her challenge to the others. Despite the noise of the wind and burning tents, I overheard enough to confirm this. The rest of the tribe dropped their weapons, surrendered their belongings, and fled without looking back."

Farah followed, her voice trembling with emotion. "It's true. We were left behind, chained, while the camp burned and the rest of the men ran away after her threats. They did not even look back to save us from our burning tent." She cast a grateful look towards Aluriel, then ran to hug her again.

Finally, Nadiya stepped forward, her tone measured. "I confirm their words. She fought for us, and her power was enough to break their spirits. Kharesh's men were terrified, and they surrendered without hesitation as soon as they heard her challenge them all. They brought what she demanded as reparation, and then fled into the night"

Khalid nodded at each testimony, his gaze sweeping over the crowd. "With these affirmations, we now turn to Zahara. Before the gathered witnesses, and under the gaze of the Stars, do you swear that the words you have just spoken are the whole truth?"

The crowd fell into a stunned silence, shock rippling through their ranks. All eyes turned to Zahara, their expressions betraying a mix of awe and disbelief. Even Khalid's stern visage softened with surprise as he processed Zahara's words. Zahara stood firm, her tone unyielding. "This is true. I swear it by the Stars above, by the Sands below, and by the Desert Spirits. I witnessed it myself. If anyone doubts Aluriel's claim, let them speak now."

Layla, Farah, and Nadiya repeated Zahara's statement in turn, word for word.

No voice rose in dissent. The weight of the women's words lingered in the air, leaving both the townsfolk and their new Khan challenger to regard Aluriel with newfound respect and reverence.

Khalid stepped forward, his expression now grave as he addressed Zahara directly. Speaking in Lughat al-Barbar, his voice rang clear and ceremonial. "On pain of death, Do you swear by the Stars above, the Sands below, by the Desert Spirits, and by the Blade Dancer Himself, that this elf challenged Kharesh's entire tribe and all their warriors to a free-for-all fight and stood her ground as a Shieldmaiden?"

Zahara raised her head high, her voice unwavering as she spoke with ritual clarity. "By the Stars that guide us and the Sands that cradle us, I swear this truth. I witnessed her stand unyielding, her courage unmatched, and her power undeniable. With my own eyes, I saw her challenge the entire tribe, showing no fear, and not one dared rise to her challenge. May my words be weighed in truth by the Stars above and the Sands below. May the Desert spirits torment me and the Blade Dancer himself cut me down if my tongue lies."

One by one, Khalid asked the same question of Layla, Farah, and Nadiya, and they all repeated the same oath. For some reason, a flash of what seemed like amusement – or perhaps relief – briefly washed over Nadiya's face after she'd spoken the last sentence.

The townsfolk held their silence throughout, save for Yousef who had been quietly translating the exchange into the Common Tongue for the two outsiders. Khalid lifted his arms slightly, continuing in his ceremonial tone. "By our customs, Zahara, Layla, Nadiya, and

Farah have sworn by the Stars, by the Sands, to the Spirits, and to the Blade Dancer. Their words are sacred. They are binding. If anyone here doubts them, let them step forward now."

Once again, no one stepped forward. A ripple of awe passed through the townsfolk as the gravity of the words settled over them. Khalid turned towards Aluriel, who was a few paces away, next to Ian and Yousef. His gaze, sharp as ever, now held a glint of newfound respect. "Then it is decided. You are a Shieldmaiden by right." With these words, the ceremony was concluded. The townsfolk erupted in loud cheers. Khalid stepped down from the podium, approached Aluriel, and explained: "This is not a title bestowed by decree: it is one you earned, Aluriel, through your words and deeds alone."

As the murmurs ripped through the settlement, Khalid began to lecture Aluriel. "A Shieldmaiden," he explained, "is a woman, regardless of her race or origin, who has become so powerful that she may challenge an entire tribe to a ritual all-against-one fight. If she wins, or if no man dares to fight her, she earns the right to form her own small, matriarchal tribe. This tribe may consist of a maximum of five women and five men, along with their natural descendants, who shall be left unharmed and welcomed through all Barbarian lands, provided they spread no hatred and raise arms against none, save in self-defence."

He continued, explaining the consequences of Zahara's bold declaration. "Upon a Shieldmaiden's peaceful death, her eldest male son is granted the right to challenge for leadership first, as per the usual laws of succession. However." And here, Khalid's voice grew heavier. "If her death comes by the hand of a barbarian man, and the Shieldmaiden had broken no Laws to provoke this, leadership passes to her daughter, or to the daughter of any of the original

Spearmaidens, or finally to any woman in the tribe who remains unchallenged, and the tribe remains a Shieldmaiden tribe. Such are our laws, and they are as ancient as they are binding."

Aluriel was reeling, trying to grasp the avalanche of information that had been heaped upon her sleep-deprived mind since she step foot into this town.

Khalid raised his hands to quiet the murmuring crowd and shouts to regain their attention before continuing to speak to Aluriel. "By your actions and by our women's sacred oaths, you have earned this title. With it comes respect and protection within our lands. You may travel safely to the borders of Varthia and through all Barbarian lands at will, knowing no harm shall come to you here."

The townsfolk ushered them towards a large tent, offering it for their rest. "You are heroes," Yousef said, gesturing for them to enter. "Please, take what you need. You are safe here. Lulu'a welcomes you."

Ian wasted no time, unstrapping his armour and collapsing onto a pile of cushions with a groan. "I could sleep fer a week," he muttered before drifting off almost instantly.

Aluriel, however, felt restless. She stepped outside. Though just past its peak, the winter sun hung low in the sky, casting long shadows and offering little warmth against the desert's chill. The pool of the oasis shimmered invitingly, and without hesitation, she stripped off the ill-fitting robes and cast them aside unceremoniously before wading into the water. The coolness was a pleasant shock to her skin, and she sighed deeply, submerging herself fully and drinking whilst underwater.

As she floated on her back, her thoughts wandered. The faces of the women she'd freed lingered in her mind, a mix of triumph and guilt intertwining. *I did what I could, and now this further weight is on my shoulders? Surely 'Shieldmaiden' isn't just some title they hand out for fun? What will I be expected to do?* she wondered. Yet another trigger for more spiralling. *Elenwen. The exile. The lightning again. The whispers. The butterflies. The Lady of Twilight. Or madness? Hafez. The potion. Now this. Shieldmaiden!* The ruminations returned. Circling. Unwanted. Unbidden, as always. The whispers never left her. Underwater, in the silence, they seemed to amplify. She clenched her fists as if to hold onto something, but the water simply swirled around her hands.

When she finally sauntered out of the water, the golden sands of the desert lay quiet under the waning sun, broken only by the bustle gathered near the unlit bonfire at the heart of the settlement. She headed back to her tent, overwhelmed by fatigue. She lay down onto the bedding that had been prepared for her, uncorked one of Hafez's brilliant blue potions and drank it in a single gulp.

A peaceful, dreamless sleep took her immediately. She did not even have the time to notice what the potion tasted like.

Aluriel awoke hours later, her body rested and her thoughts soothed by serene anticipation. The potion she had taken hours earlier had blocked out the incessant whispers and granted her a rare, peaceful sleep, despite the hustle and bustle of the barbarian town. Even in darkness, the whispers had not yet returned. Someone had covered her naked body with a sheet, and laid a robe and a cloak next to her bedding. The robe was simple, made of fine white cotton, and hastily stitched together, but it fit her size, at least. The cloak was made of wool, and looked thick enough to ward off the freezing cold of the desert nights.

A brief note in Common Tongue read:

"Sorry they're not as elegant as a Shieldmaiden deserves, but I had little time to make them. I hope they fit you.

– Amira (Khalid's wife)"

Leaving her tent, Aluriel stepped into the freezing desert night. She glanced at the sky, noting the position of the stars. Two hours remained until the midnight ritual would begin. Around her, the townsfolk moved with purpose, carrying final offerings to the towering bonfire. Each held small slips of parchment, scrawled with prayers, wishes, and fears, meant to rise with the smoke and reach the Stars above. The air carried the mingling scents of roasting meat, spices, and the faint tang of incense, promising a night of reverence and celebration.

Throughout the day, Khalid, the Vice Sharif of the Guild of Alchemists, had been preparing the sacred ointment with great care. Now, he stood at the bonfire's edge, cradling a vessel of the amber, musky blend in his hands. Its sweet, intoxicating aroma wafted through the air as he stirred the viscous mixture. His movements were precise, deliberate, and almost ritualistic, as he prepared for the pivotal moment to come.

As the appointed hour approached, Yousef, the young Khan challenger, arrived astride his giant goat. The animal held its head high, as if sensing the gravity of the moment. Dismounting by the totem, which represented the Desert Spirits, Yousef raised his scimitar high in one hand, the blade catching the light of the rising stars and moons. With his free hand he touched the ground and bent one knee, a gesture that symbolised bravery on one side and obedience to the Laws on the other. The gathered townsfolk fell silent as Khalid stepped forward to address him.

"What brings you here?" Khalid's voice rang out, clear and resonant, carrying across the gathering.

Yousef's reply was equally steady. "I seek anointment as the Khan of these people gathered around me, and of the Southwestern Sands."

"Have you fought all challengers?" Khalid asked, his tone probing.

"There were none," Yousef replied, his gaze unwavering.

"Have you let your brothers and sisters who wished to leave depart in peace and with your blessing?"

"Their blessings are upon me, as are mine upon them."

"Have you let your brothers go even if they were angered?"

"Yes. One cursed me. I wish them peace and prosperity."

"Will you uphold the Laws?"

"I will."

"Will you defend the Tribes?"

"I will."

Satisfied, Khalid spoke: "I now place the rune of the Challenger on your forehead. Return in one full turn of the first moon: if you still stand undefeated, and the Stars have borne witness to your strength, you shall be anointed as Khan of the Southwestern Tribes." Then, with solemn gestures, he anointed Yousef's brow as the young Khan repeated the ritual gesture of bending one knee while raising the scimitar high, as tradition demanded.

Khalid and Yousef turned to Aluriel. "Let the Shieldmaiden step forth, that she may be anointed before the very Stars that witnessed her deeds!" Khalid called out.

Aluriel stepped forward in ritualistic movements, the weight of the title settling on her shoulders. Khalid painted a single stroke on her forehead. "We honour a new Shieldmaiden," he proclaimed, then passed her the brush. Together, they held it as he said, "A

Shieldmaiden anoints her own rune. Let this rune of your creation be the mark of your newborn tribe!"

Khalid had explained earlier that a Shieldmaiden could anoint one rune of her own invention, and then anoint it again for each year she survived thereafter. Each rune carried a wish, and brought its bearer a little closer to making it real. Aluriel's thoughts were clear as she painted a rune on the palm of her left hand, silently wishing for control over lightning. The mark glowed blue for a brief moment before fading, leaving a tingling warmth in its place.

As Aluriel stepped back, Zahara moved forward, kneeling before her mother and asking for her blessing in Lughat al-Barbar. Upon receiving it, Zahara stood tall and turned to Aluriel. "Shieldmaiden, with my mother's blessing, I ask to stand beside you, as one of your Spearmaidens."

Khalid leaned in to quietly explain the significance of the request. After a moment of thought, Aluriel nodded. Zahara bent her left knee in deference, a sign of respect that carried the weight of her commitment.

Moved by the gesture, Aluriel unsheathed the magical scimitar she had taken from Kharesh and presented it to Zahara. "Take this, Spearmaiden, as a token of our allegiance. Let it be a reminder that no one will ever torture you or enslave you again. May it serve you well." Khalid translated for her.

The crowd murmured their approval as Zahara accepted the blade, her hands trembling slightly. "Thank you, Shieldmaiden." Her voice was low and quivered with emotion.

Aluriel smiled softly, then dipped the ceremonial brush into the sacred ointment. She stepped closer to Zahara, her gaze steady.

"Khalid has told me of the tradition," she said, her voice carrying a solemn weight. "Women who join a Shieldmaiden's tribe are granted the title of Spearmaiden, and bear the same rune she bears, a mark that bestows a gift as long as the Shieldmaiden lives."

Aluriel carefully painted the rune on Zahara's forehead, the strokes precise and deliberate. The rune responded much as it had with Aluriel. Zahara's wish took shape in Aluriel's mind, becoming crystal clear. So clear, it felt natural to speak it aloud: "May your strikes always be swift." As she intoned the words with quiet power, the rune flared brightly blue for a heartbeat, then left a faint glow for a few more seconds. Zahara touched her forehead, stunned that Aluriel had reached into her thoughts and silently learned her strongest wish.

The crowd watched in reverent silence, the significance of the act not lost on them. Zahara bowed her head. "Thank you, Shieldmaiden. I will bear your gifts with pride and purpose."

Yousef, watching the exchange, stepped forward and spoke. "A Shieldmaiden and her Spearmaidens deserve armour befitting their titles," he declared. "I promise hardened leather armour to be crafted for Zahara and whatever kind of armour you desire, Aluriel. Name it, and it shall be yours if we have it, or we will make it if we do not."

Aluriel considered for a moment before replying. "I wish for padded robes, such as those I have seen some of your warriors wear. The ones that look exceptionally resistant, yet allow for nimble sword fighting and archery. And I would like them to be red and blue."

Yousef nodded. He knew exactly the kind of robes Aluriel was talking about. "It shall be done," he promised, his tone resolute. The gathered tribe cheered, their voices roaring like a rising tide beneath the stars.

With the ritual finished, the crowd began dispersing. Amira, Khalid's wife, approached Aluriel and introduced herself. She was a small olive-skinned woman, nearly middle-aged, and bore her years with grace and beauty. Aluriel learned she was a skilled tailor, and thanked her for the simple tunic and the cloak she had hastily stitched together for her. She took Aluriel's measurements, and when the time came to measure her height, neck, and shoulder size, she had to stand on a crate. Dismounting it, she smiled. "You really are very tall. One hundred and ninety-eight centimetres!"

Aluriel smiled at her. "I can't help it. I was born that way... but as some humans like to say, the best wine comes in small barrels. Just like you."

Both women chuckled warmly.

***

Soon after, the banquet began in earnest. Long tables were laden with marinated grilled meats, flatbreads, and light, refreshing beer. The food was served communally, the townsfolk helping themselves freely. Ian, though unimpressed by the light beer, nevertheless took great delight in the grilled meats, devouring them with gusto whilst muttering about "proper dwarven ale" under his breath. Aluriel, meanwhile, particularly enjoyed the beer. Slightly smoky, slightly salty, much like the kind served in Al-Hadiqa, she found it a perfect complement to the spices on the meats and the soft, warm flatbreads. She savoured the meal, appreciating the care that had gone into its preparation.

As laughter and music filled the air, Yousef and Khalid approached Aluriel, inviting her to join them in Yousef's private tent. Inside, the atmosphere was quieter, the air thick with fragrant shisha smoke. They sat around a low table, sharing food and drink as the conversation turned towards the future and Aluriel's role as a Shieldmaiden.

Khalid, ever the scholar of Law, began to explain. "You may not realise it, but you are the first elven Shieldmaiden, Aluriel. No elf – whether a high elf, a sea elf, a wood elf or, Stars Above, a dark elf – has ever earned this title. No dwarf or half-elf has, either. The title carries immense honour, but it also carries great responsibility. Your tribe will live for as long as you do, for a Shieldmaiden's tribe exists only as long as its founder lives. Only if you were to die at the hands of a Barbarian man having broken no Laws, leadership of the tribe passes to one of your daughters, ensuring continuity, and the tribe remains a Shieldmaiden tribe."

Aluriel listened in silence, her expression gloomy as the words sank in. Her thoughts swirled.

*For as long as I live, and all of my descendants, and those of my spearmaidens?*

Her mind was already racing. An elf's lifespan was long, possibly tens of centuries. Just how large could her tribe grow over such a time frame? The thought made her shudder.

*I'm a lesbian... but maybe one day I'll want a child. Maybe I'd let a man fuck me again, just the once, if I really wanted one. If I even can bear a child. I wasn't supposed to exist myself!*

*I'll keep it small,* she resolved. *I have to keep it small.*

*I hope Zahara's not already pregnant.*

Khalid continued, as if sensing her hesitation. "But the shape your tribe takes is yours to decide. Each member who joins does so by your choice and yours alone."

Yousef leaned forward and spoke warmly, "And remember, Aluriel, you have earned this. The people here respect you, not just for what you've done, but for what you now represent. Now, as a newly anointed Shieldmaiden, you will anoint me together with Khalid in one turn of the first moon's time. No one will dare to challenge me, and if they do, they will regret it!" he laughed, with a wide grin.

"One turn of the first moon? That's... thirty-four days!" Aluriel burst out. "I can't stay here five weeks. I have to reach Vashlin!"

Khalid interjected, his tone as clipped as ever when he explained the finer points of Law. "While the choice would, in principle, have been yours to make... Aluriel, you must understand: the ritual you completed now binds you to this role under our Laws. To reject it earlier would have been an insult. To renege on it now would be seen as a rejection of the Law itself, which carries grave and severe consequences. I speak only as an advisor, but I urge you to weigh this decision carefully. It would be wisest to accept your new role and remain here for these weeks. It will take almost that long to prepare the armours for you and Zahara. And remember, she is now under your care and your protection."

Aluriel nodded slowly, her resolve firming. "If Zahara wished to cast her lot with me, who am I to refuse? But I will not let this tribe grow uncontrollably. It will remain... manageable. And I will wait until your anointing, but then I won't delay my trip further."

Yousef and Khalid exchanged a glance, the meaning of which Aluriel could only guess, but something in their faces hinted at approval. Yousef smiled. "Then may your tribe be strong, Shieldmaiden. Know that you, Zahara, and Ian will always be honoured guests in my tribe and hold a seat at my table. And all who belong to your tribe shall have free passage throughout Barbarian lands. At dawn, messengers will ride to all corners of the Great Desert with a drawing of you, a summary of what happened, and an invitation to the new Khan's anointing."

Yousef, as if struck by an afterthought, added, "You should also know, Aluriel, that the three more women you may anoint into your tribe as Spearmaidens will be your closest allies. Their anointment will signify not just membership but a shared bond of purpose, ensuring their protection as part of your Shieldmaiden tribe."

Aluriel tilted her head, curiosity flashing in her eyes. "What happens if I anoint Ian?" She giggled, twirling a strand of hair around her fingertips.

Khalid stepped in to explain. "If you did anoint him, it would signify marriage to the Shieldmaiden or one of the Spearmaidens. However," he added, his tone pragmatic, "provided no more than five men accompany you, no one will question you. A Shieldmaiden is allowed to travel with up to five men of her choosing. These men are afforded the same safe passage, so long as they travel under the Shieldmaiden's protection."

Aluriel's thoughts flickered bemusedly. *What's less likely? Ian wanting to marry Zahara, or Ian wanting to be anointed into a barbarian tribe led by a young half-Sea Elf woman?* The absurdity of the thought almost brought a faint smirk to her lips, but she managed to keep her expression neutral.

She decided to press further. "How do marriages work among the tribes?" She leaned in, genuinely curious.

Khalid tilted his head thoughtfully. "Barbarian marriage customs are... complicated," he began, his voice carrying the weight of centuries-old traditions. "If I were to explain the Marriage Laws in all their intricacies, I'd be talking until dawn, and likely a few more days thereafter. I'm actually writing a tome on it, collecting the past rulings of all the councils, and all the particular cases in recorded and oral history. I've written several volumes so far. It will probably take twenty-seven in total to finish it, if I live long enough. If you could read Lughat al-Barbar, I would offer..." he trailed off. "But as for you," he smiled as he resumed, "you'll no doubt be happy to hear the path is simpler." He drew a long drag on the shisha, exhaling fragrant smoke. "For a Shieldmaiden tribe, special rules apply. A Shieldmaiden may marry one man of her choosing, so long as he agrees. It is customary for the Shieldmaiden to make the first move and ask the man. While unmarried, Shieldmaidens and Spearmaidens may have intimate relations with whomever they wish, and they are expected to raise any offspring of such unions within the tribe."

After a moment, he added, "once a Shieldmaiden or Spearmaiden has married, they may share their husband intimately with the other four, as long as all agree. This arrangement fosters unity within the tribe and ensures its stability. The children are raised collectively by the entire tribe."

Yousef, stepping in, added, "Other tribes would universally honour a Shieldmaiden and grant them safe passage, at least as they would to a neutral or friendly Barbarian tribe. However," he added with a knowing smile, "in practice, no neutral tribes exist. Only alliances or enmities. Save, of course, for bands of bandits who prey on travellers too foolish to know better." *Or capture two Elemental Mages who burn them all to dust, he thought to himself,* but refrained from saying the words.

He paused, thoughtful. "Shieldmaidens are often called upon when two or more tribes want to end a feud and solve matters diplomatically. Their neutrality and the reverence they're shown make them trusted mediators." His expression saddened slightly as he continued. "A pity there was no Shieldmaiden when Kharesh took power and began his conquest. He was a brutal warrior, yes, as brutal as a fighter should sometimes be. But he was honourable and obeyed the Laws. Yet, over the years, he became... cruel. Almost as if he wished to raze villages and massacre peaceful people for the pleasure of it."

Aluriel tilted her head, curiosity flashing in her eyes. "Why Shieldmaidens? What makes us the ones tribes turn to if a tyrant rises?"

Yousef turned towards Khalid, bowing his head ever so slightly. "Perhaps our Vice Sharif would tell you the ancient tale. But first..." He flashed a curious smile. "I must ask, Aluriel... what did you wish for when you painted your rune?"

Aluriel hesitated for a moment, then smiled. "Control over lightning."

Khalid's eyes glinted with interest. "A fitting wish, given the circumstances. Perhaps tomorrow, you can try it out in the training tent. Its warding runes would prevent any accidents from a misfired bolt."

Aluriel nodded in agreement, intrigued by the offer.

Khalid clapped his hands lightly, gesturing to the group. "But before we delve into tales, let us refill our drinks and plates. Come, let's go find Zahara and Ian. This tale is best told in good company."

Zahara and Ian were busy eating from their plates and chugging beer from their drinking horns, but when Aluriel called them, they rose and joined the others around the low table in Yousef's tent. Two guards sat nearby with plates and drinks of their own, keeping watch whilst quietly enjoying the feast and chatting amongst themselves.

Khalid gestured towards Zahara and spoke, his tone reverent. "Before we begin, let me introduce Zahara properly. She is the daughter of Rafiq, a great warrior renowned in this tribe and beyond for his skill and strength. From a young age, Zahara was relentless in her training and pursuit of martial skill. She showed remarkable talent, enough to earn her the rare honour of being trained as a warrior, an honour given only to the most gifted women who prove beyond doubt they truly belong on the battlefield."

He paused, his gaze shifting to Zahara. Her strong musculature, honed from years of relentless labour and combat training, was evident even under the bright, traditional women's festive garb she now wore. Her rugged hands, marked by calluses, rested calmly on her lap. Her dark hair, now clean and woven into a solitary braid, framed her round face marred by countless scars. Aluriel had noticed many of her scars before, but was astonished at just how many more she had missed, now that her outfit exposed more of her skin. "Her path was not without hardship. She challenged Kharesh to a duel, and though she fought valiantly, she was defeated. For eight long years, she endured the shame and hardship of slavery... until Aluriel came to free her."

Zahara lowered her gaze briefly, then lifted her chin. "And now, I stand free, thanks to you, Shieldmaiden. That is a debt I will not forget." The words were simple, but the depth behind them was profound.

Khalid smiled faintly, leaning forward to add a small chunk of charcoal to the shisha. The smoke thickened and swirled around them. "And as we enjoy this quiet moment, let me share with you the tale of the first Shieldmaiden: Khadija. Because now," he continued, "You too will live in our songs and tales, Aluriel. That cannot be undone."

"Then the songs and tales about me must be mistaken..." she replied, even though she did not quite believe it.

"Many centuries ago, all barbarian tribes were torn apart in a blood feud between two great factions. Both were too proud to offer peace. Neither could afford further losses, for the war had raged for years and left both peoples starving, with most of their men dead. And it was then that Khadija rose."

Khalid inhaled deeply, letting the sweet smoke curl around him. "And so began the legend of Khadija," he said, voice dropping to a solemn hush. "The first Shieldmaiden..."

Aluriel leaned forward. *Whatever her story is, I need to hear it.*

# ✦ Interlude - The Tower of Philosophy ✦

## *Sergei*

The room was dimly lit, at the top of the Tower of Philosophy, itself the summit of Vashlin Keep, partly carved into the mountain behind it. A wide window offered a view over the sprawling fortress city below. It shimmered in the moonlight, its buildings and roads veiled beneath a canopy of evergreen climbing plants. Snow was falling, settling on rooftops and the canopy above the streets, occasionally dropping in clumps when the plants failed to bear the weight. The ground itself was paved and drenched in water: the vast river from Steelforge, too warm to linger in, steamed as it rushed downwards, bisecting the Great Staircase that split the city in two. Some of its flow was diverted sideways through underground canals that wound throughout the city in a marvel of Gnomish engineering. They warmed the city's homes as a shield against the bitter cold. In the freezing air, the steam would rise so thick and high that the bridges above were barely visible. The high walls and battlements, bathed in three moons' light, cast long shadows across the courtyard. Dragon-piercing ballistas dotted the walls, always manned and primed to fire. The vibrant foliage added an almost ethereal quality to the scene. Lanterns dotted the parapets, their flickering flames casting a faint glow against the starlit sky. Within the chamber, a soft, otherworldly glow emanated from the crystal ball on the ornate table at the centre. Within the sphere, mists shifted and danced, their light refracting into subtle patterns of colour, violets, blues, and greens swirling in a hypnotic display. Occasionally, the light would coalesce into brief, fleeting shapes before dissolving back into mist, lending the artifact an air of living mystery. Sergei sat reclined in a heavy, cushioned, massive armchair. Built to bear his weight alone, it groaned softly as its fabric and old wood strained under his immense bulk. His pale skin, almost translucent, reflected the faint light. His light-blue eyes scanned the swirling mists within the crystal with intensity. Short blonde hair, meticulously combed, crowned his clean-shaven face, and his wizard's robes, deep crimson with golden trim, impeccably tailored to his impressive frame, gave him an air of refined menace. Despite his enormous size, his movements were uncannily fluid and quick.

A knock on the heavy oak door pulled him from his trance. Sergei sighed and called out, his faint accent lending a soft cadence to his words. "Come in, old friend."

The door creaked open to reveal the High priest: a gaunt man in his fifties, with pale skin that contrasted starkly with his short white beard. His hair, once as long and blond as a High Elf's when Sergei had first met him, was now streaked with white and neatly tied into a short ponytail. His piercing green eyes missed nothing, reflecting the sharp intellect behind them, as if clarity might make amends for all that he had failed to protect. Yet, every glance bore grief, old sorrows unhealed and sacred, almost as if they were memories of a world he'd left behind. His left hand, crafted entirely of silver, rested at the end of his wrist, its polished surface glinting faintly in the dim light. The hand seemed almost alive, twitching occasionally, as though it harboured thoughts of its own. Strapped to his belt were a revolver gun and twin, sleek warhammers, adding an aura of martial readiness to his otherwise scholarly appearance. He was dressed in flowing gray robes adorned with glyphs from many schools of magic woven alongside sacred symbols and runes from all known Gods, in bold defiance of them all: a blasphemy only the most devout clergy of the Void would dare commit. To wear them in Vashlin was no issue. Elsewhere, such robes would invite trouble. He stepped into the room, closing the door softly behind him.

"Sergei," the High Priest began, his tone neutral, though Sergei had known him for far too long to be fooled by his attempt to conceal curiosity. "Any news? Or are you simply staring at that crystal for entertainment again?"

Sergei gestured lazily to the crystal ball with a faint smirk.

"As for entertainment..." He chuckled, pointing at the crystal ball. "I knov exactly vhich high-ranking paladins and priests of the Peacemaker are gay, and they don't knov I vatch them vhen they... give into temptation."

"You know, you should tell me their names, just in case I need leverage, but watching them? Not my thing. How about Aluriel?"

"She lives." Sergei's voice carried a note of satisfaction, laced with his faint accent. He scribbled a list of names on a piece of parchment and handed it to the High Priest. It was a little longer than he had expected. "Don't get any of them impaled, if you can. I like vatching them, you knov?" He laughed for a moment. Then, he turned serious again. "About Aluriel... Through this"- he pointed at the crystal ball again -"and her bracelet, I feel her lifeforce. Aluriel grovs stronger... her pover is rising."

The high priest's eyes narrowed slightly as he approached the table.

"Interesting. Predictable, though. But last I heard, she had no powers at all?" His tone settled into his usual scepticism.

Sergei leaned forward, his blue eyes glinting. "No povers? Perhaps no povers she can control. Not before yesterday. But nov... She is starting to control them," Sergei's eyes narrowed slightly as he gestured to the crystal. "I can feel her pover rising vhen I connect to her. It is like a drop of snov, da? Small, but given time, it can grov into a slavine. And she has so much pover hidden vithin her."

For a moment, silence hung between them, broken only by the soft hum of the crystal ball. Then Sergei spoke again, his voice reflective. "Do you remember that night? At Steelforge's gates?"

The high priest nodded slowly. "How could I forget? Thalorin, taking that arrow for Aeliana... nearly bled out while finishing the spell. It was a miracle he survived."

Sergei's eyes flicked to the high priest. "A miracle, da... but more so, Aeliana's sheer villpover. She already spent everything she had, her magic... so she used her own lifeforce, her own blood. Channelled it into healing him until the gnome healers arrived. That fool of a voman nearly killed herself. No vonder they felt... a connection. No vonder vhat they felt for each other right after. No vonder they fucked." Sergei's hands mimed the act in a vulgar gesture.

The high priest's expression darkened, his voice tinged with wonder, unusually so. "I've never seen anything like it. A High Elf and a Sea Elf... that their union bore fruit should have been impossible. And yet..."

"And yet it vasn't," Sergei murmured, his gaze drifting back to the crystal ball. "I have a theory about that... Perhaps it vas through Aeliana's... blood magic, if you vill allow me the term, that she vas able to conceive that night. The prophecy speaks of one 'Born of a union impossible'. Aluriel fits that description all too vell." He leaned back in his chair, his tone sceptical. "But I vonder... is she truly the one?"

The High Priest's reply was firm, almost ritualistic. He drew a slow breath, and recited:

"Born of a union impossible, beneath the rarest skies,

A journey marked by madness, a wisp of mist, and lies.

A myriad shards of power, each hidden in the storms,

To butcher or to falter, just as the world transforms.

Twilight calls in riddles, death whispers through the flame,

From blood her wings awaken, rebirth without a name.

In shadow's darkest hour, when decay rules its throne,

Shall rise a blaze forgotten, and claim fate as her own." He recited, voice stern, then let the words hang there for a moment.

"Like every scholar worth their salt, I know this prophecy well. Like every other scholar, worth their salt or not, I don't know what it all means. Though, decay ruling its throne, that is definitely grim," he added. "Aluriel... she's been watched since the day she was born. If she shows any sign of being the one the prophecy speaks of, I will know." He paused, staring directly into Sergei's eyes, before continuing. "And if she is... You and I both know it means the world is on the brink of chaos. And there are forces at play who will stop at nothing to end her."

Sergei chuckled softly, though there was little mirth in it. "Perhaps. But the die is cast, my friend. Aluriel is on her vay here. Vhatever she brings, let us hope it's good for Vashlin."

The high priest's gaze hardened. "If the prophecy is true, Sergei, much more than just Vashlin is at stake."

"And something tells me Aluriel vill be in the middle of it all." Sergei pointed to a small hourglass resting on his desk. "See how the sand flovs upvards? It started the night Aluriel vas born," he muttered. "But I didn't turn it. Every hour, it turns *itself*."

The base of the hourglass bore an inscription in a script even Sergei could not understand. Whenever he or the High Priest tried to read it, the glyphs rearranged themselves.

A heavy silence fell over the room, broken only by Sergei's sudden sigh. "It's been too long since I've heard from Vladimir." The High Priest did not mind the sudden change of topic. Sergei would do this whenever he had nothing more to say, or simply wished to say no more.

The high priest raised an eyebrow. "You cannot locate your brother?"

Sergei shook his head, his pale fingers steepled before him. "Not with magic. I have tried... even asked Yesod to assist me. An old friend in Zahira... and occasionally more," he added with a faint smirk. "Even he failed."

"Occasionally more? When's the last time you managed to see your dick with that huge belly of yours? How do you even know it's still there?" The high priest teased him. Sergei chuckled, retorting, "Oh, vhenever I need to find it, I can alvays ask your hand to *give me a hand*."

"You do that and I'll make it chop it right off. See if you can get a *silver* dick!" They laughed for a moment, before their expressions turned sombre. He frowned, his voice dropping. "About Vladimir... well, where the hell is he? And what the hell is he up to?" He leaned back, his expression darkening further. "You know Vladimir... he has a knack for finding trouble. Let us hope he has not stumbled into something dangerous again."

Sergei's blue eyes glinted in the dim light. "Qvestions without ansvers, my friend. Bah. They are like tiny pebbles in your boot. Small, but maddening. Vladimir's silence... it feels vrong. It's unlike him to vanish vithout leaving some clue. I do not like unansvered questions."

The high priest sighed, his silver hand twitching slightly as if echoing his unease. "When we find answers about Vladimir... let us hope they are not bad news."

He moved to one of the chairs by the wall and sat down heavily, the wood creaking slightly. Rummaging through his bag, he retrieved a finely carved pipe and a pouch of halfling pipe-herb. He packed the pipe and lit it, the flame briefly illuminating his contemplative face. Sweet, sticky smoke - somewhat psychoactive - soon filled the room. He took a long drag, exhaling slowly as he stared into the distance.

"Here," he said after a moment, offering the pipe to Sergei. "You look like you could use a distraction. Pretty damn good batch, if I say so myself!"

Sergei raised a pale eyebrow but took the pipe with a smirk. "Distraction, da? Let's see vhat you find so special about this batch." He inhaled deeply, the sweet smoke curling from his nostrils as he leaned back. "Ah... sweet, with a bite," he remarked, a faint smile playing on his lips. "Halfling craftsmanship never disappoints." He puffed some more. "This batch... is quite potent, da."

The high priest chuckled softly, the smoke swirling around him. "You could smoke ten of these pipes and not experience even the faintest hallucination, Sergei. Your... metabolism sees to that."

Sergei nodded with a smirk. "It has its uses. You, of *all* people, vould know," he said, exhaling smoke like a man savouring secrets.

"But yes, this year's crop is exceptional. Never seen pipe-herb so plentiful, and of such good quality..."

The conversation drifted into a more solemn tone as the High Priest leaned forward, resting his elbows on his knees. "What of Aeliana? Have you kept track of her other children?"

Sergei nodded slowly. "Ilinur and Girfila. They are still in Varthia, living as adventurers. Both of them are as vild and stubborn as their mother. They tread dangerous paths, but I suspect they prefer it that vay."

The high priest exhaled another stream of smoke. "Aeliana's lineage remains remarkable. Ilinur and Girfila inherited her light, no doubt..."

A pause.

He tapped his pipe against the edge of the armrest, once. "I trust they've stayed clear of Varthia's worst cruelties?"

Sergei gave him a sideways glance, one eyebrow faintly raised. "You ask that every time."

A brief smile flashed across the High Priest's lips. "Humour an old man." He exhaled a plume of smoke.

"They're vell." Sergei glanced at him sidelong. "So far... so good."

The high priest nodded, a bit too quickly. "Good. That's... Very good..." He trailed off, his face now more relaxed. "But what were we saying... Aluriel? Aluriel is... Different."

Sergei's pale fingers tapped lightly on the armrest of his chair. "Different, yes. Perhaps that is what worries me most. Tell me, dear friend, did Aeliana ask you to go help Aluriel?"

The high priest leaned back, his green eyes narrowing slightly. "Matter of fact, she did," he admitted, his tone calm but edged with practicality. "But if the Varthians, or the Barbarians for that matter, recognised me, it would mean fight after fight after fight on my hands. So much blood, spilled for nothing. My presence would be a magnet for chaos, not protection. Varius himself wouldn't kill me. If he has something close to a friend, despite all our differences, I would be it. And he values his own life too much. But the rest of his Peacemaker followers... They'd love nothing more than a piece of the Void's High Priest, consequences be damned."

Sergei needed no explanation of what the high priest meant. To kill a devout follower of the Void would, inescapably, later result in the killer's own death through a series of nested coincidences, each with vanishingly improbable odds.

"Ian," the High Priest continued, "as a dwarf and a priest of the Tireless Forger, has the best chance of taking her through Varthia unscathed. Dwarves, especially Dwarven priests, are generally respected there. So we both agreed to ask him."

Sergei frowned, his concern etched deep into his features. "Even so, things could still go vrong. Is there not something more you can do to ensure she makes it to Vashlin in one piece?"

The high priest stood, his silver hand twitching slightly as though echoing his thoughts. "I've already been working on it," he said, his voice carrying a note of finality. "And it's about time I went and had some words with the Baron."

"Please tell me you're not getting that jester priest involved... Vhat vas his name... Kalogerus?"

"Whether I do or not, he will involve himself, eventually, if only out of sheer boredom. Better he does so with my... guidance."

"You still trust him?" Sergei frowned. "After how you say he betrayed your best friend? His own friend?"

The high priest didn't answer immediately. He puffed at his pipe some more. Finally, he took one last slow puff, then spoke.

"I trust him to be himself. Which is to say... not at all."

The High Priest strode towards the door purposefully. As he exited Sergei's room, he caught the attention of a guard stationed nearby.

"Prepare my carriage," he ordered. "And have a couple of escorts ready, whoever's the Paladin and Battlemage on duty tonight. We leave for the border immediately."

His silver hand detached briefly, picking up one of his warhammers.

"Not yet, Hand." The High Priest whispered. "We're still in my tower, and really, I don't expect we'll get into a fight at all tonight. No one would dare attack my carriage within Vashlin. Varthians know better than to cause trouble in the Baron's tavern, and the Baron knows better than to cause trouble with me".

The hand fastened the warhammer onto the high priest's belt, briefly raising a middle finger before reattaching itself to his wrist, protesting loudly even though it had no mouth, "And here I was hoping to get into a fight. It's been years since you took me into a proper fight!"

*Don't worry, Hand. Chances are there'll be plenty of fighting, real soon,* the high priest thought, knowing that the hand heard his thoughts, too.

"Good. About bloody time! Thought you were trying to waste away into an old bag of bones without me, you stubborn bastard!" The hand responded, cackling in his thoughts.

*Maybe that's not such a bad idea,* the High Priest mused dryly. *You were less cranky when we fought together...*

As the High Priest's carriage rode into the distance, Sergei got up and stretched. "Time for some food," he murmured to himself. Pushing a book in one of his libraries revealed a hidden elevator. He entered it, and rode all the way down.

Some time later, he returned the same way. He was sated, his stomach was full, and his cheeks looked a few shades rosier.

Meanwhile, puffing away in the comfort of his carriage, the high priest thought to himself. *I might have an even wilder theory about how she was conceived. Too wild even to tell Sergei. But what if that orc sorceress was the one to start it all...*

# Chapter 7 – Khadija's tale

Khalid leaned back, drawing deeply from the shisha, its embers glowing faintly in the dim light of Yousef's tent. The group sat in a loose circle around the table, most having brought a plate of food or a goblet. The guards by the entrance were whispering quietly to one another, relaxed, but still vigilant.

"Now," Khalid began, his speech slightly slurred from one goblet too many. "Before I tell this tale, I will light this magical incense. I haven't got much left, probably just enough for tonight, and it's quite tricky and time-consuming to make more. But it will make all of us in this tent understand each other, no matter what language we speak, for as long as it surrounds us. So, fetch yourselves enough drink, relieve yourselves if you must, because once I begin, the flaps will stay closed until the tale is done."

He went to get more beer and relieve himself. When he returned, he placed a hanging incense burner onto a hook at the tent's apex. Once everyone else was back, including Ian, who carried a whole keg of beer with a roast chicken balanced on top, mumbling how he "dinnae ken hou lang the tale would tak," he began sealing the tent.

Amira had joined them as well. She had heard the tale before, but saw it as a chance to get to know Aluriel better.

Khalid ensured all the flaps were sealed, lit the incense burner and said, "Listen closely. This tale is no jest. It is no idle boast. It is the truth of our people. The truth of Khadija, the first Shieldmaiden." He tapped the shisha water-pipe, letting the ash fall into the tray below, and added a couple more pieces of charcoal. "Long ago, many centuries past, the tribes were broken. Divided. Blood stained the sands, and the war seemed endless."

"War for what?" Aluriel interjected in Elvish, leaning forward. In her native tongue, her voice sounded so much more melodic and fluid, yet still her curiosity all the same.

Khalid turned his gaze to her. "War for pride. For insults long forgotten. For who had more goats or whose warriors deserved the fairer women. It had started long before, as many wars do, with jealousy of one chieftain who saw his love interest wed to another chieftain. His pride simply could not bear it. Conflict escalated, and soon all tribes were drawn in, on one side or the other, each for reasons that seemed valid at the time." He took a long drag on the shisha and exhaled a thick cloud of smoke. "But with the passing of each year, the reasons were slowly forgotten. Pride and animosity, however, burned ever hotter. And pride, Shieldmaiden, is harder to slay than any warrior."

Aluriel nodded, her lips pressing into a thin line. *Pride has broken more than just tribes,* she thought, as a flicker of her own past surfaced before she pushed it away. **NOW** *is not the moment for endless rumination!* She steeled her mind as best she could, forcing it to listen – to truly listen – to Khalid.

Khalid continued. "The war left all of our ancestors starving. Most men were dead, and those who lived had naught left to fight for. It was then that Khadija stepped forward. A warrior like no other. Fierce, swift, unmatched with the scimitar. She saw the truth, clearer than any of us: the war itself was killing us faster than any enemy ever could."

"Was she a Chieftain's dochter?" Ian asked, his Dwarven accent cutting through the air as he tore a piece of roast chicken with his teeth. "Or just a woman wi' a knack fer fightin'?"

"She was no daughter of any chief," Khalid replied with a faint smile. "Her father was a smith, her mother a weaver. Khadija made her name by her blade, not her blood."

Yousef nodded thoughtfully. "She carried no lineage, but she earned respect. That is what matters among us. As the Blade Dancer teaches..." He paused to draw on the shisha. "At the end of a fight, all that matters is who stands, and who has been cut down." He exhaled a puff of fragrant smoke as he spoke, which made his voice sound strange.

Khalid took another puff from the shisha and released a sweet-smelling cloud before continuing. "Khadija, she went alone to the leaders of the warring tribes. Eighteen of them. She carried only her scimitar and her voice. Among us, it is said that to strike a lone woman who comes in peace brings misfortune, perhaps even a curse on their whole bloodline. Even enemies know better."

"And they listened to her?" Aluriel asked, latching onto Khalid's every word.

"They listened because she gave them no choice," Khalid said, chuckling faintly. "She spoke plainly, fierce as a storm. She told them to meet at a neutral oasis, under the palms and before the Blade Dancer. Swore on the sands and the stars that if they came, she would bring peace."

"And they came?" Zahara asked.

Khalid nodded. "Oh, they came. Starving men will clutch at any hope, even when pride blinds them. They swore oaths not to raise arms against each other at the oasis. But when the talks began, their pride flared like wildfire. Voices raised, threats were spat, but no blood was shed, for their oaths held them back."

Ian downed his second goblet of beer and, after a loud burp, asked: "Did Khadija nae lose patience?"

Khalid leaned forward, letting the sweet smoke from the shisha swirl around his face. "She did. But her patience was a hawk's patience, waiting to strike."

He paused to tap the ashes free before continuing in a hushed tone, as though conjuring the memory...

"When their bickering reached its peak, she rose and silenced them all with a challenge."

He leaned forward, conveying Khadija's words as best he could. "'*If even one of you can cut me,*' she said, '*I will surrender. But if you cannot, then you will surrender to me, and I will lead these talks.*'"

Khalid drained his goblet of beer, refilled it, and continued.

"For Khadija understood what few ever do: That ruling through death may win fear, but leading with mercy wins the people's hearts. And that is what keeps legends like hers alive even today."

"And then what?" Aluriel asked, her voice barely above a whisper, afraid of the possible answers.

"The first leader, a man swollen with arrogance, stepped forward," Khalid said, his tone growing rougher, more animated. "He thought her an easy target. But Khadija, she moved like the wind. In mere moments, his blade had flown off, and hers was at his throat. She did not kill him. No, she let him step away, ashamed, but breathing."

Ian let out a low whistle. "A bold lass, that one."

"Bold and deadly." Khalid glanced at Ian in response. "Two more came at her together, thinking numbers would sway the fight. They too were disarmed, their blades sinking into the sand. Khadija never took a scratch. The others, seeing her skill, hesitated. Three more stepped forward, and met the same fate. Then four. Then the rest, they all attacked together. When the last one finally surrendered, she stood, undefeated, before them all."

"She beat eighteen warriors on her own?" Zahara asked, her mouth agape.

"She did," Khalid said firmly. "Not a single man cut her. And when the last of them recovered his blade and sheathed it, she stood tall and told them this: *'You have been bested. Now you will listen. Together, we will find peace, or together, we will fall.'*"

Aluriel's gaze dropped to her hands, noticing a faint tremor. *Could I ever face so many without freezing?* Fear and unease squeezed through her chest. The memory of unleashing her own lightning against Kharesh flashed through her mind, as guilt and pride, in equal measure, assaulted it in turn. *I was desperate, not confident. Khadija chose to stand alone.* She forced a slow breath, trying once again to steady the tumult within her.

"And did they listen?" Ian asked, his voice breaking the heavy silence.

"They listened." Khalid nodded. "For days, she led the talks, hammering out agreements like a smith at the forge. And when it was done, she made her final demand: that she be allowed to form her own tribe. A Shieldmaiden tribe, she called it, led by her and four other women warriors, each from one of the other tribes. They would defend the peace and uphold the laws."

"And they agreed?" Zahara asked, wonder blooming in her voice.

"They did," Khalid continued, "but this was no small thing. A Shieldmaiden's tribe is unlike any other. It has peculiar rules and traditions, forged by Khadija herself and upheld by every Shieldmaiden since. A Shieldmaiden's tribe is always matriarchal, led by the Shieldmaiden and joined by four Spearmaidens she anoints. These women can be of any tribe, any race, they could be born free or they could have been a slave. Khadija made that clear. Their unity represents the peace they fought for."

He leaned forward, letting the shisha's smoke swirl around him. "Succession, too, is unique. But we have already told you these rules *ad nauseam,* to borrow a Varthian expression. The thing to understand here, though, is this: a Shieldmaiden's violent death, but also a Spearmaiden's, especially if at the hands of a Barbarian man, becomes a rallying cry: not merely a demand for justice and a call to arms for all Barbarians, but rather a relentless cry for vengeance. One that summons blood and blades from every corner of the Great Desert until such vengeance is carved in blood. Until the Stars Above remember it."

Khalid paused, glancing at Aluriel. He had already told her this, but drink made him ramble. "And a new Shieldmaiden is not chosen. It is not a title given, but one earned. It requires strength, honour, and the recognition of the Gods. It's rare, but a woman of any background, any bloodline, can rise to the position if she proves worthy. Khadija's own legacy ensured that no woman would be excluded simply for who she was or where she hailed from."

He drew from the shisha, then exhaled. "The Shieldmaiden became a symbol of unity, a reminder that peace was worth fighting for."

Yousef leaned back, a faint smile on his lips. "Khadija's name lives on, not just in our laws but in our hearts. Every Shieldmaiden since carries a piece of her spirit."

Khalid nodded solemnly, his gaze shifting to Aluriel. "And now, you, Aluriel, carry her legacy. May you wield it with the same strength and honour. And remember," he added, his tone growing heavier, "the legacy of a Shieldmaiden is not just one of battle. It is one of unity, of peace forged in the fires of conflict. One day, you may be asked to mediate between tribes as Khadija did, to lay down your blade and your lightning and pick up the burden of peace. When that day comes, may the Blade Dancer, the Stars, and the Spirits not only guide your hand, but also steady your heart."

The incense felt strange to Ian. Whilst he had continued speaking as he always had, trying to speak as close to the Common Tongue as he could, he was amazed at how he now understood Aluriel's Elvish, and especially Lughat al-Barbar. Shaking his head in wonder, he let out loudly in full Dwarvish: "Foo can a leid soun sae thrawn an' unfreenly fin ye dinna ken it, yet sae bonnie an' poetic fin ye dae?"

Aluriel understood it perfectly, as she had understood Khalid's tale and felt much the same thing. "I agree. Lughat al-Barbar sounds so harsh to an outsider's ears, to an elf like me, almost unfriendly, as Ian was saying. But now that we can understand it through magic, we can feel its beauty, its poetry. It flows in ways I never thought a language could. It's... beautiful."

Zahara was the first to reply, "Your languages are beautiful too. I never thought I could understand Dwarvish, or Elvish. Tomorrow, it will all sound foreign to me, like a dream fading away, and we will speak as if we were strangers again." She paused, the melancholy evident in her voice. "But tonight, and the story..."

Aluriel caught Zahara's quiet sorrow, rose to her feet, and hugged her. "Zahara... My Spearmaiden... We may go back to translators and using gestures. We will need to learn each other's languages, in time. But we will *never* be strangers again."

Amira, who had been silent throughout, cleared her throat and spoke. "Aluriel, your language is beautiful, and the tales about Elven grace are not merely tales. But more than that, you have a beautiful soul. Don't let darkness snuff your light out." She turned to Ian. "And you, Ian, I'd never seen a dwarf before. Now I know you can eat and drink like five men, but also that your heart is kind, beneath the coarse exterior. It's a secret you can no longer hide from me. It is an honour to know you both."

She turned towards Khalid, "You used that incense to make us feel that there is truth in unity, in understanding each other, is that not so?"

Khalid smiled. "I thought it would help bring us closer. A glimpse into another's language is like a glimpse into their soul. Almost." He puffed again on his shisha, remaining silent.

Yousef leaned forward, breaking the silence. "Khalid, there's one more thing we must do before she leaves us. Not tonight, perhaps not even tomorrow, but before she goes, in a moon's time."

Khalid raised an eyebrow, intrigued. "What is it, Khan?"

Yousef gestured towards Aluriel. "She has earned more than just our respect. Let's see to it that she is given a teleporter wand and a scroll for fire messages. She'll need them in the weeks ahead."

"A wise suggestion." He turned to Aluriel. "I have a teleporter wand stashed away. It was passed on to me by Rashad al-Amin, the late Vice Sharif of Lulu'a, and to him by his predecessor. It will take you directly to the city of Zahira, by the coast, close to the Varthian wall. All you must do is wield it in your hand and break it. It's a one-time use, so save it for an emergency or if you are urgently summoned by an officer of the Guild of Alchemists." He paused, drawing a rolled up parchment from his pack. "The scroll is simpler. If someone sends you a fire message, it will start to emit smoke, and the words will appear. Trust me when I say that the smoke... the smoke, you will notice for certain. You don't need to know how to send one, only how to read. I, or anyone else wishing to send you a fire message, needs of course to know how to do it, and also to have touched your parchment once." He held the parchment out for Aluriel to touch.

"Touch it now, for the future. I suspect you will one day learn to send messages yourself, Shieldmaiden," he reassured her. Aluriel complied and touched it.

Ian raised his hand slightly. "Actually, I've got a fire parchment too. Means I could send messages tae Khalid, or tae ye, Aluriel, if the need arises. Once we get tae Vashlin, I'll try an' teach ye tae write through 'em." He touched Khalid's parchment, then offered his own for the others to touch.

Aluriel raised an eyebrow at Ian, her smirk returning. "Oh, wonderful. What could possibly go wrong?" she said, her tone dripping with mock concern. Khalid chuckled at the exchange but said nothing. Then she crossed her arms. "Good that you'll be teaching me, because I wouldn't know where to start." She winked at Ian as she spoke, but the sarcasm in her voice had gone.

Khalid laughed, evidently well beyond tipsy. "That's why you have us. The wand and scroll will be ready for you tomorrow in my tent. Or whenever I manage to find the stuff, anyway. Yousef, I trust that will suffice?"

Yousef nodded solemnly. "It will. These tools will serve her well."

He then turned to Aluriel, with a serious expression. "Before the night ends, Shieldmaiden, is there anything you will need? Supplies for your journey?"

Aluriel considered for a moment. Then it came to her: Arrows.

"Arrows, please. I'm short on arrows." *Only eighteen left. Six fell out when I was dragged across that camel's back. Twelve plus six. Twelve plus half twelve. That will not do. Three times twelve, that would be right.* "Eighteen of them, if you could, please…"

Yousef nodded immediately and summoned one of the nearby guards. "Go find Rashid al-Sahmi," he instructed, "and ask him to prepare a bundle of his best arrows for the Shieldmaiden in the next days and weeks, whilst their armours are being made."

As the guard left, Yousef walked to one of his chests, unlocking it with a small bronze key. He rummaged briefly before pulling out six gleaming silver arrows. Turning back to Aluriel, he handed them to her with care. "These are not just silver-tipped arrows," he explained. "They are entirely made of silver, shaft and all. Enchanted. Particularly potent against undead and demons. May you never have need of them, but if you do, they will not fail you. Just practice with them a bit first. Their weight makes them fly differently from wooden arrows."

Aluriel accepted them with a nod of gratitude, and brushed her fingers over the polished, shimmering shafts. "Thank you, Yousef. I'll put them to good use if the time comes." *Twelve plus half twelve plus six. That's more comforting. Not perfect. But more comforting.*

Khalid broke the comfortable silence. "It's unusual to see someone who looks like a sea elf using a bow and arrows." His tone was curious rather than accusatory. "Most would expect you to wield something more... aquatic. Like a trident, for example."

Aluriel gave Khalid a genuine smile as her fingers idly traced the edge of the carpet. The beer had gotten to her head, just enough to make her tipsy. "It's not a typical skill for sea elves, I suppose," she admitted. "But I wasn't raised among them. And I am only one half of a sea elf. I learned archery because... well, because magic didn't come easily to me. It still doesn't."

Ian snorted, then laughed. "Arrows don't run out o' magic power, there's that." Aluriel and Khalid laughed at the remark, but as the remark and their laughs seemed to lighten the mood on the surface, Aluriel's mind ruminated yet again: *But arrows can run out. And you've got twelve plus six plus six more. That is not ideal. Not terrible, but not ideal. If you lose one, that'd be twelve plus five plus six. That would be a bad omen!*

Growing thoughtful, Aluriel continued. "I was young. Still trying to fit in among my mother's people, trying to prove I could be like them. But no matter how hard I tried, I couldn't grasp Druidic magic. The forest's heartbeat they spoke of, the connection... it always felt just out of reach."

"And so you turned to the bow?" Zahara asked, pausing her eating for a moment.

Aluriel shook her head. "Not immediately. At first, I tried harder. I stayed after lessons, practised until my hands were raw, and my knees sore from kneeling on the forest floor. But it was all in vain."

Her gaze drifted to one of the lanterns. "One evening, after yet another day spent failing to grasp nature magic, I was alone in the woods, and I was... crying. I felt so... small. Like I didn't belong. That's when Rhovan found me."

"Who's Rhovan?" Yousef asked, leaning forward with interest.

"A young ranger, a wood elf." Even the memory of him was enough to warm her tone. "He is one of the kindest elves I've ever known. He saw me crying and asked what was wrong. When I told him of all my struggles, he didn't laugh at me. He simply sat down next to me. Said, 'Magic isn't everything.' He sat in silence a little longer and then remarked that if anything, it was *he* who should feel *tiny* sitting next to me."

Ian burst out laughing first, and then the others joined in. Aluriel was, in fact, at least a head taller than all of them even when they were all sitting.

"And that was enough to inspire you?" Khalid asked.

Aluriel smiled, and her eyes betrayed a touch of humour. "Not quite. He offered to teach me something different. He led me to a clearing where a target was set up, and handed me his bow. I'd never held one before, and my first few shots were... less than impressive." Aluriel downed her beer, and giggled at the memory.

Ian refilled Aluriel's beer and guffawed. "Let me guess. Ye couldn't hit the broad side of a barn."

Aluriel laughed, nodding, then gulped some more beer down. "Not even close. The first arrow vanished into the trees, and the tenth barely grazed the target. But Rhovan was patient. He helped me adjust my stance, taught me how to correct my grip, and overall, he kept encouraging me. Told me this was something that anyone could do, with enough practice. Thanks to his encouragement, I didn't give up. At first, I didn't notice it. But slowly, I started to improve."

"And you found you had a knack for it?" Zahara asked matter-of-factly.

"Not at first," Aluriel admitted. "But I kept at it. Rhovan made it feel... possible. He never compared me to anyone else, never made me feel like I was failing. In time, I began to enjoy it. I wasn't great. Not like him and all the other wood elf snipers, who could hit a sparrow in the eye mid-flight... but I got better."

"Why didn't you stop once you learned?" Yousef asked. "Surely you could've tried something else. Some other form of combat, maybe?"

Aluriel shrugged. "Because it gave me something I didn't have before. The sense that I could do something. A sense of control in my small accomplishment. A sense that even though I wasn't great, I could continue to improve. It wasn't magic, and it didn't make me stand out from anyone else, but it was mine. And I'm useless with a sword! Believe me, he tried to teach me that, too."

Ian grunted and took another swig of beer. "Sounds like this Rhovan bloke kent fit he was aboot."

"He did," Aluriel agreed softly. "He taught me how to fire the bow, how to move quietly through the forest, how to track, all the trails winding through it, including the ones we took to get here... He even tried to teach me swordplay, but... well, let's just say I liked the bow better. Which is to say, I'm useless with a sword, like I just said. I keep it because it is my mother's."

Zahara interjected. "Useless, you say? Maybe I could teach you a trick or two. But tell me, did Rhovan ever say why he helped you?"

Aluriel hesitated, her fingers brushing over her bow, which lay beside her. "I think he saw something in me that I didn't see in myself. He once told me I had a spark inside, something within me that made me different. And while everyone knew I was different, for him it wasn't something bad. At the time... I struggled to believe him."

"And do you believe it now?" Zahara's question hung in the air, and the tent fell silent as Aluriel pondered her next words.

She looked down at her hands, then back at her companions. Her voice was steady, yet betrayed vulnerability. "I don't know."

Yousef grinned and rose to his feet. "Shieldmaiden, you should believe it. I believe it, and I've known you just a day. But for now, let's rejoin the others. It's almost time for dancing. And the incense's effects are about to fade."

The group rose, their conversation lightening as they returned to the bonfire. Soon after, some of the Barbarians brought out instruments and drums. They began to sing and play with an infectious, lively rhythm. The melodies carried into the night air, and the Barbarians began to dance in quick, spirited steps. Ian and Aluriel were drawn into the circle, and whatever reluctance they might have initially felt was quickly swept away by the energy of the gathering.

A storm of drums and horns filled the night air, the flames of the bonfire casting long shadows of those who danced around it. Partners whirled and clapped, as swirls of sand danced around their spinning feet.

Aluriel, though unfamiliar with the dance, caught on quickly and found her pace easily. Her movements were nimble, her steps flowing naturally, and her hips swayed in a way that felt oddly intuitive. Swept along by the music, lost in the frenzied dance, she almost did not notice when Zahara took her hands. Their gazes locked. The world around them seemed to slow in that moment. Aluriel felt heat rise to her cheeks, unsure if it was from the bonfire or Zahara's touch.

The dance held a subtle sensuality, until a quick drumbeat signalled a partner swap, and they were gone from each other's reach, the tension between them lasting just long enough to linger. To hint at, perhaps, something slightly deeper.

A few more guards stood watch by the edge of the gathering, drinking beer and exchanging quiet words as the celebration continued late into the night.

Aluriel, now an unwilling part of their history and their future, sat quietly. As she gazed up to the stars, she could feel the weight of Khadija's legacy wash over her like the desert night's cool embrace. *These laws... they are ancient, intricate, and deeply respected,* she thought, her gaze drifting to the embers of the bonfire. *But how am I to uphold them when I don't even know the first thing about them?* The weight of her title made her heart flutter, reminding her of the responsibilities she had taken on. Responsibilities whose full extent and implications she did not even know.

She clenched her fists lightly, resolve building within her. *I'll ask Khalid in the morning. Or, well... whenever I get up. It's morning already. He can guide me through this maze of traditions.*

# Chapter 8 – Yousef's Anointing

The days following the feast in Lulu'a passed in a blur of discovery and activity for Aluriel. Slowly, almost imperceptibly at first, the weather began to warm. Ian and Zahara kept busy around the village; Ian helped where he could, and Zahara soon resumed her martial training. Meanwhile, Aluriel spent most of her time with Khalid, exploring the limits of her new rune's power. The teleporter wand and fire parchment were delivered as promised; later, eighteen exquisitely crafted arrows arrived, but Khalid seemed far more interested in her rune and the control over lightning it granted her.

The day after the celebration, Aluriel woke up groggily sometime in the afternoon, and made her way to Khalid's training tent. Inside, the air was thick with incense that curled upwards from four braziers. The smoke caught the glow of the warding glyphs as they pulsed gently. Each wisp glowed in turn, in hues of red, gold, green, and blue, and at the apex of the tent they all merged into a swirling, ever-changing rainbow of smoke that circled lazily overhead. Aluriel's violet eyes glowed in response to the magic, casting their own hue into the mix, creating a mesmerising, slow-turning kaleidoscope of colour. Khalid gestured to a simple wooden dummy set up in the centre. "This tent will keep us safe from any mishaps," he said reassuringly. "Now, Shieldmaiden, show me what you can do."

Aluriel hesitated, looking at her hand. The rune she had painted the night before seemed to pulse faintly, as if waiting for her command. "I've never tried to control it," she admitted. "When it's happened, it's... it's not something I've done intentionally."

Khalid nodded thoughtfully. "Then it is time you learned. Start small. Focus your mind on the feeling, on the storm that lives within you. Do not force it. Guide it."

He paused, and looked straight into her eyes, gently placing a hand over her arm. "I will be brutally honest. I cannot channel lightning myself. I cannot teach you to do something I have never done myself. But what I will do for you, to the best of my ability, is guide you so that you may grasp that power from within yourself. Think not of me as a teacher you must learn from, but as a fellow mage, a fellow traveller who will help you find your path."

*If only they'd treated me like this back home,* she thought bitterly, *maybe I wouldn't even be here.* She took a deep breath, and raised her left hand. Closing her eyes, she imagined the crackle of energy, the flash of lightning. At first, nothing happened. She felt foolish, standing there with her hand outstretched.

"Patience," Khalid said softly. "The storm will not answer if you do not call it with purpose."

Minutes passed before she felt it: a tingling warmth in her palm. Slowly, it grew stronger, and eventually sparked into a tiny arc of lightning that swirled between her fingers. She gasped in a mixture of awe and fear as her eyes sprang open, marvelling at what she had just done.

"Well done. Now, direct it towards the dummy. Slowly."

She turned her hand, the arc sputtering before lashing out at the dummy barely a handspan away. The bolt struck its shoulder, leaving a tiny scorch mark. It was not much, but it was more than she had ever managed before.

"Good!" He gave her an encouraging smile. "You've made the first step. Now, refine it."

The training that followed was gruelling. For hours, Aluriel worked to direct the lightning with precision. At first, the bolts were wild, striking the ground or missing the dummy entirely. Khalid stood by, offering advice and encouragement. "Focus on your breathing. The storm must be controlled, not unleashed without thought."

Her failures were frustrating, but each small success pushed her forward. By day's end, she managed to reliably strike the dummy's torso from a foot away. The training left her drained, but for the first time, she felt a glimmer of control.

The second day brought new challenges. Khalid introduced the idea of touch. "The storm does not always need to leap from you," he explained. "It can flow directly from your hand to your opponent. Try it."

Aluriel approached the dummy and placed her palm against its wooden shoulder. She closed her eyes, focusing on the tingling energy in her hand. The first few attempts resulted in... nothing, but eventually, a small jolt passed from her hand to the dummy. Aluriel gasped, pulling her hand back as the wood crackled faintly.

"Good," Khalid said with a smile. "Now again. And again. Until it is as natural as breathing." Aluriel steadied her breathing, but in the back of her mind, those distant whispers stirred like an uneasy reminder that her journey wouldn't be confined to these desert sands forever.

As Aluriel took a break from her gruelling practice, she stepped out of the tent, and the chill of open air prickled her sweat-lined skin in a welcome respite from the tent and the lightning's heat.

Wandering near the practice grounds, her gaze fell upon Zahara, her scimitar flashing under the fading sunlight. Zahara moved with a grace born of years of training, her strikes fluid and precise as she carved through both imaginary opponents and training dummies. Aluriel paused, watching in admiration.

"You're relentless!" Aluriel called, her voice exhausted but tinged with respect. Having a Shieldmaiden in their town meant that there was always someone nearby, eager to translate whatever she said. Zahara turned, her braid swaying with the motion, and grinned.

"So are you, Shieldmaiden," Zahara replied. "But relentlessness is how we hone our edges."

Aluriel nodded with a warm, genuine smile. *I could learn a thing or two from her persistence*, she thought before heading back into Khalid's tent to resume her training. *But instead, my persistence gets me nowhere. I am no closer to getting a straight answer from these whispers than I was back in the forest. Every night, the same dreams, the same circle of butterflies, scrawls in pencil in the centre, and nothing to make of it. You're just mad, Aluriel. Shieldmaiden or not, that won't save you from madness*, she thought bitterly.

The next day, Khalid had to attend some judicial business, and Aluriel took a long break. She found herself sparring with Zahara. The two women exchanged techniques, their movements blending into a dance of fluid swordplay and strategy. Aluriel's strikes with her mithril short sword were clumsy at best, and Zahara quickly noticed the imbalance.

As before, someone appeared immediately, eager to be the interpreter. "You've got potential," Zahara said, lowering her blade after a particularly intense exchange. "But your swordsmanship needs work. Once you control that lightning of yours, no one will stand against you."

Aluriel exhaled sharply, wiping sweat from her brow. "The lightning is my strength, but this sword feels more like a burden than a weapon."

"Then don't try to make it your primary weapon. Use your sword defensively: to block, parry, and take advantage of openings. Reserve your sword strikes only for when the opportunity is perfect. Let the lightning be your main weapon."

"I remember when I first picked up a scimitar," Zahara continued, brushing droplets of sweat from her forehead. "I thought sheer strength would suffice. It took me years to learn that timing, precision, and speed matter more than raw power."

Aluriel considered her words. "That... makes sense. I've been trying to force my sword to do what it can't. Maybe if I focus on my strengths, I can build from there."

Zahara grinned. "Exactly. Defence first. Then, when you see the moment, strike like the storm you carry within you." Aluriel pondered the words whilst walking back to Khalid's tent for more practice.

One afternoon, a couple of days later, Khalid upped the stakes. He gestured towards the dummy, muttering an incantation under his breath. The wooden figure jerked to life, its movements jerky at first but soon smoother, like a warrior finding their rhythm. "It will dodge and block now," Khalid said with a smirk. "Let's see how you handle something that dodges and tries to get away from you. Once you master this, we might see what happens if the dummy tries to fight back!"

Aluriel squared her stance, realising this was going to be an even steeper learning curve. The animated dummy shifted, sidestepping her first bolt with ease. Her next attempt hit the ground, as the lightning fizzled out before reaching the dummy. A little frustrated, she gritted her teeth and tried again, and then again, and then again, refusing to give up.

"Focus!" Khalid called out. "Breathe. Anticipate its movements."

Hour after hour, day after day, Aluriel worked to outmanoeuvre the dummy, her muscles burning with the effort. Each failure only fuelled her determination. Over the following five days, she began to anticipate its dodges, her bolts striking closer and closer to their mark. When she finally hit the moving dummy squarely in its chest, Khalid let out a triumphant laugh. Aluriel's heart pounded as the dummy jerked to a stop. She watched the smoke rise from the blackened spot on its chest, and allowed herself a single breath of stunned relief: this was real control, not accidental fury.

"Well done, Aluriel!" Khalid exclaimed. "Now again. And again. Precision comes with repetition."

Each day passed like a blur, yet brought incremental progress. Aluriel's range improved, and she was now able to hit a dummy from just over a metre away. One day, Khalid introduced multiple moving targets, animated wooden spheres that bobbed and weaved unpredictably. Aluriel struggled at first, her frustration mounting as she missed more often than not. But she adjusted her stance, her breathing, and began to strike the targets with more consistency. By the end of the day, she had hit three in a row, a feat that brought a rare grin to Khalid's face.

Whenever she took a break, she often sparred with Zahara, who focused on teaching her to use the short sword to block and parry.

Yousef stopped by most evenings to check on her progress, often staying to observe. "You're getting there," he said one night, watching her with quiet pride. "The progress is slower than I expected, but your determination is what impresses me."

Aluriel gave him a wry smile. "Progress isn't slow, Yousef. I'm just learning to respect the storm. That takes time."

Amira would visit often, bringing them food and drinks, and offering words of encouragement.

Layla, Nadiya and Farah also came around to check on her every now and then, expressing their gratitude again and again. Farah had grown significantly, even in that short time frame. She was a little taller, her face a little fuller, and her limbs somewhat less wiry. *Guess that's what getting properly fed and cared for does to you*, Aluriel thought.

By the third week, Khalid armed his dummy with a club and had it time its strikes, creating a rhythm she had to follow whilst maintaining precision. "The battlefield is chaos," he explained. "You must learn to wield your lightning as second nature, even under duress."

Aluriel's inner monologue carried her through these exhausting sessions. The whispers and her usual ruminations never went away. *I'm a failure. I hurt Elenwen and now I'm only here, respected and revered, because of something I unleashed by accident and some words I said to bluff and save my life. I do not deserve to be a Shieldmaiden. And why can't I make these thoughts, these incessant whispers go away?* she kept thinking. However, interspersed with them, new thoughts began to appear. *I have to get this right. I can't rely on instinct alone anymore. If this is to be my power, I need to own it.*

More days passed, and eventually Aluriel was able to defeat the dummy even when it fought with verve. Her lightning could hit a target three metres away now, and it would pack quite a punch. It was not the explosive power she had unleashed upon Kharesh, but it was steady progress. One evening, she even managed to hit all seven spheres, from quite a distance. The bolt had landed with surprising ease, as if the storm had anticipated her intent and strangely obeyed. But it did not happen again.

"Control," Khalid reminded her as she celebrated the small victory. "It is control that will make you strong, Shieldmaiden. Not power alone. While we're here, there's something else I want to teach you. A few phrases in Lughat al-Barbar. Ones that could save your life."

"Such as?"

Khalid began to speak slowly, spelling out each syllable carefully. "First, how to announce yourself as a Shieldmaiden. Say, 'Ana Shijalaqa,' which means, 'I am a Shieldmaiden.'" He waited as Aluriel repeated the phrase, her pronunciation halting at first but improving with each attempt.

"Good," Khalid said with a nod. "Next, 'Ana taht himayat Naqib al-Kimya.' 'I am under the protection of the Guild of Alchemists.' This one is important. It will grant you safe passage in most lands controlled by our tribes. Of course, being a Shieldmaiden, that is already granted to you by our Laws. But, the day may come when you need help outside of our lands. The Alchemists' Guild has embassies in many places. Varthia, Vashlin, Steelforge, and even a new one, just established in Grul zur'Ghrub, to name a few. There's even one in

Sevarinel, no jest. You may need to seek help, or refuge, one day. The Guild's protection extends to you even beyond the borders of the Tribes' land."

"Sevarinel?!" Aluriel replied, stunned. "That's the Sea elves' capital. Under the sea! How do you even..."

"We have ways to manage," Khalid said, grinning. "Mind you, many Alchemists there are Sea elves themselves... yet they too need to do alchemy in air. Mixing ingredients and potions underwater just does not work. But let's not get derailed. Here, take this."

He handed her a pin with the symbol of the Guild. In place of the stars above the ring, however, there was some writing in Lughat al-Barbar. "This pin identifies you as an honoured guest, under our protection. I've had another made for Ian."

Aluriel practised the words, her tongue tripping over the unfamiliar sounds. She smirked. "I'll need more practice if I want anyone to actually understand me."

Khalid chuckled. "Practice will come with time, but the effort will be respected. Words carry weight, Aluriel, but the conviction behind them matters more."

As the sun set on yet another day of training, Aluriel sat on the floor of Khalid's tent, her muscles aching but her heart light. "I never thought I'd feel like this," she admitted. "Like I could actually... wield it. Thank you, Khalid. For all your time and efforts."

Khalid nodded with a kind expression. "You are most welcome. You have taken the first steps, Aluriel. The path is long, but you walk it with your own purpose. That is what matters."

By the time their armours were ready, Aluriel had not only gained some confidence in her abilities, but also a newfound respect for the power within her. Her padded robes were flawless, light yet durable, allowing her to move freely whilst providing just enough protection. They were crimson red with blue trim just as she had imagined them. Zahara's leather armour glinted with its polished studs, a masterpiece of craftsmanship the tribe's artisans were especially proud of.

For the following week, the Barbarian settlement buzzed with activity in the crisp stillness of the fading winter. The air was sharp with the anticipation of early spring, the scent of burning incense mingled with the earthy aroma of freshly turned soil. Wild desert flowers had begun to bloom near the oasis and the sky above was painted in hues of purple and red whenever the sun began to set. The days had grown longer, and Aluriel now felt her skin sweating under the Sun. She kept training relentlessly, even when Khalid was not around to guide her.

On the night of the anointment, all four moons hung low on the horizon, foreshadowing what would be an unusually bright night.

Barbarians from every corner of the sands had come, some trudging through weeks of travel, others riding horses and camels laden with gifts. Ornate weapons, bolts of richly dyed fabric, and casks of rare spices and oils were piled in a communal offering near the centre of the village. The clang of metal echoed as warriors sparred in the distance, eager to display their skills as an honour to Yousef. Two challengers had come to face Yousef in a ritual duel for the title of Khan. Yousef had defeated both honourably.

The anointing would begin when the moons were at their peak, and as the hours dwindled, the gathering swelled. Fires dotted the settlement, their flickering warmth inviting clusters of Barbarians who sang, laughed, and shared stories. Children ran around, darting between tents, laughing and mingling with each other and visitors alike.

Eventually, it was time for the ritual to begin, and the crowd stood in a large circle around the totem and the unburned bonfire. As he did before, Yousef arrived astride his giant goat in front of the totem, with the unlit bonfire towering behind it. He dismounted and bowed to Khalid and Aluriel.

"You have returned." Khalid's voice was steady and ceremonial. The words were old, unchanged for generations. Ritual bound them to their ancient form.

Yousef nodded, his voice equally ritualistic. "I have returned. The people have come. They deserve a leader who carries their hopes and burdens with honour."

"Have you been challenged since you last stood here?" Khalid asked the ritual question.

"Yes. Two came, and each I bested," Yousef answered.

"And what is become of them?" Khalid continued.

"They bent the knee and live among us as brothers," Yousef replied.

Khalid placed a hand on Yousef's shoulder, his grip firm. "You have proven you can bear the title of Khan. Remember, tonight you are not just taking on a title. You are becoming a symbol. You are taking on a weight."

Aluriel stood next to Khalid, her violet eyes scanning the crowd. She adjusted the folds of her newly acquired padded robes, their intricate embroidery glowing in the torchlight. The armoured robes Aluriel had requested were typically white, but Yousef had Amira make hers of blue and red fabric as she asked as a special mark of honour. Blue, to symbolise her growing mastery of lightning, and red, for the fire she summoned when Kharesh and his tents had burned. She drew in a slow breath, filling her lungs with smoky air.

As the moons reached their apex, the crowd began to quiet, their murmurs fading into an expectant hush. Khalid stepped forward. He raised his hands, his voice carrying over the gathering like the crackle of the bonfire they would soon set ablaze.

"Brothers, sisters, children of the sands!" Khalid began, his tone rich with emotion. "We are gathered standing over the Sands, under the watchful gaze of the Blade Dancer, the Desert Spirits, and our ancestors, under the light of four moons and of the Stars Above, to anoint Yousef as our Khan. He has proven his strength in battle, his wisdom in counsel, and his compassion in leadership. Tonight, he takes upon himself the mantle of responsibility for all our tribes."

A cheer rose from the crowd, but it was quickly stifled by Khalid's raised hand. "But this is not a victory. It is a beginning," Khalid continued. "And it is not upon me alone to bestow this honour. Shieldmaiden Aluriel, step forward."

Aluriel's heart quickened as she moved to Khalid's side. She felt the weight of a thousand gazes, the mixture of respect, curiosity, and scepticism pressing against her like a physical force. She lowered her chin, meeting Yousef's eyes with a steady gaze.

Khalid handed her a ceremonial blade, whose curved edge gleamed under the moonlight. The blade was ancient, etched with runes that seemed to shimmer faintly as she held it. She took a step closer to Yousef, her voice clear and unwavering.

"Yousef," she began, "by the traditions of the Shieldmaidens and the laws of the Sands, I recognise your strength, your honour, and your willingness to serve. Do you swear, under the gaze of the Blade

Dancer and the Desert Spirits, Under the light of the Stars and the Moons, to lead with justice, to protect the weak, and to uphold the Laws of your people?"

Yousef dropped to one knee, his head bowed. "I swear it."

"Do you swear to carry the burdens of leadership, even when they weigh heavier than any blade? To act not for your own glory, but for the well-being of all tribes?"

"I swear it."

"Then, take this blade, to remind you of your oaths." Aluriel placed the ceremonial blade into his hands and stepped back. *I didn't think I could do even that small part of the ritual. Memorising the whole thing in Lughat al-Barbar? I was sure I'd screw it up. But, I didn't. That's... something.*

Satisfied, Khalid raised his hands, intoning a chanted invocation in Lughat al-Barbar. His voice resonated across the gathered crowd as he called upon the Stars, the Moons, the Sands, and the Blade Dancer God himself to witness the anointing of a new Khan. The murmuring crowd fell silent, their gazes fixed on him as he spoke. Once the invocation ended, Khalid turned to Yousef and motioned for him to disrobe. The young Khan complied without hesitation, his muscular frame gleaming under the moonlight. Khalid then dipped a ceremonial brush into the thick ointment, lifting it with reverence as he began the anointing.

With steady hands, he painted a rune on Yousef's forehead and intoned, "May your mind always be true."

He marked each eyelid with precision, speaking, "May your eyes always see true."

The brush moved to Yousef's lips. "May your lips only speak with honour."

Onto each ear, Khalid traced symbols. "May your ears always hear true."

A delicate symbol was drawn on Yousef's nose. "May your nose always smell true."

Moving to Yousef's arms, forearms, back, and the palms of his hands, Khalid spoke as he painted, "May your arms always strike true."

He traced runes across Yousef's chest and abdomen. "May you always stand true."

He traced runes over his manhood. "May your loins bear plentiful fruit."

Finally, he anointed Yousef's thighs, legs, and feet. "May your legs always step true."

Once every rune was placed, Khalid stepped back in a rehearsed, ritualised motion. He took three deliberate steps backward, then knelt on one knee, then the other, before slowly placing his forehead to the ground. His hands rested on the sand, palms facing up, revealing the tattoo of the Blade Dancer God's rune etched into his left palm. The crowd fell silent, their reverence palpable. "Arise, friend and Alchemist," Yousef said, reaching down to take Khalid's hand and help him to his feet in an equally ritualised manner.

Together, they lifted a torch – Khalid with his left hand, Yousef with his right – and brought its flame to the pyre. The offerings ignited and the bonfire roared to life, sending sparks spiralling towards the Stars Above. The crowd erupted in cheers, their voices filling the night as the flames consumed the parchments, carrying prayers to the Sky.

"Then rise, Yousef, Khan of the tribes of the South-West," Khalid declared, his voice ringing with finality.

The crowd's cheers roared even louder, their voices booming into the night. Musicians struck up a triumphant melody, and the whole settlement stirred with joy and celebration.

As the noise swelled around her, Aluriel found herself smiling. For a moment, the doubts that usually plagued her were silent, replaced by a quiet sense of belonging. The weight of Khadija's legacy still lingered, but tonight, it felt shared.

Yousef walked over to Aluriel and their gazes locked. "Thank you, Shieldmaiden," he said, his voice sincere. "Your presence means more than I can say. I owe this night to you."

Aluriel inclined her head. "You'll make a fine Khan, Yousef. Just remember... the Moons are watching."

"Then I'll try my best to be the Khan they deserve to watch."

They shared a deep, genuine smile. Then, uncharacteristically, Aluriel spread her arms wide and hugged him briefly.

Then, Yousef turned to the crowd, addressing them as their newly anointed leader. Aluriel stepped back into the shadows, her place in the celebration earned but distant. The firelight flickered against her features as the sounds of revelry filled the air, the four moons above bearing silent witness to the rise of a new Khan.

The night was another one of celebrations, even grander than the celebrations the month before. Exotic drinks were brought from every corner of the desert and some lands beyond, and Aluriel even recognised some Elven wine, no doubt brought from nearby Al-Hadiqa. She drank it, and the taste of the home she'd lost filled her with nostalgia for a moment. Roast meats were handed out. Piles of flatbreads, baklava, and other sweets Aluriel did not know were left there for the taking. Aluriel tried them all. The frenzied dancing and the music went on for many hours. Aluriel drank and danced, and when she danced with Zahara, again she felt a tingling in her chest when their gaze met and their hands locked. She was not sure if Zahara felt the same or if it was the drink that made her imagine it.

When the last reveller had fallen over drunk or returned home, Aluriel was in her hut, preparing to sleep. The whispers and the dreams had not given her too much of a reprieve during her forced wait in Lulu'a, and yet this night they assaulted her with a vengeance. The butterflies, the whispers, the circle, all now carried a sense of urgency, as if the time for action had come yet again.

The next day, not wanting to overstay their welcome, the trio prepared to leave. They filled their waterskins and tried to purchase necessary supplies, but to their surprise, the townsfolk insisted on filling their pack beasts with provisions to the brim. When Aluriel and Ian offered payment, the townsfolk waved them off. "You've given us hope, Shieldmaiden," an elder said, his voice quivering. "Let us give you this in return."

Though reluctant, Aluriel accepted it all with a nod, her heart heavy with both gratitude and the responsibility that came with her title. As they set out, they went for a final round of farewell. All the townsfolk expressed their gratitude and respect to Aluriel, and she felt more prepared than ever for the journey ahead.

Nadiya also left with them, saying she would ride with them a while, then go visit her family.

As she and her newfound allies left the settlement, astride their goats and with camels in tow, Aluriel felt something she hadn't allowed herself to feel in a long time.

A glimmer of hope.

# Chapter 9 – The Varthian Wall

The journey to the Varthian Wall stretched across five weeks, an arduous ride through unforgiving desert sands. Late winter had given way to mid-spring, and the heat was beginning to be intolerable, especially for Aluriel. She did not dare imagine what this place was like in the summer. They were well-prepared, their pack beasts were laden with supplies and waterskins filled to the brim. Their status as official guests of the Guild of Alchemists, along with Aluriel's title as Shieldmaiden, ensured that their stops at oases along the way were welcomed with warmth and hospitality. They travelled mostly at night, when the desert's chill lent some mercy to the endless sands. By day, they rested wherever they could find shade, or built it with a tent. Even in spring, the desert felt like a furnace, especially to Aluriel, whose body seemed to consume as much water as any of the camels they kept in tow. The local alchemists offered them shelter and a chance to rest, often curious to hear tales of their travels, and even more curious to hear about how a creature such as Aluriel managed to become a Shieldmaiden. Aluriel was conflicted about this, as she became a Shieldmaiden inadvertently, and certainly not by choice. Whilst this had given her great benefits in crossing the barbarian lands, she couldn't help but wonder what obligations, expectations, or hurdles this title might impose upon her later. And most of all, she felt inadequate, knowing she had earned it all with a desperate bluff she improvised to save her life.

The oases were tranquil sanctuaries, dotted with date palms and small pools of shimmering water. There, the air was filled with the scent of flowering shrubs, and the calls of desert birds rang in their ears. Each stop provided a reprieve from the searing heat, and the group took these moments to replenish their strength.

Nadiya had left them at some point, as she had said she would. Aluriel gladly left her a camel to ride, with enough provisions secured in its saddlebags. Zahara and Aluriel spent much of their journey teaching each other their languages. Zahara's rich Barbarian tongue, full of sharp consonants and fluid vowels, contrasted with Aluriel's lilting Elvish, whose musical tones seemed to flow like water. Their exchanges were often punctuated by laughter at mispronunciations and shared stories of their pasts. Bit by bit, they began to understand each other, forming a bond that deepened with every passing day.

Despite her growing connection with Zahara, Aluriel's thoughts often drifted back to her title as Shieldmaiden. *Why me?* She wondered as she gazed at the tranquil waters of the oasis. *I never asked for this. The people welcome me as if I've earned it, but all I've done is survive. What will they expect of me when the time comes to act? Will I be a failure yet again as I've always been?* She shook her head, frustrated by the weight of expectations that seemed to grow heavier with each passing day.

Ian, for his part, seemed content to enjoy the hospitality, though under his gruff demeanour, his sharp mind never stopped turning. As he sipped from a cup of spiced tea one evening, he glanced at Aluriel, who was seated a short distance away, her expression distant. *Lass is carryin' a burden she doesnae need tae bear alone,* he thought. *But ye cannae tell her that. She's as stubborn as a mule in a thunderstorm.* He smirked to himself, finishing his tea, and deciding it was best to let her sort her thoughts on her own terms.

Through the last week of travel, the terrain began to change. The endless dunes of the desert gave way to rocky plains, and the air grew cooler as the altitude increased. In the distance, the Varthian Wall loomed. When it finally came into view, Aluriel was awed by the sight of a massive structure of stone and mortar that stretched for miles, dividing the desert from the fertile lands beyond. The architecture of the wall was imposing, fortified enough to withstand a full-scale siege, complete with battlements and watchtowers that stood as bulwarks of civilisation against the wilderness of the desert.

From the rocky hill where the desert gave way to stone, Aluriel could briefly catch a glimpse beyond the Wall. Her keen darkvision painted the world in muted colours: not the bright hues of daylight, but a strange, shifting tapestry of faint blues, deep purples, and shimmering silvers. She could make out what lay beyond the wall even before the Sun rose, every shape illuminated in the eerie glow she was accustomed to. Behind the wall, rows of well-armed Varthian soldiers were patrolling methodically. Tents and supply depots stretched in orderly lines from the base of the wall, bustling with activity and organisation, even well before dawn. The Varthians clearly did not like to be surprised.

On the trio's side of the wall, chaos seemed to reign. Tents and huts of Barbarian warriors were scattered unevenly across the dusty plains, their colours and designs as varied as the tribes they represented. Yet despite the apparent chaos, their numbers matched – if not outnumbered – the Varthian forces, with warriors lounging by fires, sharpening weapons, and speaking in low, deliberate tones. Zahara, observing the scene, gestured towards the camp and muttered in her broken Common Tongue, "Varthians... they try fight us. They want our land. Fail too many times. Too many times, Barbarians take revenge. Now... they build wall. Keep us out."

Over on the Varthian side, the buildings near the wall reflected a different architectural inspiration: rectangular stone structures with red-tiled roofs and wide porticos supported by large columns. The air felt heavier there: not with dust, but with structure and order, in place of the chaotic freedom of the desert. Aluriel found herself both impressed and unsettled by the transition, her fingers brushing the edge of her saddle as her gaze took in the disciplined symmetry of the land. *This place feels wrong*, she thought, a shiver running down her spine. *Too clean. Too controlled. It's as if the desert's spirit has been crushed beneath all this stone.*

To stymie her spiralling thoughts, she recounted her arrows. *Eighteen elven arrows. Six silver arrows. Seventeen Barbarian arrows. Seventeen?* **SEVENTEEN?!** *Where did the last one go?* She recounted them again. *Forty-one arrows. Eighteen elven. Six silver. Seventeen Barbarian. That's twelve plus six plus two half-twelves plus five. That's Forty-one. FORTY-ONE! A number that cannot be divided! A prime number!* Aluriel clearly began to panic as her thoughts spiralled into her usual ruminations, made heavier by an impending sense of doom that came from having an amount of arrows that was *clearly bad*.

Amidst her silent panic, as they approached the wall, the group encountered two gaunt figures stumbling through the rocky terrain. The men were ragged and thin, their tunics torn and their sandals barely holding together. Ian's sharp eyes spotted them first, and his voice carried a note of caution. "Varthian deserters, mair than likely," Ian muttered.

As the group drew near, the men raised their hands in a gesture of surrender. Their eyes were sunken, their voices hoarse as they pleaded for water. Aluriel eyed them coldly, her hands tightening on her reins. "They're not our problem," she said firmly. *Bad omen. Forty-one arrows. Bad omen. This encounter will not end well,* her mind was howling.

*The lass... I've never kent her tae be sae cold. Fit's wrong wi' her?* Ian wondered silently.

Zahara, riding beside her, frowned. "They desperate, Aluriel. We have enough, we share."

"They're Varthians," Aluriel countered icily. "They chose their path."

"Now they choose live," Zahara said, her voice steady. "You and I, we choose live too, no?"

One of the two, his voice trembling, fell to his knees and pleaded. "Anyone with a heart would desert if they were forced to follow the Peacemaker's paladins and inflict suffering on innocents. They demand not loyalty, but obedience bought with fear. We had no choice... but to flee. And for that, we are called cowards. Traitors."

Aluriel sighed heavily but relented. Dismounting, she led one of the camels forward and handed the men enough water and provisions to reach the nearest oasis. She also pressed a few coins into their hands. "This will get you started. Then you can find some work there," she said curtly.

Zahara, dismounting as well, approached the men and handed each of them a scimitar looted from Kharesh's camp. "You need this," she said, her speech clipped and accented. "Desert... no good, for protection." The men looked at her with wide-eyed gratitude. "Thank you," the one who hadn't yet spoken rasped. "My name is Marcus, and this is Iulius. We will not forget this kindness. How can we ever repay you?"

"If you want to repay it, there's a way. Ride to the Enchanted Forest, west of the desert. It'll take you about five or six weeks through the sands, and then... some days or weeks into the forest before a ranger spots you. The Elves will hold you and question you, but they will not kill you on the spot. Say you have a message for Aeliana, for her ears only. When they take you to see her, tell her you met her daughter, that I'm fine, and that the dwarf is fine."

"I swear on our lives, we will!" Marcus bowed deeply.

"You will?" She narrowed her eyes. "I'll hold you to that, Marcus." Aluriel took two of her camels, and gave them to Marcus and Iulius. "Here. They'll help you cross the desert. There's more provisions and some more coins in their saddlebags. Enough to get you there. Now go, make haste."

Aluriel watched them go, her mind conflicted. *Would they have helped us if the roles were reversed?* she wondered. *Or are we all just clinging to life, forced to pick between bad choices in the hope that we'll survive?* Her gaze drifted to Zahara, who was already remounting her goat. *She's right*, Aluriel admitted to herself reluctantly. *Perhaps we're not so different, she and I. We chose to live, too. In our own ways, we both did what we had to.* She shook the thought away, uncomfortable with the implications. Zahara's gentle but firm voice echoed in her mind. *And now they're choosing to live. Hm. Maybe they'll even be helpful, if they do what they promised.*

The trio forged ahead, the Wall growing ever larger on the horizon. By the time they reached its gates, the first light of dawn was breaking, painting the rocky plains with a pale golden hue as the world bloomed into full colour. The gate itself was a massive iron construct, flanked by guards clad in chainmail that sparkled in the newborn light. Their helmets bore crests of crimson plumes, and their tunics were spotless, despite the dust of the desert.

Ian dismounted first, his posture calm as he approached the guards. "We seek passage into Varthia," he said, respectfully but firmly. The guards regarded him with deference, noting his dwarven priestly garb and the fire emblem on his chest.

"You may pass, Priest of the Tireless Forger," the guard said. His gaze shifted to Aluriel and Zahara, his expression hardening. "But not them."

Aluriel stiffened, her hand instinctively drifting towards her weapon. "And why not?" she asked.

The guard's eyes narrowed. "A sea elf in barbarian garb and a barbarian woman? We've heard tales of you. A Shieldmaiden, they say. Your kind has no place in Varthia."

All stood silent for a moment. After a brief pause, one of the guards spoke, "wait here. I'll call my officer."

Moments later, a man clad in more elaborate armour, his helmet adorned with two additional crimson crests, approached. He eyed Ian with a mixture of respect and caution and greeted him with a crisp military salute. "Priest of the Tireless Forger: I am Captain Cassius of the Varthian Army. How may I assist you?"

Ian bowed his head slightly, attempting to speak Common Tongue at his best. "A pleasure to meet you, Captain. I am Ian Redhammer, Priest of the Tireless Forger. I request passage for myself and my companions. We travel on an urgent mission, and their presence is vital."

The officer's gaze shifted to Aluriel and Zahara, lingering on the former's distinctive features and the latter's countless scars and slave mark burned onto her flesh. He maintained his deference towards Ian but shook his head slowly. "I'm sorry, noble priest, I truly am. I would love to help you, but the orders I received were absolute. Barbarians, particularly those of... unusual origins, are not permitted entry until further orders. There have been reports of a clan war and a new large clan taking hold, as well as a new Shieldmaiden... whatever that is. This is not the time to let any potential trouble in."

"Surely an exception can be made," Ian pressed, his tone even. "Ye ken fine well these lasses are nae threat tae yer lands." His Dwarven dialect returned for a moment. He continued, "These women are under my protection and integral to my purpose here."

The officer's expression softened, but his resolve remained unyielding. "I respect your position, but my orders are absolute. They cannot pass."

Ian made one last attempt, his expression neutral but his tone sharp. "They're me servants," he said. "If ye deny them entry, I'll hae tae find somewhere tae sell them – or dispose o' them – in the nearby capital. I'll return once it's done."

The guards exchanged glances with their captain, their expressions firm but respectful towards Ian. "Do what you must, noble priest," the Captain said politely but firmly. "But they will not cross this gate. I am sorry. I truly am."

"Well, then," Ian answered, bowing his head slightly, "We'll be off. The Law is the Law, and must be respected."

"Well said," Cassius replied. Then, addressing the two soldiers, he added, "Make sure that when he does come back, he is given no further trouble."

"Yes, sir!" The two soldiers replied in unison, saluting Cassius.

Ian nodded curtly and led the group away. Once he had remounted his goat and they were well out of earshot, he muttered to himself, "Bluidy fools. They'll let me in 'cause I've got a shiny rune an' a fine enchanted hammer, but turn awa' two lasses who could tak' on their entire platoon. Typical Varthian arrogance."

"Let's get goin'," he said aloud. "We'll regroup in Zahira an' sort this oot."

The group turned their mounts towards Madinat al-Fakhri Zahira, the Barbarian capital, rising on the horizon as the sun climbed higher. The short ride to the Radiant City of Glory was silent, each member of the group lost in their thoughts. The massive gates of Varthia had denied them entry, but Zahira held the promise of refuge and a chance to plan their next move.

Just under a half hour later, the gates of Madinat al-Fakhri Zahira came into clear focus. The city's towering white walls gleamed in the crisp morning light, their smooth surfaces looking unblemished, despite the passage of time and the many conflicts Zahira had faced.

Aluriel straightened in her saddle, projecting determination. When it was their turn to approach the checkpoint, she spoke the phrases in Lughat al-Barbar that she had learned from Khalid, painstakingly etched into her memory. The guards at the gate exchanged glances, their expressions shifting from suspicion to recognition. With a respectful bow, they stepped aside and gestured for the Shieldmaiden and her companions to enter.

"Welcome, Shieldmaiden," one of the guards said. "Stables are there." He pointed towards a large structure to Aluriel's left, its wooden beams sturdy and its roof shaded by palm fronds.

The stable worker, a wiry man with sun-worn skin, took the animals with care, murmuring softly to calm the camels and goats. "They'll be well fed and watered," he assured them, gesturing them forward. "Thank you, good Sir," Aluriel said as she nodded, her eyes already wandering to the vibrant cityscape beyond the gates.

The streets of Zahira were paved with smooth, interlocking stones of black and white, their patterns forming intricate geometric designs that sparkled faintly in the soft morning light. The buildings, mostly crafted from pristine white marble, stood tall and proud. Aluriel and Ian paused, stunned by the grandeur of Barbarian architecture, to admire its soaring domes and solemn arches. This place was vastly different from the villages and settlements they had visited in the desert. The scent of spices and roasted meats filled the air, mingling with the soft murmur of flowing water from fountains scattered throughout the city. Small patches of earth dotted the city, where grass and blooming flowers showcased the beauty of spring.

Ian let out a low whistle as they wandered through the streets. "Weel, this is a sight, nae doubt!" Ian commented loudly, as his eyes kept sweeping over the bustling streets and the elegant facades of the buildings.

Zahara, scanning the skyline as she turned her head, pointed to a massive structure near the city's north-west border. Its dome was topped with a glistening brass telescope that caught the sun's rays like a beacon. "That... important place," she said haltingly. "Stars... they watch from it. Alchemist... Their home."

"An observatory," Aluriel said thoughtfully. She glanced at Zahara and smiled. "They study the stars and skies. And the main Guild of Alchemists... their headquarters, it seems."

The trio continued their stroll through the city, their footsteps echoing on the polished stones as they ventured into a bustling market. The atmosphere of the souk immediately enveloped them. Vendors called out their wares in melodic tones. Stalls overflowed with vibrant silks, glinting jewellery, and exotic spices that filled the air with tantalising scents. Fresh fruits adorned one of the first stalls they passed. Other stalls offered copper pans and clay tagines, rows of painted dishes, and hand-carved utensils stacked high like miniature towers. One stall displayed brushes and jars of powdered pigment, whilst another offered charcoal sticks, quills, and parchment rolls. A third offered animal feed. And there were far too many more for Aluriel to thoroughly inspect each one of them.

A barber worked beneath a canopy, expertly shaving a client whilst a young boy fanned the air. Nearby, a toothless antiquarian guarded his collection of cracked statues, scroll fragments, and various oddities. Aluriel whispered to Zahara, pointing subtly towards the stall, "I want to check this one out. Please, be my interpreter. I'll point at things when I want more information, and if I want to actually buy something, I'll say 'This one' in Elvish. You do the haggling, and when you tell me the deal's finalised, I'll pay."

They headed for that stall, unsure of what they'd find. Of the myriad of items, each labelled in a handwriting so spidery it seemed older than the wares themselves, most were useless to her. But she found a spyglass and a compass, both of Gnomish manufacture, and a sextant. After some expert haggling by Zahara, she bought all three. To Aluriel, it sounded like an extended exchange of insults, followed by a pantomime of Zahara turning to leave and the seller calling her back to offer a better price. *So this is how Barbarians really haggle... Wonder how much I overpaid our goats...*

In an Alchemist's booth, bottles of ink and vials of perfume stood side by side with healing potions and salves, and countless other ingredients and concoctions whose purpose Aluriel could not dare even guess. She stopped there, too, and purchased three more healing potions. They were expensive but, no doubt thanks to Zahara's haggling, they cost her far less than they would have had she walked in alone, speaking a foreign tongue.

In his stall, a scribe was offering to compose letters for coin, whilst a shoemaker hammered leather soles against an anvil. Rows of boots and shoes in every colour and size surrounded him. Noticing how Zahara's boots were basically in tatters, Aluriel pointed at the stall and told Zahara, "You need new boots, for sure. Let's get you some."

Zahara frowned. "But I have no money..."

Aluriel reassured her, "I have plenty of money. Between what my mother gave me for the journey, and all the gold I looted from Kharesh and his men... *I've placed a generous share of Kharesh's gold into Layla, Farah, and Nadiya's possessions, and I placed your share at the bottom of your pack when you weren't looking. Still, I have plenty left. Shoes and boots won't bankrupt me.* "So, don't worry and find yourself a pair of boots or three. As usual, you haggle, I pay."

Zahara walked out wearing a new pair of polished leather boots, and a pair of running shoes now tucked inside her satchel. Aluriel had also insisted she treat herself to a pair of elegant low-heeled shoes. Zahara was reluctant to accept them, feeling she did not deserve such luxury. But Aluriel had been unwavering. "Either you try these on and find a pair that fits, or I'll guess and leave you with elegant shoes that don't," she'd said. Zahara relented.

"Thank you, Aluriel," Zahara said, with a sincere smile born of genuine gratitude. Aluriel had also bought a pair of boots for herself. The ones Aeliana gave her for the journey were still in good shape, but, as a precaution... *Besides, they say a girl can never have too many shoes.* And so, she bought not just the boots, but also a pair of elegant, low-heeled shoes to match Zahara's.

A fortune teller behind a table covered in purple velvet fanned out her tarot cards with slow, deliberate grace. Cages of brightly plumed birds hung from tentpoles, their songs rising, blending with the calls of the vendors and mutters of haggling voices. A myriad of lanterns swayed gently overhead, catching the sun in their coloured glass, ready to be lit up after dusk.

A group of con artists was deceiving a visitor they managed to tempt with a game of three-card monte. Another group nearby was doing the same, this one with balls and cups.

But the trio's noses commandeered their attention with a sweet, irresistible scent, and they found themselves moving towards it. On the way, a fletcher had a stall, and Aluriel bought exactly one arrow, which immediately felt like it restored her sanity. Or, at least, some of it. Perhaps, at the cost of the fletcher's, whose puzzled expression needed no words.

Following the scent led them to a stall, where a cheerful halfling with a plump, rosy-cheeked face and a spry demeanour caught their attention. "Bonjour, mes amis!" he greeted them with a wide smile. "You look like you could use something sweet, oui? Jacques will make you ze best crêpes in all of Zahira!"

Aluriel exchanged a glance with Ian, who chuckled. "Weel, I'll nae say no tae a sweet treat," he said.

"And perhaps, good sir, might you be kind enough to point us towards the docks?" Aluriel interjected.

"Mais oui! Certainly!" Jacques set to work, his nimble fingers expertly flipping delicate crêpes on a hot griddle. He drizzled them generously with honey and handed the golden creations to the trio. "Et voilà! Ze taste of paradise."

As they sat on the cushions in the stall, the first bite melted in their mouths, the sweet honey perfectly complementing the soft, warm crêpes. Zahara's eyes widened, and she nodded enthusiastically. "Good... very good!".

"Aye, this is somethin' special," Ian added, his voice full of appreciation. Aluriel simply nodded, too engrossed in her second bite to speak.

They devoured the crêpes quickly and found themselves ordering seconds, to Jacques's delight. "Ah, you have ze good taste! Eat, eat! Life is too short to be hungry, non?" he exclaimed, gesturing flamboyantly.

As they finished their second helping, Jacques leaned on his counter, his curious eyes studying them. "You are travellers, yes? From far away? You must tell Jacques ze stories! But first... more crêpes? Or perhaps a galette?

"Galette?" Ian asked, raising an eyebrow.

Jacques' smile widened as he gestured to the griddle. "Ah, oui! Ze salty cousin of ze crêpe. Let Jacques make you one with ham and cheese. If you do not like it, it is free of charge."

Ian grinned. "I'll tak' yer word fer it, laddie."

Jacques quickly prepared the galette, folding the savoury filling into the thin, golden-brown batter before handing it to Ian with a flourish. "Et voilà! Try zis."

Ian took a large bite, his eyes widening in delight. "By the Forger, this is braw!" Ian exclaimed between bites, tearing through it with gusto.

Jacques clapped his hands together. "Ah, Jacques is ze master of ze griddle! Shall Jacques make ze same for ze ladies?"

"Yes, please," Aluriel said enthusiastically. Ian liking something didn't necessarily mean that *she* would, but it did smell great. Zahara said nothing, but nodded with the same enthusiasm.

Jacques handed them each a galette, and soon the trio were enjoying the savoury treat, their hunger finally sated. "Good... very good," Zahara managed to say, despite her mouth being full.

As they ate, a small figure slipped behind them, blending into the crowd. Quick as a shadow, the man reached for Aluriel's coin purse, his nimble fingers extracting a handful of coins before disappearing into the throng of passers-by.

Unaware of the theft, the trio thanked Jacques warmly. But when Aluriel reached for her coin purse to pay, her expression darkened. "Some of my coins are missing," she said in an annoyed tone, almost sharp with irritation.

Jacques' cheerful demeanour faltered for a moment before he sighed. "Ah, zis is unfortunate. Ze markets have ze thieves, no matter how bright ze city. If you find ze thief, tell ze guards. Ze penalty is ze loss of a hand."

Aluriel's eyes narrowed as she scanned the bustling market, frustration bubbling beneath her calm exterior. Zahara and Ian exchanged looks but quickly realised the futility of chasing a thief in such a crowded place. The vibrant chaos of the souk offered too many shadows and nooks for the thief to vanish into unnoticed.

"Ah, forget it," Ian muttered, tightening his grip on his own coin pouch. "Naebody's catchin' him in this lot."

Aluriel sighed but nodded reluctantly. "You're right. Let's just be more careful." *Good thing I'd packed the pillagers' heap of gold coins at the bottom of my bag,* she thought. *The thief got little more than pocket change, in comparison.*

Ensuring their coin purses were secured, they turned back to Jacques, who nodded encouragingly and began giving them directions.

"Merci for ze visit," Jacques said warmly, gesturing in the direction of the docks. "If you ever find yourself in Lunith, north-west of Varthia, just outside ze Varthian border, you must visit my cousin Pierre. He has a crêpes shop, just like mine, mais oh, mon Dieu! much, much bigger! A whole patisserie! With ze tables and ze waitresses! Ah, tell him I sent you! He will treat you well, oui? Now, for ze docks, follow ze main road until you see ze fishmongers. On ze way, you will pass a flower shop. Ze best flower shop in Zahira! And after that, ze fountain. Turn right there. Just don't linger near ze alley by ze brothel. It's not ze place for travellers like you. You cannot miss ze sleek, shiny boats!" His gaze lingered on Aluriel for a moment before his eyes lit up with recognition. "Mais you... you look like some of ze elves I see at ze docks! But... a bit different, non? Are you one of zhem?"

Aluriel's heart leapt at his words, and began pounding with excitement. "There are Sea Elves here?" she asked eagerly. "I'm half Sea Elf myself."

Jacques clapped his hands together with delight. "Ah, merveilleux! Ze sea elves, zey are down by ze docks, oui!" He gestured animatedly, repeating the detailed directions with great enthusiasm.

"Thank ye kindly, we'll dae just that," Ian said with a nod. "Let's get tae it, then." The trio said their goodbyes and made their way through the bustling market.

Guided by Jacques' directions, the trio took the main road lined with the same polished black-and-white paving stones that adorned the rest of Zahira. Small shops and street vendors dotted the path, their voices rising in a cheerful cacophony. A fishmonger stood near the entrance of the street, his stall laden with an impressive array of freshly caught fish, their scales glistening like gems under the sunlight. The sharp scent of brine and saltwater filled the air.

Aluriel paused briefly, observing the fishmonger deftly cleaning a large tuna. *Such precision in a task so mundane*, she thought. *Even here, there is beauty in the ordinary.*

Further down the road, a flower shop bloomed with vivid colours, its shelves overflowing with pots of fragrant blossoms. The shopkeeper, an elderly woman with kind eyes, was weaving a garland of jasmine as they passed. Zahara stopped for a moment, inhaling deeply and murmuring, "Flowers... like desert's rain."

Aluriel paused as her gaze fell upon a single red rose with thick, velvety petals. She reached into her pouch and handed a few coins to the shopkeeper, who smiled warmly and wrapped the stem in a small piece of cloth. Turning to Zahara, Aluriel held out the rose with a soft smile.

"For you," she said simply.

Zahara's eyes widened, and a faint blush crept across her cheeks as she accepted the rose. "Beautiful," she said haltingly. Her fingers brushed against Aluriel's as she took it, lingering just a heartbeat longer than necessary. "Thank you."

Aluriel gave her a warm smile before they continued onward. As they neared the fountain Jacques had mentioned, its crystal-clear water sparkled in the sunlight, cascading from an intricately carved marble statue of a warrior raising a shield. Aluriel bent down, cupping her hands to drink from the cool, refreshing stream. The water soothed her parched throat, and she let out a sigh of contented relief. *A moment of peace amidst the chaos,* she thought. *Perhaps Zahira is not so different from the places I once called home.* But the truth gnawed at her, as inescapable as it was relentless. *Home?* she wondered bitterly. *Did I ever have one? Too High-elven for my father, too sea-bound for my forest, and now... even the Barbarian tribes took me in only because of some sacred words and a ritual I didn't understand.*

Her fingers brushed the edge of her bracelet, one of only two reminders of her family. *And yet,* she thought, glancing at Zahara and Ian, *we are a tribe now. Small, strange, but bound by choice, not tradition. The joke's on me, cast out for not belonging, only to bind myself to others in a way no one expected.*

Her gaze flicked to Ian and Zahara, who were patiently waiting nearby for her to finish drinking. By now, her seemingly bottomless thirst for water no longer surprised either. *I've been running for so long. Will I ever stop?* the thought lingered as she straightened – her thirst finally sated – and rejoined her companions.

Just past the fountain, they turned onto a narrower street leading towards the docks. The buildings here were simpler, the white facades giving way to rougher stonework. The sea's scent grew stronger, mingling with the aromas of fried fish and the warm spice of roasted nuts from nearby stalls. A figure emerged from an alley: a cloaked and hooded woman, her face obscured by an ornate mask. The sharp click of her high heels echoed in the narrow passage as she moved with exquisite grace, her long cloak swaying slightly with each step. She stopped before a brightly painted door on the opposite side of the street, its frame adorned with hanging beads that clinked softly in the breeze and a red lantern above the door frame. Without hesitation, the woman pushed the door open and slipped inside.

Unbeknownst to Aluriel, the woman climbed to a room on the top floor and stood by its wide window overlooking the street below. She positioned herself quietly behind the curtains, watching as the trio continued their walk towards the docks.

"Looks like this here be the *Sauna* the halflin' was tellin' us aboot," Ian muttered, his tone neutral but his pace quickening. "Best keep movin'."

Finally, the harbour came into view, bustling with activity. Ships of various sizes rocked gently in their berths, sails furled and ropes creaking as sailors moved purposefully about. The sleek, flowing designs of several vessels stood out, unmistakably the handiwork of Sea Elves. Aluriel's heart lifted at the sight.

"If there's Sea Elves here," Ian said, his voice low but hopeful, "this is where we'll find them."

# ✦ Interlude – The Courtesan ✦

## Ludmilla

She walked with confidence into the brothel by Zahira's docks. The Madam knew better than to question her, for whenever she graced her establishment with her presence, customers would rush in, and so would the money. So she gladly pocketed a small coin purse that Ludmilla placed into her hands without a word.

Today, she had no time for... customers.

Ludmilla had frequented brothels for as long as brothels existed. She could only charge her magical powers through draining others' sexual energy, like the rest of her kin. Other than for temporary exhaustion, her lovers were unharmed... save for the few she had already meant to harm after the act.

This brothel was a dingy establishment by the docks in a Barbarian city, and unless she had drained her magical reserves to the point of desperation, none of the customers here would have been her first choice. She much preferred liaisons with kings, rulers, high priests, and most of all, wizards. They smelled better, had more energy for her to drain, and could pay her far more handsomely. This place, however, had one thing going for it: a room with a large window, thick curtains, and a full view of the docks. After some conversation here and there, Aluriel and her two companions approached one of the ships, sat down, and started drinking and conversing with a sea elf captain. She pulled her magic spyglass out of her purse. This spyglass not only let her see at a distance, like any good spyglass was meant to do. It also let her hear quietly, in her mind, what the ones it observed were saying.

Aluriel was beautiful. Restless. Broken in all the right places. Ludmilla tilted her head. **So that's what a phoenix looks like before it remembers the fire.**

She could have approached them. Stepped out of the shadow. Played the stranger, the saviour, the temptress. But the time wasn't right. Not yet. She still needed to be certain. And besides, Varius was watching Aluriel too. Through her. *How delightful, to be paid a fortune to do things I would have done anyway,* she mused silently. *They turned her away at the Varthian gates, and so she's trying to see if she can get through by sea. But the blockades from the Eastern Varthian navy... Aluriel could swim unnoticed. Ian alone would be allowed through. But Zahara? Zahara couldn't do either. Aluriel going through all that trouble to get her through as well? Hm. She must be more important to her than I'd thought. This... is a complication. So now, she will go to Yesod at the guild of alchemists, and then, through the Sunless Depths,* she thought.

Ludmilla waved, the motion so fluid it might have been an illusion itself. Her fingers traced a swirling glyph mid-air, and reality bent.

The room dissolved into leaves and wet silence. The air here was different. **Denser. Wilder. Hungrier.**

The demiplane of Mist did not resemble a forest so much as the dream of a blind artist. Someone who had never seen a tree, and tried to imagine it. The boughs glistened like bone wrapped in velvet. Petals of flowers hanging in mid-air opened and closed in time with her breath. The soil pulsed softly, like a heart. Impossible floral shapes rotated as they flew through the air. Clouds felt upside-down.

Home.

She stepped forward, breathed it in. Just long enough to catch the scent of her kind.

"Back so soon?" One of her kin asked. He, too, like all Mist Elves in their true form, carried the stunning beauty of an angel, though none of them had ever truly been elves. Mist Elves was just the name lesser races, mortal races had given them, on the rare occasions they encountered one.

"Yep. But not for long." She flew a short distance, then she started weaving the next spell, sharper this time. She heard her kinsman say,

"You're getting too attached to that Earth! Your flaming sword's been planted in the ground, gathering dust for what, centuries? Millennia?"

Damn right she was getting attached. If HE knew why, HE would be, too.

"And in all that time, nobody touched it?" she replied. "Good. That means I can leave it there a few centuries longer." And with another motion of her fingers, she was gone. Like every other mist elf, she had one. To fulfil their purpose, should the time ever come again. She could not take it outside of their demiplane, but she did not need it.

Not on Earth.

She appeared in a room heavy with drapes and incense. Gold gleamed in half-shadow. Pillows. Wine. The sound of water trickling through a marble fountain. A luxurious bed with bedposts made of solid gold, and crimson silk sheets.

Varius's bedchambers.

She made no announcement. Only let the veil of illusion fall from her cloak, revealing bare shoulders kissed with shifting runes, eyes that knew too much, and a smile practised to perfection. Her features quickly morphed to those Varius remembered. She donned the black lace lingerie that had been left for her. Expensive lingerie, gifted by Varius each time, meant to be worn by her, and destroyed that same night by the fury of his passion.

She rang a bell, and a servant quickly came. "Tell him I'm here."

The servant required no introduction and no further explanation.

She would let him think she was his.

Let him believe his coin bought her loyalty.

Let him take her body, and think it power over her.

Let him ask her to watch Aluriel again. And when he did, she would agree.

After all, she intended to follow the phoenix anyway.

# Chapter 10 – The Sharif

The harbour bustled with activity. The air was thick with the tang of salt, and the creak of ship masts swaying gently in the breeze. Among the throngs of sailors and merchants, Aluriel's eyes were drawn to a sleek vessel docked nearby, its hull shimmering with the telltale elegance of Sea Elf craftsmanship. The ship seemed to ripple like the waves, and its design flowed seamlessly as if it were an extension of the ocean itself. A group of sailors worked deftly on the deck, their dark blue skin and white or blue hair stark against the bright midday sun. Gills, much more formed than her own, adorned their necks.

Aluriel felt her breath catch. They were unmistakable. True Sea Elves. All of them stood a little taller than her.

She hesitated, her pulse quickening as curiosity and apprehension swelled up within her. *What will they think of me?* She wondered. *Will they see me as one of their own, or something less?*

Ian nudged her gently, his voice low. "Weel, lass, ye've been searchin' for this. Best not stand gawkin'."

"Right," she murmured, steeling herself as she approached the ship. Zahara followed closely.

One of the sailors looked up, and his violet eyes – identical to Aluriel's, save for the glow – narrowed slightly as his gaze landed upon her. He set down a coil of rope, stepping closer to the gangplank. "Well now, wot 'ave we 'ere?" he said, his accent rough and lilting, carrying the unmistakable tones of a Sea elf. "Ain't you a sight? You look a bit like one o' us, you do, but... not quite, eh?"

The others on deck paused their work, and their gazes fell upon her with a mix of curiosity and cautious scrutiny. Aluriel's silvery white hair caught the sunlight, looking exactly like some of theirs. The sailor tilted his head, his tone polite but guarded. "An' who might you be, then?"

Aluriel hesitated, then drew herself up. "My name is Aluriel. My father... is Thalorin."

A ripple of murmurs spread among the crew. One of the older sailors, his hair a deep indigo streaked with silver, stepped forward, his face stunned as if meeting a legend. "Thalorin? The mage, you mean?" he asked, his words spilling as quick as rain. "The one what...? Cor Blimey, you're really 'er!" He trailed off, his eyes widening slightly. "Bleedin' Abyss, it's you, ain't it?!"

"Me?" Aluriel asked, her heart pounding. "What do you mean, me? Of course I'm... Me... I mean, I'm just, I am me!" She stammered the last words, awkwardly pointing at herself.

The older sailor exchanged glances with his comrades. "There's a tale, lass. About Thalorin takin' up with a High Elven druidess. Folk said it'd come to nowt. Sea Elves don't 'ave children with other kinds. But you... you is proof otherwise."

Aluriel felt a strange mix of pride and discomfort as their eyes lingered on her, studying her intensely. *So even among them, I am an oddity worthy of gossip,* she thought. *A living exception to their rules.*

One of the younger sailors, a wiry man with hair the colour of storm clouds, muttered, "Ain't never thought I'd see the bleedin' day. Thalorin's own, strollin' 'round like it's any ol' dock."

"Oi, enough o' that," the older sailor said sharply, though his tone held no malice. His words carried the rough lilt of a pirate, softened by centuries of travels. He stepped forward, his manner softening.

"Name's Captain Leorin. Kin to Thalorin, are ya? Well, you're proper welcome 'ere."

He reached into a pouch at his belt, withdrawing a brass necklace with a small cat pendant. "'Ere, take this," he said, holding it out to her. "Bit o' luck fer ya. From one o' the sea to another. Keep it close, mind the water, and mind the moggies, right?"

Aluriel accepted it with trembling hands, her voice barely above a whisper. "Thank you," she said, as she placed it around her neck.

Leorin's smile was warm. "Come aboard, you and yer mates. We'll wet our whistles, aye? Reckon there's tales worth hearin'."

Ian's eyes lit up as soon as he saw Leorin tap a keg. "Proper dwarven ale?" He exclaimed, unable to contain his excitement.

Leorin chuckled. "Cor blimey, mate. We gets stuff from all over, we trade stuff from all over, booze an' all. An' the best bit? We get to drink it too! Come on, then."

The trio followed him up the gangplank. Aluriel's mind swirled with questions and emotions. As they settled into a quiet moment aboard the ship, Ian leaned closer to Aluriel and Zahara, his voice low but animated.

"Ye ken," he began, gesturing towards the various cats scattered about the ship and docks, "followers o' the Lady o' the Abyss, aye, they've got a soft spot fer cats. They say the Lady hersel' loves 'em, sees 'em as sacred wee guardians. That's why ye'll find cats bein' nurtured an' cared fer by Sea Elves. It's like they're protectors in their own way."

Aluriel glanced down at the cat who, moments earlier, had jumped onto her lap, now purring deeply, and stroked its ears. *Guardians of the sea,* she mused. *Even something as small as this creature holds significance here.*

Captain Leorin overheard Ian's explanation and chuckled. "The dwarf's got it spot on, 'e 'as. We look after our own, right, an' that includes the moggies. Ain't just us sea-farin' folk. Funny thing, the Barbarians, they say prayers to the Lady o' the Abyss sometimes too. Prayin' fer water, they are. They got cats as well, though not 'alf as many. Can't see too many moggies wantin' to roast their whiskers in the middle o' the bloody desert, now can ya?" He grinned wryly. "Still, the ones they've got? Spoilt rotten, just like ours.

The cat shifted slightly, leaning into Aluriel's touch as if to prove the captain's point. Aluriel felt a flicker of ease settle over her, as the soft purring gently soothed the whispers and eased her swirling ruminations. She glanced down at the pendant around her neck and noticed something she hadn't before. Every Sea Elf she could see there wore a similar pendant, and each one was shaped like a cat. Some were sleek and poised, others playful, and each shimmered faintly in the light, as if reflecting the ocean's vitality. Aluriel's fingers brushed against her own pendant, feeling its warmth.

On the dock below, a Sea Elf crouched near a stray cat, offering it a piece of fish. The cat accepted it with a contented purr, whilst two kittens darted out from behind a barrel, tumbling over each other in play. The sight brought a genuine smile to Aluriel's lips. *Even here, amidst the salt and spray, life flourished in unexpected ways.*

Captain Leorin cleared his throat. "Most of us live under the waves," he resumed speaking, his voice shifting into a proper yarn-spinner's rhythm. "Aye, ocean's where we belong, no doubt there. But we don't all stay under, see? Some like me an' me lot, we live aboard ships, or ports where the water's close. Them deepwater folk, they call us *surface elves*, like it's a bleedin' shame." He paused to shrug his shoulders. "Few o' us, the adventurous lot, daft enough to wander too far inland. It's rough, that. We need the water, right? Not just fer swimmin', drinkin', bathin', breathin' proper..." As he mentioned drinking, he refilled his goblet, then stopped speaking for a moment to gulp down some more ale.

"Still, ye get a few mad buggers what made it work. Built a half-sunk temple out at Vashlin Lake. Big ol' puddle it is, a great body o'freshwater, way inland. Blendin' their lives with the surface folk. It ain't common, but it happens. An' that lot there at the lake? They don't speak common like us, mind. We learned it from the sailors and dockworkers. That lot? They yap like them posh Vashlin mages, they do!"

Aluriel tilted her head, curiosity replacing some of her unease. "And yet you choose to live above the waves."

Leorin gave a wry smile. "Aye, we do. Someone's gotta trade with surface folk, don't they? Ain't all of us cut out fer life under the deep. There's freedom up here, even if it ain't always easy. Still got the sea at our backs whenever we need it, don't we?"

Her thoughts raced. *If some Sea Elves can live above the waves, then perhaps... perhaps my need for air won't be an obstacle. Perhaps I could... belong here.*

Leorin kept questioning her. "Where did you live, lass? How did you end up in this port?"

Aluriel hesitated, glancing at Ian and Zahara before speaking. "I grew up in an ancient enchanted forest, far to the west. My mother is Aeliana, a High Elven druidess. My father, Thalorin, visited me occasionally. He would teleport to visit when he could. But... he was always a fleeting presence."

Leorin's expression showed a trace of sympathy in his eyes. "The forest, eh? That's a long way from the sea, lass, innit? An' yet here ye are."

Aluriel nodded. "I had no choice. Circumstances forced me to leave. I journeyed with Ian and Zahara across the desert, all the way through the barbarian lands, and eventually, here."

Leorin's eyes widened in disbelief. "The whole flippin' desert? By the Abyss, I wouldn't make it a mile! Not even with all the water a thousand bleedin' camels could carry." He shook his head, incredulous. "Lass, you've got more grit in ye than I reckoned, that's fer sure."

Ian smirked, crossing his arms. "Aye, she's tougher than she looks. Desert's nae place fer the faint o' heart."

Leorin laughed heartily. "No wonder Thalorin's daughter can make it here. You're full o' surprises, Aluriel, you are."

The unexpected compliments made Aluriel smile. She felt a flicker of hope, not just for acceptance, but for understanding. Aluriel hesitated before adding, "Though I probably wouldn't have dared make the journey in the summer. The desert's harsh enough in the winter, but under the summer sun? I doubt we would have survived."

"We reached Zahira after being turned away at the Varthian border," Aluriel continued. Her tone held a trace of frustration. "I could swim across the border, even with the strong currents, but Zahara... she wouldn't make it."

Leorin's brows furrowed. "Turned away, eh? That's a bleedin' shame. Varthians, eh? Always makin' it 'ard. Right pain in the bleedin' neck, they are. You sure there's no way 'round?"

"None that I've found," Aluriel said, shaking her head. "And Zahara can't be left behind. She's... important." The last word came out with an unexpected conviction that Aluriel felt burn inside her chest as she glanced towards Zahara.

Leorin studied her for a moment, lighting his pipe before nodding. "Aye, I see how it is. I'll think on it. There might be a way... There might not. Leorin leaned back on his seat, a grin full of salt and smoke curling on his lips. "Aye, that lot across the ocean – Eastern Varthia – they ain't too chummy with this side, not since Varius went and crowned 'imself Emperor o' bloody everything. Got naval blockades stretchin' tighter than a kraken's arse all round the coast, they do. An' lemme tell ya, love, the Lady o' the Abyss – aye, the Goddess herself – She hates that bleedin' bastard. Y'know why? 'Cause the sod tortures moggies. Aye, *Cats,* mind ye! *Eats* 'em too, like it's a delicacy. Right foul, innit? So She stirs the waves, sinks his ships, turns his winds sour... Does everythin' but drown the git outright. Drown 'im she would, too. Problem is..." He spat overboard. "The bastard don't sail. He *flies.* Sits astride that great lizard o' his, wings spread wide, glidin' right over her waters like he's mockin' Her. If it were up to Her, he'd be fish food by now, but dragons don't drown easy."

He gestured towards the ship's interior. "You're welcome to stay here, rest for a bit. We've got spare bunks, and you've more than earned some sleep."

Aluriel hesitated, torn between the comfort of the ship and her duty. *It would be easy to rest here,* she thought, *to accept kindness after so long on the road.* But the weight of responsibility won out. Her expression turned resolute. "Thank you, Captain, but I can't. If I don't present myself to the Sharif today at the Alchemists' Guild, it'll be taken as an insult."

Leorin inclined his head, then nodded in understanding. "Fair enough. Duty calls, don't it? But remember this, love: our ship's always 'ere for ya, right?"

With grateful smiles and a promise to return, the trio took their leave, heading towards the towering observatory where the Sharif awaited.

By the time they reached the observatory, it was mid-afternoon, and the sun had warmed the air enough to make their foreheads glisten with sweat. The structure loomed above them, an elegant blend of stone and brass, with its towering dome reflecting the sunlight. Intricate carvings adorned the entrance, depicting constellations and alchemical symbols intertwined.

A young attendant, clad in the traditional white robes with golden trim, greeted them at the door. Recognising Aluriel and Ian's pins and the latter's priestly armour, he bowed deeply and ushered them inside without delay. The air was rich with the aroma of spiced coffee, curling incense, and the faint metallic mustiness of well-used alchemical tools.

The trio was led through winding corridors until they entered a spacious chamber bathed in golden light from a series of arched windows. A young tabby kitten hopped around the room, its playful antics drawing smiles from them before it leapt onto the lap of the man seated on an ornate divan. The Sharif, stroking the kitten as it purred contentedly on his lap, was surrounded by trays of dates, sweets, and steaming coffee. Yesod was a tall, corpulent man in his forties, his robes embroidered with alchemical symbols in shimmering gold thread. He, too, wore the emblem of the Guild of Alchemists, but instead of the six stars on Khalid's emblem, his emblem sported seven. His round face was framed by a neatly trimmed beard, and his eyes sparkled with warmth and curiosity.

"Ah, welcome!" Yesod's voice was rich and melodious, almost mellifluous. His hands gestured expansively as he rose to greet them, carefully holding the kitten in his arms so that it did not wake. "You honour my observatory with your presence. Please, sit, sit! Have some coffee, some sweets. You must be weary from your journey."

His charm was undeniable, his manner effusive without being overbearing. Ian's brows lifted as he took in the lavish spread. "Well, ye don't see hospitality like this everywhere," he muttered, though his tone was one of approval.

Aluriel inclined her head respectfully as she took a seat. "Thank you, Sharif Yesod. Your kindness is most appreciated."

Zahara, less accustomed to such formalities, followed Aluriel's lead, her movements slightly hesitant but respectful. Yesod's gaze lingered on her for a moment, his expression curious but kind. "And you must be Zahara, the warrior I've heard tales of. It is a pleasure to meet you."

He turned to Ian, his smile broadening. "And a priest of the Tireless Forger graces my halls! Truly, I am blessed today."

Ian nodded, one hand already reaching for a piece of baklava. "Aye, blessed wi' fine coffee, sweets, an' nae shortage o'kindness, it seems. Thank ye, Sharif."

Yesod laughed, a roaring, genuine sound that echoed through the chamber. "Eat, drink, rest. Then we shall discuss what brings you to Zahira and how I may assist. But first, while we eat and drink," he looked at Aluriel, "you must tell me everything!"

The coffee, once served, tasted sweet, rich, and almost chocolatey. It was a signature drink of the Alchemists' Guild, as Yesod proudly explained. "Did you know? It was Alchemists centuries ago who first invented this drink," he said with a beaming smile.

"Yesod," Aluriel said, her voice steady despite the storm of thoughts brewing beneath her calm exterior. "Your hospitality is remarkable. As all the Tribes' has been. When I left the forest, I sure did not expect this kind of welcome."

The Sharif inclined his head with a gracious smile. "It is my pleasure, Aluriel. Hospitality is the heart of our people, especially for those who carry stories worth hearing. And your story," he looked straight into Aluriel's eyes, "Shieldmaiden, is one that is definitely worth hearing!"

At his words, Zahara shifted slightly in her seat, casting a glance towards Aluriel. It was a look of quiet encouragement, a nudge to share the weight they carried together. Aluriel hesitated, fingers tracing the edge of her cup as she gathered her thoughts. *The journey was long, but the tale is longer,* she mused. *Where do I even begin?*

"Yesod," she said finally, setting the cup down carefully. "Since you asked, I suppose you want to know about Kharesh and his men." Aluriel hesitated before recounting the ordeal, her voice steady despite the pain of the memory. "I was exiled from the Elven forest. Ian arrived to guide me, and we were making our way to Vashlin. When we entered the desert, we were captured by Kharesh's tribe. At first, he..." Aluriel hesitated a moment. "He tried to sweet-talk me, promising safety if I agreed to his... terms. When that didn't work..." she paused, her eyes narrowing, "he tried to whip me into submission." Her face grew gloomier. Re-telling the story made the memory of her trauma surface again. "That didn't work either. So he had me pinned down, ripped my tunic and tried to take what he wanted by force."

A silence fell over the room as Ian and Zahara exchanged dark looks. Aluriel continued, her voice quieter now. "I've never felt such rage. It wasn't just anger... it was like something deep inside me snapped. Before I knew it, there was this white-hot surge, and a chain lightning shot from me, killing a dozen or more of his men. But it drained me completely, I could barely stand."

She looked away, her hands tightening in her lap. "With nothing left in me, I bluffed. I challenged them to test me if they dared and let my lightning fry them all, or give us their supplies and flee with their lives. And... somehow, they obeyed. They fled like I was a demon, leaving most of their water, their camels, their slaves," she said, nodding at Zahara briefly "and even a lot of gold and other spoils. I still don't understand why."

Yesod's eyes widened, his expression shifting from shock to fascination. "Chain lightning? And you survived that?" He leaned back, and let his booming laughter roar again across the room. "Oh, Aluriel, you're a marvel! Challenging an entire tribe with no plan, no power and just sheer audacity. The Blade Dancer surely delights in you!"

"Yes, Kharesh was a powerful and brave fighter," Yesod added, his tone turning thoughtful. "He was honourable once, when he ascended. I don't know why, what changed. Perhaps it was time. Perhaps pride. Perhaps something he picked up along the way. It didn't happen overnight, but slowly... he became cruel. Far too cruel a Khan for the welfare of the Tribes. I believe the Blade Dancer put you on his path to stop him and restore some balance to the desert tribes."

"It was just a bluff to save myself. I didn't think it would work, let alone have all these... *consequences*!" Aluriel retorted.

Yesod's eyes widened, and then he burst into deep laughter yet again. "You bluffed! Challenged all the Khan's chosen warriors with no idea of the ancient Laws you were invoking? Marvellous! Simply marvellous!"

Aluriel flushed slightly but managed a small smile. "It's not so funny. I'm terrified. I have no great power to back up the title that's... that's been saddled upon me. If my mettle were truly tested... I'd fail."

Yesod's laughter softened to a chuckle, and he leaned forward, his tone mellifluous and reassuring. "Oh, my dear Shieldmaiden, the Blade Dancer would not have allowed you to take the title if it were not meant to be. The gods see further than we mortals do. Your potential will be revealed when the time is right, when the Gods choose the moment. And, my dear, you are deserving of that title. You survived. Kharesh is dust. As the Blade Dancer teaches, that is all that matters."

He gestured to a small side table and picked up a bowl of sand. Holding it in his hands, he turned back to Aluriel.

"For instance, have you not noticed yet? The Blade Dancer's blessing gives every Shieldmaiden some measure of power over earth."

Aluriel blinked, bewildered. "Earth magic? I... I don't think I have any such power."

Yesod smiled knowingly. "Allow me to demonstrate. Shieldmaidens receive more than just a title and some runes, Aluriel. Watch carefully."

He guided her hands over the bowl, his own movements deliberate and slow. For a moment, Aluriel marvelled at the tiny grains swirling before her eyes, forming a tiny tornado that made the bowl glow in an almost hypnotic dance. *Perhaps there is something to this... saddle, after all,* she thought, a faint flicker of pride sparking within her.

Ian cleared his throat, breaking the moment. "Well, unless Aluriel learns enough earth magic tae tear down that bloody wall herself, we've got a problem, Sharif. We're trying tae reach Vashlin, but we've got tae cross Varthia first. The border guards cannae let Aluriel and Zahara through."

Yesod stroked his beard thoughtfully. "Ah, yes. That is... normal. You see, whenever there is a shift in the balance of power among the desert tribes, skirmishes and raids almost always follow. It's an old cycle. New tribes form, eager to prove their mettle. And who better to test it against than the Varthians?"

He gestured expansively. "In Zahira, we even have a festival each year to celebrate the warriors' achievements. Each brings forth the helmets of every Varthian they've slain that year. The victors are rewarded handsomely: a night with their choice of the finest prostitutes and slaves."

Zahara stiffened slightly and her gaze turned blank. For a moment, she froze.

Chains.

Hunger.

Thirst.

Freezing cold.

Scorching heat.

Her captors, laughing after beating her.

After raping her.

The mention of rewards chilled her to the bone, and though her voice kept steady, her face could not lie. "Not all traditions are good ones," she said quietly, lowering her gaze.

Ian scowled. "Festivals celebratin' death, aye? Though I s'pose the Varthians are nae better wi' their barbaric executions. At least the barbarians' traditions come wi' one bonus: dead Varthian soldiers"

Yesod guffawed, spreading his hands wide. "It is barbaric, I admit, but tradition holds strong. We are *Barbarians*, after all!" His gaze lingered a moment longer on Zahara. "Zahara, my dear, you seem quiet. What do you think of all this?"

Aluriel, catching the tension flickering across Zahara's face, interjected, to shield her from Yesod's probing. "So, Sharif, about these rewards… what would happen if one of the winners were, say, more attracted to men?"

Yesod's laughter faded into a chuckle, and his expression turned contemplative. "Ah, well, that is a delicate matter. You see, our customs are not… forgiving in such cases. Homosexuality, at least between men, is heavily frowned upon. Technically, illegal. A gay man would never be allowed to become a warrior. Such men take different paths. Merchants, tradesmen, Alchemists like myself, or any other trade that does not require them to bear arms."

He sighed, a faint trace of sadness in his eyes. "Their liaisons are consumed in secret, hidden away. It is unfair, it is unjust, but it is the way of our people. Even the bravest man could not defy such expectations without consequence."

Aluriel tilted her head, now even more genuinely curious. "And what of gay women? Are they treated the same way?"

Yesod's expression did not change, and his voice remained contemplative. "With women, it is... slightly different. Such relationships are more common, especially among the harems or brothels. While still technically illegal, punishments are rarely enforced, if ever at all. You see, the attitudes of straight men towards such liaisons are driven less by disgust and more by their... lustful imaginations."

He let out a quiet chuckle. "The hypocrisy is not lost on me. Still, it creates a certain leniency that does not exist for men. In many ways, it is a matter of societal convenience rather than acceptance."

The conversation lingered in Aluriel's mind as the group finished their coffee and prepared to depart. Yesod's words about traditions, hypocrisy, and the shifting dynamics of the desert tribes painted a vivid picture of a world both rich in culture and fraught with contradictions. Zahara had grown quieter, her thoughtful gaze fixed somewhere beyond the ornate windows of the observatory.

"Yesod," Aluriel said after a pause, "you mentioned that knowledge might help us navigate these challenges. Where would we start?"

The Sharif's face lit up with renewed energy. "Ah, I thought you'd never ask! The Alchemists' Guild prides itself on its libraries, with texts and tomes spanning centuries of our history and magic. There, you might find insight into the deeper mysteries of the desert and the Gods' influence, or even answers to questions you've not yet thought to ask."

He gestured grandly towards a side door, the brass handle gleaming in the sunlight. "This way. It's not just a library; it's a sanctuary for those who seek understanding. You may find something of use for your journey."

With Zahara at her side and Ian offering a gruff nod of encouragement, Aluriel followed Yesod down a winding corridor. The air grew cooler, and the faint scent of parchment and old ink wafted towards them. As they entered the grand library, the sight of towering shelves filled with ancient scrolls and leather-bound tomes took her breath away.

She didn't know what she would find. But now? she wanted to look.

# Chapter 11 – Sex and Magic

"I'll see ye in the morning," Ian called back over his shoulder, his dwarven accent carrying down the hallway. "Try not tae get intae trouble withoot me."

Satisfied, Yesod chuckled, his voice warm and melodic, and opened a carved wooden door within the grand library, ushering Aluriel and Zahara inside. "This is my *private* library," he said nonchalantly. The room was spacious yet intimate. Its walls were lined with shelves, which overflowed with books and scrolls. A large desk stood in the centre upon which sat an astrolabe, a magnifying glass, a mortar and pestle, and a collection of quills and inks. Outside, the sunlight was fading into dusk, and the light of one of the moons filtered gently through a stained-glass window, casting intricate patterns across the room. The faint scent of old paper mingled with the aroma of sandalwood incense, giving the space an aura of magical serenity.

"Please, make yourselves comfortable," Yesod said as he began looking into the shelves. His fingers ran along the spines of several books before he pulled out two tomes, turning to Zahara first. He handed her a slim, leather-bound volume. "This is for you, Zahara. A dictionary between Common Tongue and Lughat al-Barbar, complete with common phrases and notes on grammar. It should help with your studies."

Zahara took the book carefully, opened it hesitantly, and flipped through the delicate pages filled with neat columns of translations. "Thank you," she said haltingly, in Common Tongue. Her voice was soft but sincere, and her accent lent her gratitude a quiet, earnest weight.

Yesod then turned to Aluriel and handed her a slightly thicker tome. "And this is for you, Aluriel. A book on Barbarian laws and customs, written in Common Tongue by Louis Dumont, a travelling halfling writer. I must warn you, it is written from an outsider's perspective. While factually accurate, his tone may come across as... detached."

Aluriel accepted the book with a nod, running her fingers along its worn spine. *Another book to add to my growing collection of knowledge I never thought I'd need,* she mused wryly. The weight of the tome reminded her of just how much there was to know about Barbarian customs. *Barbarian laws... maybe understanding them would help me navigate their world. Or maybe it will just remind me of how far removed I am from any place I can call home.* "Thank you, Sharif. I'll read it carefully."

"Good," Yesod replied, his tone warm. "You'll find it enlightening, I think. Now, if you don't mind, I have something I'd like to discuss with Aluriel privately. Zahara, feel free to peruse the library while we talk. You'll find plenty here to intrigue you."

Zahara nodded, already leafing through the dictionary, her lips moving as she tried out some unfamiliar words. Yesod gestured for Aluriel to follow him to a smaller alcove within the library, where a pair of comfortable chairs sat near a low table. A small tray with a teapot and two cups rested nearby, the faint steam curling upward and dissipating in the warm light of a brazier.

Once they were seated, Yesod leaned forward slightly, his expression gentle but inquisitive. "Aluriel," he began, "forgive me if this seems forward, but I couldn't help but notice something about you. May I ask... are you gay?"

Aluriel stiffened, her grip tightening slightly on the armrest. Her thoughts raced. *Why would he care? Does it matter here? I've worked so hard to keep this hidden all through the desert trek.* She glanced at the stained-glass window, as if to evade Yesod's gaze. "That's a rather personal question," she replied, her tone guarded.

"It is," Yesod admitted, his voice calm. "But please, understand that I mean no harm. Here, within these walls, you are among friends. And anything you say will remain strictly between you and me."

Aluriel hesitated, studying his face. There was no mockery there, only genuine curiosity, and a touch of kindness he didn't bother to hide. Finally, she sighed. "Yes. You're right. I am. What gave it away?"

Yesod's smile widened, his tone softening further. "Thank you for trusting me with that. You have nothing to fear here. Here in the Alchemist's Guild, your secret is safe. I mentioned it before, Alchemy is one of the few paths where gay men and women are… tolerated, so you will find many more inside these walls. But beyond these walls, I would advise caution. This city… this world… are not always kind to those who stray from its rigid norms. And in Varthia, the strictness is even more pronounced. Their laws leave no room for deviation, and the consequences can be severe. Be especially mindful there, Aluriel, the Varthians' so-called 'corrective therapies' are even worse than what Kharesh tried to do to you."

She nodded slowly. Some of the tension eased from her shoulders, if only a little. "Thank you, Yesod."

"No thanks needed, my dear," Yesod replied, leaning back in his chair. "We all carry burdens. Sometimes heavier than most can see. And some carry burdens so crushing, they grow blind to the weight upon their shoulders. If nothing else, know that you will always find allies here." He paused, a faint smile playing at his lips. "And believe me, Aluriel, recognising such things about others... well, let's just say it takes one to know one."

The warning sat heavily on Aluriel's chest. *As if I needed yet another reason to tread carefully in Varthia,* she thought bitterly. Ian had already warned her of this. But hearing it from Yesod felt different. Not a grim warning from the gruff, old dwarf, but a gentle caution from someone who genuinely understood. *They see me as a Shieldmaiden now, but what would they see if they knew everything?*

The silence lingered for a moment, until the soft clink of Zahara turning a page broke it. Yesod reached for the teapot, pouring a cup of the steaming liquid and sliding it towards Aluriel. "Here," he said, his voice lighter now. "A drink for thought. You've had a long day."

Yesod leaned back, his expression contemplative. "You have much ahead of you, Aluriel. I sense you are destined for extraordinary things. But destiny, I've learned, often walks hand in hand with peril. Be cautious, but do not let fear rule you. There is strength in embracing who you are."

Aluriel met his gaze, the sincerity in his words sinking in. "I'll keep that in mind. And... thank you. For everything."

He nodded as he rose, his faint smile widening, his voice returning to its usual tone. "No need to thank me. Your company is a pleasure, my friend! Now, take your time in the library. Enjoy it! I have other duties to attend to, and I shall leave you and Zahara to explore." He waved with both hands towards the shelves. "The books here may not answer all your questions, but they will at least guide you towards the right ones. If you do find one that calls to you, do feel free to borrow it."

After a few moments, Aluriel and Zahara began exploring the library, wandering through the rows of shelves filled with tomes and scrolls. The books were a mixture of Common Tongue, Lughat al-Barbar, and Elvish, their spines reflecting the rich diversity of knowledge housed within the observatory. Zahara paused often, flipping through books written in her native tongue, her lips moving as she sounded out unfamiliar words. Aluriel allowed her fingers to trail across the aged leather covers, occasionally pulling one free to glance at its contents.

In one alcove, Zahara stopped abruptly, her fingers brushing against a slim, weathered tome. She pulled it free and, flipping through the pages, called out softly, "Aluriel!" Her face shone with excitement. "Look!" She held the book out, revealing dense text and diagrams written in Lughat al-Barbar.

Aluriel peered over her shoulder, recognising the shapes of rocks and flowing sands depicted alongside what appeared to be instructions. "This looks like... basic earth magic?" she murmured, curiosity sparking in her voice.

Zahara nodded, her expression determined. "It... it is. I help. Translate for you."

Aluriel smiled, touched by the offer. "Thank you. Let's borrow it. Yesod said we could." They carefully tucked the tome into Aluriel's satchel, deciding to ask Yesod in the morning.

In one of the shelves near the back of the room, they found a large, roughly drawn map, unfurled across the pages of an ancient tome. Aluriel leaned in, her eyes scanning the faded ink lines that detailed the regions surrounding Zahira.

"Look here," Aluriel said, pointing to the coastline marked with tiny symbols of harbours and trade routes. "It seems we could sail into Varthia by ship," she murmured. "This must be what Captain Leorin meant when he said there might be a way."

Zahara, standing beside her, frowned thoughtfully, then nodded. "Sea good," she said, conveying agreement in her halting, broken Common Tongue. "Safer than wall. But... there is block..."

Soon after, an acolyte arrived to escort Zahara and Aluriel to their quarters. The walk through the observatory's halls was brief, and when the acolyte finally opened the door to their room, both women paused, momentarily taken aback by the sheer luxury. The room was spacious, exquisitely styled in the traditional grandeur of Zahira's finest architecture and hospitality. Intricate arabesque patterns adorned the walls, whilst soft, colourful carpets softened the polished marble floor. A low darkwood table rested in a corner, surrounded by plush, crimson velvet cushions trimmed with gold. Overhead, a delicate filigree lantern hung from the ceiling, casting a delicate, dappled glow across the room. A balcony, veiled by a set of drawn curtains, offered its guests a breath of fresh air or a glimpse at the stars if they wished. A large bed, draped in silk sheets embroidered with elaborate floral designs, stood against one wall. A burner filled the air with the sweet, soft scent of incense. Beyond a marble archway, on the side opposite the bed, a sunken bath of smooth marble steamed gently, perfumed water bubbling beneath another lantern's glow.

Aluriel's eyes widened, and her mouth opened with surprise as she stepped inside. "Wow!" she murmured. "They've spared no detail." She glanced at Zahara. "We might as well enjoy it while we can."

Zahara nodded silently, her eyes darting around the room, unused to such finery. Aluriel made her way to the bath, disrobing and slipping into the warm water with a groan of pleasure. The heat seeped into her muscles, soothing the day's fatigue.

Zahara lingered by the doorway, hesitating. "You... you enjoy," she said haltingly, her voice uncertain.

Aluriel glanced over her shoulder, her tone light. "There's room for six people at least, Zahara. So, plenty of room for you too. You look like you could use it as much as I do," she replied, beckoning her forward.

For a moment, Zahara hesitated further, but then nodded, and slowly stepped forward. She undressed and eased into the bath opposite Aluriel, allowing the warm water to envelop her. She exhaled softly, her body relaxing. The two sat in silence, the warmth of the bath and the soft glow of the lantern creating a momentary sanctuary from the world outside, with all its cruelty and intrigues. After a few minutes, Zahara moved closer, her presence gentle but deliberate. Her hands rested lightly on Aluriel's shoulders.

"You tense," Zahara said softly.

Aluriel glanced over her shoulder, surprised but not resistant. "I suppose I am," she admitted, letting out a quiet laugh. "Guess I have been, ever since I've left the enchanted forest."

Zahara began kneading the muscles at the base of Aluriel's neck with surprising skill. Her fingers worked with a firmness that melted the tension in Aluriel's shoulders, drawing a purr from her lips. The sensation was soothing, but as the minutes passed, something else stirred within her... a warm, unfamiliar tingling.

A feeling that hadn't touched her for what felt like ages.

Arousal.

Zahara's hands slid lower as she moved to massage Aluriel's back. The strokes were slow and sensual, and she lightly scratched her skin at times, making Aluriel tingle. She closed her eyes, breathed out a sigh of pleasure, and surrendered to the experience. She leaned back slightly, her own hands finding their way to Zahara's thighs, mirroring the earlier touch. Her fingers pressed gently into the tense muscles she found there.

"You're good at this," Aluriel said softly, her voice tinged with curiosity. "Have you always been this... skilled?"

Zahara smiled, sighing under Aluriel's touch. "I learn. Good hands important for many things."

Zahara wasn't exactly her type. Short, muscular, stocky, and olive skinned, she differed vastly from what Aluriel had once been taught to admire, the ingrained concept of beauty of tall, blonde, blue-eyed High Elves. Yet, she could not deny her own desire, her arousal, or the understated flirtation that had been blooming between them.

And Damn it, Zahara's hands were making her desires simply burn.

So, tempted to throw caution to the wind, Aluriel chuckled lightly, as the fear of rejection blunted her desire. Ultimately, desire won. "Zahara... Do you like women?" she asked, in a faltering tone.

The question lingered in the air, a fragile yet electrified silence neither dared disturb. Zahara's hands stopped briefly on Aluriel's back before resuming their deliberate movements.

"Yes," Zahara said quietly, her voice steady but layered with emotion. "Always, a bit. But... eight years... Kharesh... his men... I cannot let man touch me again."

The admission was raw, and Aluriel turned around to meet Zahara's gaze. Their eyes locked, and neither dared to look away. The desire between them was unspoken, undeniable, and had only grown from the moment of the first spark, when they had danced around the fire in Lulu'a. Aluriel leaned forward slightly, cradling Zahara's cheeks gently between her hands.

"You're safe here," Aluriel murmured, her voice barely above a whisper.

As their gaze remained locked, the distance between them closed, as if moved by a magnetic attraction. Their lips met. Just a gentle peck at first. But, an instant later, it deepened into a desperate, raging kiss. Their eyes closed. Their lips and tongues locked. It felt inevitable. It felt destined to happen. It felt exhilarating. It was not tender love. It was brutal, raging passion.

The world outside the bath faded. Everything blurred, leaving only the warmth of the water and the intensity of the kiss.

Their breathing grew heavier. Their bodies pressed closer. Their hands began to caress each other, and with each touch the flames of desire burned brighter.

Aluriel kissed Zahara's nipples. Zahara's hands found hers and squeezed them, caressing her with a hunger of her own. She felt Zahara's nipples harden under her tongue's gentle licks even as her own stiffened under Zahara's fingers. Soon, Zahara was panting, reaching for Aluriel's lips again, thirsty for another kiss. Aluriel clawed her back with one hand, pulled her head closer with the other, sealing their lips once more. With restraint discarded, they would now test the fierce limits of the inferno of desire they were unleashing.

Aluriel's fingers traced the curve of Zahara's spine with a light touch, then moved on to caress her, as if to map every contour of her body. The water in the bath was kept warm by some alchemical device somewhere. The air between them was thick with the warm, perfumed vapours, and the surging tension that neither could ignore any longer. Zahara's hands, damp and warm, wrapped around Aluriel's waist, pulled her closer. Their inner thighs touched, and they began grinding against each other. The movement was slow and deliberate at first, becoming more frantic, more intense, as each thrust brought pleasure and awakened even more desire. The sensation was electric, sending jolts of pleasure through Aluriel's body. She gasped, a crescendo of passion that grew more insistent, more deliberate, more spontaneous. Zahara's lips moved to Aluriel's ear, as if to confess something she dared not say aloud. "You feel good," she whispered, her voice low and rough with desire. "Much good."

"You feel amazing too," Aluriel managed to say before her body forced a moan out of her. She bit Zahara's neck as their tangled bodies took over, overriding what little hesitation might have remained. Aluriel could feel the water around them, warm against her skin but doing nothing to extinguish the fire building inside her. Her hands wrapped around Zahara's back, gripping tight as she pulled her closer, their bodies pressed together from chest to thigh. Their hips met at the pulsing centre between their inner thighs where desire burned fiercest, and began to rub and grind in a special kind of kiss. Neither was thinking anymore. There was no room for thought. Just rhythm. Friction. Need.

Aluriel's fingers dug into Zahara's buttocks, guiding their hips in synchronised rhythm. Their minds were fractured. Lost in passion. But their bodies knew where to press, how to grind. Each clitoris knew how to kiss the other and escalate the shivers into jolts and shocks of pleasure.

Zahara's body answered every touch. Urgent. Eager. Resounding with shared need.

Zahara's lips found Aluriel's again, her kiss fierce and hungry, as if she were trying to devour her whole. Aluriel responded in kind, her hands moving to the spot between Zahara's legs where her desire throbbed in anticipation. Entering her with her thumb, as far as her webbed fingers allowed. Curling it inside her in a rhythmic motion. She then dove beneath the surface, her tongue finding Zahara's clitoris and began to kiss and lick her in all the right places. Zahara first began to whimper and arch her back, then began shaking, moaning louder and louder as Aluriel's tongue sent waves of pleasure crashing into her. There was no gentleness in her moans, no sweetness in her grip. Only urgency. Only the ravenous roar of someone who had been starved of pleasure for too long. Her every muscle tensed with the anticipation of release, until she exploded with a scream, her mind shattering from the force of the orgasm. She slumped back into the steaming water and leant against a wall, her mind blank and unable to think, still quivering from the force of the meltdown.

As soon as her mind cleared enough to gather some thoughts and act on intent, Zahara wanted to make Aluriel orgasm. However, she couldn't hold her breath underwater as long as her. So instead, she slid her hand between her thighs and found Aluriel's vagina. She slid two fingers inside her and began curling them. With the other hand, she rubbed her clitoris. First, in circling motions. Then, sideways. Then, up and down. Until she found the combination that *worked*. Her touch was gentle, deliberate, and insistent, and soon it was Aluriel's breath that started to feel quicker and more ragged. Aluriel's moans turned fierce. Resounding. Lyrical, like a soprano singing her highest, wildest notes in her final crescendo. Zahara kissed her neck whilst her fingers relentlessly conjured pleasure. Aluriel's world narrowed to just her blazing pleasure. Her mind was drowned by her voice, which felt almost out of body, and the intense, wet sounds of their lovemaking. And as it continued, Aluriel's thoughts shattered even more. She barely knew whose body this was anymore. Hers? Zahara's? Theirs? All that existed was raw pleasure. Encouraged by Aluriel, whose moans gradually morphed into grunts and screams, Zahara continued to pleasure Aluriel with her deft fingers. As Zahara felt she was almost there, she kissed her again, stealing her breath, locking their tongues together. That pushed Aluriel over the edge. Pure pleasure reached its zenith and she began to climax, letting out a painful scream, as her whole body began shaking with release. And light. And something inside her that would not be contained.

What followed was no ordinary climax. As the wave of pleasure peaked, something deep within Aluriel – something ancient and luminous – erupted. It started as a faint tingling in her chest, growing and resonating until, without warning, her body released a radiant ball of energy. A soft, silvery light poured straight from Aluriel's heart, enveloping the two in a luminous shimmering dome, which spread outward. First, to the entire room. Then, beyond.

Zahara gasped as the light coursed through her. She clutched her chest. Recoiled with fear. For a moment, time itself seemed to hold its breath. Then, another, stronger stream of silvery light flowed from Aluriel like a river, rushing directly into Zahara's body. It shimmered like liquid silver. It flooded Zahara's body at her core, then seeped into her skin, erasing her scars as if they had never existed. From there, the stream of light spread out, coalescing into a ball that kept expanding, gaining depth and momentum as it grew.

Zahara's transformation was subtle, and yet, total. Her skin shimmered as the light found every scar, rewriting her flesh until no trace remained.

*It's as if they never happened...* she thought, a sob catching in her throat, tears welling in her eyes.

Even the memory of how she acquired them began to fade. Earlier that day – and every day before – they had been a constant reminder of each battle, and every cruelty she had to endure. Now? It felt like a distant dream, the way a nightmare fades once one awakens into the light of day.

Zahara looked at Aluriel. As this uncontrollable energy flowed out from her in all directions, Aluriel did not look like the turquoise-skinned elf she had known. She was blindingly luminous, floating in mid-air just above the water, and looked as if she were enveloped by a white-hot fire, without being consumed. Plumes of this white fire swirled around her back, almost in the shape of swirling wings. Zahara could only bear to look at her for a fraction of a second before the brilliance dazzled her, and she had to avert her gaze.

Eventually, the light receded somewhat, and Aluriel gently slipped back into the water. Zahara looked at herself, her hands shaking as they traced over her now unblemished skin. "Aluriel," she whispered, stunned with wonder. "What... what you do?"

Aluriel stared at her luminous hands, her heart racing. The magic had come unbidden, raw and pure, without her intent. It was raw power, surging through her, totally beyond her control. No way to stop it, or direct it. For what felt like ages, she was unable to speak, unable to think, a wordless vessel of magic. When this strange sensation subsided a bit, she tried to speak again. "I... I don't know," she stammered, her voice barely audible, her mind still clouded by the explosion of pleasure and magic. "I didn't mean to... I just... lost myself in the moment and it... it just happened... Are you okay?" she asked. Her heart thudded. She feared what she would hear. *I just hurt everyone I care about,* she thought gloomily for a moment.

Zahara smiled, a tear sliding down her cheek. "You make me orgasm... You make me feel thing I think was gone forever... and you heal me," she said softly, her voice filled with awe. "Aluriel, you heal me." She paused, hugging her tenderly. "No, not heal. Healed," she corrected herself.

"I... did?" Aluriel blinked, confusion scattering through her mind. "I did what? Where?" A jolt of relief, mixed with confusion, made her spine tingle. *So I didn't release another lightning?*

"My scars... My backside... my chest... my belly... my legs... Look, I feel this... This warm... light, from you..." Her eyes opened wide, showing a twinge of fear. "WHAT are you?!" Zahara cried out.

Aluriel's heart leapt. *I... Healed her? What? How?* For a moment, Aluriel was overwhelmed.

But it was fleeting, swallowed by a sudden wave of guilt. Her thoughts turned inward, unbidden memories of Elenwen surfacing and sniping at her. *If I can do this,* she thought bitterly, *why couldn't I have done it for HER? The scars I could have healed are still there, and they'll never fade.* The question gnawed at her, reawakening all her guilt.

Her gaze fell to Zahara's body. Indeed, her skin was flawless, as if her cuts and whip marks had never happened. The branding on her shoulder, the mark of a slave, had vanished. *What does this mean? This power?* She thought. *Why now? What is it trying to show me?* Confusion and wonder tangled together, leaving her untethered, adrift in a sea of emotions she did not quite know how to navigate.

As the water began to cool and the steam thinned into the air, Aluriel shifted, her fingers brushing gently against Zahara's hand. "We should get out," she murmured. Zahara nodded, her eyes heavy with the weight of exhaustion and sheer wonder.

They rose together. Aluriel grabbed a thick towel from the nearby rack, handing one to Zahara before wrapping herself in another. The scent of jasmine lingered faintly in the fabric, soothing in its simplicity. They dried off in silence. The intimacy of the moment still clung to the air with a faint hum of magic.

Once dry, they made their way to the bed without haste. Aluriel pulled back the silk sheets, and the fabric felt impossibly soft and cool to the touch as they slipped beneath it. Zahara nestled close, her head resting against Aluriel's shoulder, holding hands. Aluriel's other hand caressed Zahara's hair absent-mindedly, her thoughts drifting between the warmth of the moment and the uncertainty of what lay ahead. Slowly, Zahara's breathing deepened, her body relaxing completely as sleep claimed her. Aluriel forced a small smile, her heart heavy despite Zahara's gratitude. As Zahara nestled against her, Aluriel stared at the ceiling, her thoughts spinning. *If I can heal, why couldn't I heal the one I once loved? What does this magic want from me?*

*The one you still love,* a fleeting whisper brushed her mind, as maddening as it was undeniable, as inescapable as it was true. She tried to shove Elenwen's scarred face away from her mind. She let her fingers brush against Zahara's hand, as if to anchor herself even as her thoughts of Elenwen continued to swirl. It didn't work. *I love you, Elenwen,* her mind whispered. The magic, unexpected and overwhelming, had torn a veil she wasn't sure she was ready to walk through. But something deep inside her whispered that she might have no choice.

Yet as she lay there, her thoughts turned inward, clouded with uncertainty. Zahara was no Elenwen, Aluriel realised. That realisation gnawed at her, leaving an odd pang of guilt behind. Casual sex, as well as same-sex experiences, had been a normal part of her Elven upbringing. Even though she was scorned by her kin, many of her peers would still bed her just to *fuck the freak girl*, and then call her a slut behind her back. At first, Aluriel did let them seduce her, indulging in the illusion of being wanted by those who spat her name at day, yet moaned it in the dark when she would ride them. Fairly quickly, she realised that she had no sexual interest in men and was, in fact, a lesbian.

As she now lay in bed with Zahara, she wondered how she might see the events they shared not long before. It had begun with lust, and ended in an explosion of magic and healing. Maybe Zahara would see it as something more, something deeper. *What if she expects more than I can give?*

Her heart, already fractured from past pain, felt too broken to offer even a shard of it to another. *If it's shattered, how can I give it away?* she thought, as the weight of that truth pressed against the tender solace she had just found.

Yet, despite her inner turmoil, a faint smile tugged at her lips. *Yesod knew, didn't he? Just how much does he know?* she thought. *I'll have to thank him later. Or curse him. It's almost as if he could see something between us that we did not...* Aluriel looked again at the room. *Of course. One bed. Oh, sneaky Yesod. You're a magnificent bastard!*

"It takes one to know one," his words returned to her mind. *I see... And what exactly are you, Yesod?* Aluriel wondered.

As Zahara drifted into a deeper sleep, her head still nestled on Aluriel's chest, her breathing slowed and deepened. A radiant smile had already settled on her lips, and her arm lay draped protectively over Aluriel's waist as she softly mumbled something in her sleep.

For Zahara, the moment held a profound significance she dared not try to give words to. Having endured years of enslavement under Kharesh and his men, she had been starved of any touch that did not carry pain or powerlessness. As she lay beside Aluriel moments earlier, just before sleep claimed her, as they held hands in silence, she had found herself breathing easier than she had in years. Making love to another woman had not only awakened a dormant longing, but also felt like reclaiming something stolen. Her control. Her dignity as a woman. Her heart, so often guarded, had swelled with a fire she had not dared give voice to.

Aluriel kept staring at the ceiling, her mind too restless for slumber. The familiar whispers came, as they did every evening, low and incomprehensible at first as always, their sound like the rustling of distant leaves. But this time, amidst the chaotic murmurs, two words rose up. Two words she could hear. Two words, clear and distinct.

*"Find them!"*

The words echoed faintly but distinctly, sending a chill down her spine. Her eyes glowed violet for a moment. Her breath caught, and her hand instinctively tightened around Zahara's. The whispers faded, leaving only the sound of the soft breeze outside the window. She lay there, heart pounding, wondering what, or who, she was meant to find. *Or maybe it's my madness. The Lady of Twilight doesn't exist, and it's my madness progressing...*

As Aluriel's eyes finally closed, sleep claimed her. She found herself standing in an endless pool of darkness, a place that felt neither warm nor cold, neither real nor imagined. Then, the butterflies appeared, flitting around her before settling into a circle as they always did, brushing against her skin as more and more arrived, leaving trails of light that danced along her arms. The whispers grew louder, tugging at her mind like a thread being pulled taut. Low and incomprehensible at first, as always, but this time the rising storm of whispers swirled around her like a tempest, growing louder and louder. Her heart quickened. Her hands reached out towards the glowing creatures, but the whispers suddenly coalesced into distinct words.

*"Find them! Save them!"* They were words, spoken by a woman, or rather, by a chorus that sounded like a thousand women speaking in unison.

The words struck her like a physical force, reverberating in her chest. The butterflies flared brighter, their light intensifying until it was almost blinding. Within the circle, two faces emerged. Faint at first, like sketches drawn in soft pencil.

As the drawing sharpened and details came into focus, she recognised them instantly: Ilinur and Girfila.

She hadn't seen her older half-siblings in years.

Not since her childhood days in the forest had she seen them. The sight of their faces, serious and determined, brought a pang of both nostalgia and dread. The visions lingered for a moment longer, the whispers carrying an urgency that mirrored the command she'd heard.

*"Find them! Save them!"* The chorus said once more, as if to ensure Aluriel understood the message. Then the butterflies dispersed, fading into darkness.

Aluriel awoke with a sharp breath, drenched in sweat. Her heart was pounding against her chest, even more wildly than it did after any previous vision. Zahara stirred slightly beside her but did not wake. Aluriel stared at the ceiling, the echoes of the dream lingering in her mind.

Sleep, as always, would not come again easily for her, especially tonight.

# ✦ Interlude – The Voyeur ✦

## Ludmilla

She was invisible, crouched in the shadows above, unseen on the high balcony. She had picked the wrong moment to arrive. Hoping to seduce Aluriel, disguised as a servant, or a Lady alchemist no one would have heard of the next day, she had teleported into the room only to hear Aluriel and Zahara approaching, just a few paces away. She hid on the balcony and turned invisible. Then, the two decided to take a bath. Predictably, they began caressing each other, kissing, and then, furious lovemaking. She remained to observe them. She could tell a lot about someone by the way they had sex. But nothing in her long existence could ever have prepared her for this. Not an archmage's orgasm flooding into her, magic bursting like a star. Not an Emperor fucking her relentlessly for hours which – in fact – one had just done. Not even the ecstasy of the orgiastic rites of the Merry Gentleman Himself had made her suspect that what she was about to experience was even remotely possible.

The moment the wave of healing magic burst forth, it was like a tsunami through the Weave. Ludmilla felt it before she saw it. An orgasmic cascade of light, raw and blinding, racing across her skin like a lover's gasp. Soon, it enveloped her. She could not help but absorb it. She drank in the magic greedily, feeling it flood her with more power than she had ever tasted.

And then, for the first time ever... she had to stop.

It was too much.

So much sexual energy as to overload her. HER! It was Magic and pleasure, woven together in purity.

Uncontrolled.

Divine.

She struggled to regain her composure, lips parting as she steadied herself against the balcony's stone railing. Her glamour flickered. "Gods," she whispered. "She really is the Phoenix."

And in that moment – not when she saw Aluriel's body, not when she had heard her name – but now, Ludmilla fell in lust. And maybe, just maybe, something deeper.

Ludmilla had seen desire before. Felt it, fed on it. Gods, she had drowned in it. But this? This was something else entirely. The very act of pleasure had become divine invocation. It was not merely sex. It was a tsunami of divinity. Healing, terrifying, magnificent.

And suddenly, she felt envy.

Not for Zahara, no. The barbarian would be dust in a few decades. A candle in the wind.

No, Ludmilla envied the way Aluriel gave. So freely. So wildly. Without even realising it.

"She doesn't know what she is," Ludmilla whispered to herself, one hand tracing the curve of her own hip. "She doesn't know. Fortunately, my kin don't know either. But now... I do."

Her kin would destroy her without hesitation, and sentence themselves to another few million years of boredom. But that just would not do.

Aluriel would belong to her, and her alone.

Soon.

With one last glance at the entangled figures on the bed, Ludmilla turned from the balcony and jumped onto the streets below without a sound. Her form shifted as she walked, glamour folding over her like a silk gown, turning her once more into the perfect stranger.

The beautiful foreigner no one remembered clearly.

The courtesan with eyes no one dared meet twice.

But in her heart, the decision had already crystallised.

The others did not matter. They were supporting cast.

Ornaments. Replaceable.

Zahara, Elenwen, Ian, Aeliana. Even Varius... Each one had a role to play. But none of them could compete with her for Aluriel.

And if they tried to overstep their role?

Well.

They would be replaced.

# Chapter 12 – Before the darkness

Aluriel stirred in the soft glow of the morning, the warmth of Zahara's body still lingering against her skin. The night had been unlike any other she had experienced. Tender, overwhelming, and new, the intimacy they shared – and the magic she unleashed – still left her mind blank. *What should I even think of this?* was the first thought to stir in her sleepy mind. But as she opened her eyes and turned her head, she found Zahara still fast asleep, her breathing deep and even, her dark curls ruffled across the pillow. For a moment, Aluriel simply watched her now flawless skin and felt her heart pound with something she couldn't quite name. *Is this fear? Excitement? A mix of both?*

She slipped out of bed quietly and carefully so as not to wake Zahara, then dressed nervously. Her thoughts swirled as she left the chamber. *I need to make sense of this.* She needed guidance. Someone wiser, if perhaps only by the faster clock of human years, who could help her put her thoughts in order. *Yesod.*

A passing acolyte, startled by her sudden approach, courteously directed her to the herb garden after she inquired about Yesod's whereabouts. As she stepped into the garden, the scent of fresh herbs and damp earth welcomed her. Yesod knelt by a row of potted plants, carefully plucking leaves and flowers and placing them in a woven basket nearby.

Aluriel hesitated for a moment before stepping closer, her voice quieter than usual. "Yesod? May I speak with you?"

He glanced up, his expression friendly and kind as always. "Of course, Aluriel. You look troubled." He dusted off his hands and stood, gesturing for her to sit on a nearby stone bench.

She sat. Her fingertips twisted in her lap as she struggled to find the right words. "I... I need your advice. About something personal."

Yesod's eyes met hers, inquisitive yet kind, and he nodded encouragingly. "Speak freely. I will listen."

Aluriel swallowed, feeling the weight of her words before they even left her lips. "I... spent the night with Zahara. We... We made love." She exhaled sharply, as if saying it aloud made it more real. "I didn't plan for it to happen, but it did. And now I don't know what to think, or how I even feel."

Yesod studied her for a long moment before his smile widened, and then he let his usual booming laughter explode, roaring through the garden. "Ah. The joys and confusions of the heart." He sat beside her, hands resting atop his knees. "Tell me, Aluriel, what troubles you more... the fact that it happened, or the emotions it has stirred within you?"

Aluriel hesitated before narrowing her eyes slightly. "Did you... plan for this? You put us in a lavish room with only one bed."

Yesod let out a soft chuckle, shaking his head with amusement. "*Plan* is a strong word, Aluriel. But did I sense something between you two? Yes. And I thought it might be... beneficial to give fate a chance to light that spark, if it were meant to be." His gaze softened as he studied her reaction. "You have been alone for a long time, carrying burdens you do not always need to bear alone. Zahara, too, has been searching for something, someone, after her years of slavery. I simply gave you both the space to find out what that might be."

Suddenly realising that she was holding her breath, Aluriel exhaled, rubbing her hands together as she mulled over his words. "I suppose... I should be grateful," she admitted, her voice quieter now.

"I've spent so long convincing myself that I wouldn't... that I couldn't have..." she paused, before blurting, "something like this! And yet, it felt... right." She hesitated, then gave a soft, wry chuckle as she shook her head. "Terrifying, but right."

Yesod nodded, watching her closely. "The heart is often wiser than we give it credit for. Fear only holds us back when we allow it to." His voice took on a gentler tone. "But I sense there is more on your mind."

Aluriel's fingers twitched in her lap. "Yes," she admitted. "There is." She took a deep breath, bracing herself. "At the height of everything, when we..." she paused, the blood flowing to her cheeks making her turquoise skin look more purple, "when I... orgasmed." She spoke the word in a hushed tone. "I felt something... shift inside me. Magic surged from me, but it wasn't lightning." She turned to Yesod, searching his face for understanding. "It was healing. A wave of it, uncontrolled, and strong enough to erase Zahara's scars. The ones that had been with her for years."

Yesod's expression immediately turned sharp and focused, all traces of amusement vanishing instantly. "Uncontrolled healing?" He thought for a moment in silence. "That is no small feat, Aluriel. But"– his voice had lowered to barely more than a whisper –"I knew this already. A tremendously powerful spell shook the weave around us. It was like an earthquake. It enveloped practically the whole observatory and beyond. In the infirmary," he added, "all the sick and wounded were suddenly healed. Throughout the building, even outside the infirmary, people who had minor cuts or bruises found them gone when they woke.

He scanned the garden around them, to make sure no one was listening.

"And Sheikh Qasim," he said, his voice even more hushed. "My mentor. The former Sharif of this Guild. He was very old. Barely breathing. Bedridden, blind, waiting for his end. We did all we could to keep him comfortable. But even Alchemy, Aluriel, cannot stop all the diseases that come with age. It cannot cheat death forever. Yet when the wave of healing hit? He stood. Ate a full meal. Took a bath without help. Said he could see the sky again. Hear the wind."

He looked at her, and something close to *awe* tinged his voice. "He said he dreamed of fire, and wings of fiery light." He paused, reflecting on the words that he'd just spoken. "He is still just as old, and he's not jumping like a rabbit, I'll admit. But he is healthy again. It was a miracle."

Yesod kept scanning the garden, wary of any acolytes who might overhear.

"We searched for the source of it, my Vice-Sharifs and I. Thought maybe an Angel had come for a visit." He gathered his thoughts for a moment. "An Angel who might have come to heal someone in the infirmary for their own reasons, and then, out of kindness, also healed everyone else. Sometimes they do that, and they don't announce their arrival nor grace us with explanations." He stood up and began pacing. "We even looked into your room to make sure you were all right, and you and Zahara were fast asleep, breathing fine, so we let you be. And if you'll forgive me saying the whole, harsh truth?" He chuckled. "Chain lightning is one thing, but *this*? None of us even imagined *you* could be the source."

She nodded, pressing her hands to her thighs to ground herself as her ruminations resurfaced. *Of course, I've always been a failure so far, and I'm going mad. I'm the last person they would look for when something good happens.* "I don't know. It just... happened. I wasn't thinking about magic. I wasn't even aware I was doing it. But when it was over, she was... whole." Her voice wavered slightly at the last word.

Yesod studied her intently before letting out a slow, measured breath. "Magic – especially powerful magic – tends to manifest at moments of great emotional intensity," he began. "But what you did is not rare. It is simply unique, my friend. The most powerful of specialised healers, the High Elven priests, train for years to summon a mere fraction of that kind of power, and yet yours came unbidden." His gaze sharpened further. "This is another sign that your magic is bound to your emotions. The stronger your feelings, the stronger your magic's response. And if it is allowed to run unchecked..."

Aluriel swallowed, feeling the weight of his words, and finished his sentence: "It could be dangerous."

"Yes." Yesod's expression remained grave. "Magic without control is volatile. Even the gentlest of spells can become unpredictable if left to the whims of emotion. You must learn to master it, Aluriel, before it begins to master you."

She nodded, her jaw tightening. "And how do I do that?"

Yesod folded his arms, considering his next words carefully. "There are ways. Meditation, discipline, training with those who understand the intricacies of magic. And the sooner you find someone who can truly guide you in this, the better. I fear that if you wait too long... your magic will only grow more unruly." He met her gaze. "Vashlin or Steelforge would be best. Both are home to mages of great knowledge, who may help you shape your power into something you can wield with purpose."

Aluriel clenched her fists, frustration gnawing at her. "I don't want to hurt anyone."

"Then learn to control your magic," Yesod said firmly. "Before it chooses for you."

Aluriel hesitated, shifting slightly on the stone bench, her hands idly twisting a loose thread on her sleeve. "There's... something else," she admitted. "Something I've been afraid to ask about." She glanced towards Yesod, searching his face for any sign of scepticism before continuing. "The whispers and the visions. They've changed."

Yesod tilted his head slightly. "Changed?" he said no more, waiting for her to explain.

"They've always been there," she continued, her voice barely above a whisper. "But now they've been growing stronger. More vivid. And this time, they showed me faces. Ilinur and Girfila, my half-siblings." Her fingertips clenched the thread even tighter. Yesod remained silent, to give her space to speak. "I saw them, drawn in pencil in the circle of butterflies, as if they were standing right before me. And then... a message: 'Find them! Save them!'" She exhaled sharply. "I don't know what it means, but I can't ignore it."

Yesod's expression darkened. He looked away for a moment, his gaze settling on the rows of herbs swaying gently in the breeze. When he finally spoke, his voice was measured, his tone as neutral as he could muster.

"The Lady of Twilight."

Aluriel swallowed, nodding. "You've heard of her?"

"Yes," he admitted. "Though she is spoken of in hushed tones, even among scholars. The Lady of Twilight is a mystery, Aluriel. Her existence is debated. Most believe she is merely a fabrication, the fevered imaginings of those who succumb to their own unravelling minds. Others, though fewer, claim she is real, however... unstable."

Aluriel frowned. "Unstable?"

"If she exists, then she is most certainly mad. Every account we have – of every mage who heard her whispers – ends the same way: with them lost to insanity." He exhaled slowly, rubbing a hand over his brow. "No one who has truly heard her voice has ever remained unchanged."

A chill crept up Aluriel's spine. "But... she doesn't seem cruel. The visions she gives me.... I don't know if she's real or if I'm just... losing my mind." She did not need to ponder long before her mind screamed back, *You are going mad!* She flinched for a moment, then mustered the courage to speak the crux of her question: "But if she is real... what does she want from me?"

Yesod thought carefully before answering. "I cannot say for certain. If she is real, then she may be benevolent... at least, in her own way. But benevolence does not mean safety, Aluriel. Do not trust the whispers blindly, even if they offer you truth. The minds she touches never escape with their sanity intact."

Aluriel nodded slowly, absorbing his words. She had spent years – nay, decades – dismissing the whispers, forcing herself to ignore them. But now, they refused to be ignored. If this was madness, it was one that gripped her from the start.

Yesod sighed, placing a hand on her shoulder. "Whatever this means, whatever the Lady of Twilight truly is, tread carefully. Listen, but do not follow blindly. There is often a thin line between prophecy and delusion, and I would not wish to see you lost to either."

Aluriel straightened her shoulders. "Madness or not, I know what I saw. Ilinur and Girfila are in danger. I can feel it. I can't just ignore that."

Yesod studied her, pondering what to say next. Finally, he nodded. "I don't doubt your instincts, Aluriel. But getting to them will not be easy." He turned to pluck a few more leaves from a plant beside him, taking a moment to arrange his thoughts before continuing. "With the wall border barring you from entering Varthia, you're already facing a difficult path. And with the East Varthian Empire embroiled in war with the West, any attempt to bypass the border by sea is... virtually impossible."

"The Blockades?"

Yesod sighed. "Blockades, patrols, and the constant risk of being caught in a battle that isn't yours. If you were to attempt to sail east, you would find no safe harbour between here and the empire's heartland." He turned to face her fully, his expression grim. "There is, however, one possibility. A dangerous one."

Aluriel sighed. "What is it?"

Yesod shook his head. "Not yet. This is a conversation best had with Ian and Zahara as well." He turned, raising a hand to summon a distant acolyte who had stood out of earshot. "Go and fetch Ian and Zahara. Have them meet us in the coffee room."

The young acolyte nodded and hurried off, disappearing through the halls of the guild.

Yesod then turned to another acolyte, placing the bundle of cuttings and flowers he had gathered into her hands. "Dry these carefully. The petals will be needed for restoratives, and the roots must be separated properly."

With that, he gestured for Aluriel to follow. "Come, we'll discuss this further in the coffee room." His tone was even, but the weight behind it was clear. Whatever he was about to propose, it was not something to take lightly. "Oh, and that earth magic book you took? Keep it. The Dancer knows you need it more than I."

"Oh! Sorry! I forgot! I was going to ask if I could borrow it, but then... things happened last night. I forgot. Sorry! Thank you!" Aluriel burst out, then impulsively hugged him.

Yesod and Aluriel entered the coffee room, where the rich aroma of roasted beans filled the air. Sunlight streamed through the tall arched windows, illuminating the room in a soft golden glow. The kitten lay curled up on a pillow, its tiny body rising and falling with each slow breath.

Ian and Zahara arrived soon after, both looking somewhat groggy and bleary-eyed from their interrupted rest. Ian ran a hand through his beard as he settled into a seat, eyeing the steaming cups of coffee already prepared for them. "Aye, if we're talkin' o' serious matters afore breakfast, I'm gonna need this," he grumbled, taking a gulp.

Zahara took a seat beside Aluriel, her gaze flicking between the three of them. Though she said nothing at first, there was a quiet attentiveness in her posture, almost as if she wondered whether any of them would comment on the sudden change in her appearance.

Yesod leaned forward. Calmly, seriously, he began to speak. "Thank you both for coming. There is something urgent we must discuss." He glanced briefly at Aluriel before continuing. "Aluriel has received a vision. One she believes is tied to her half-siblings, Ilinur and Girfila. She is certain they are in danger."

Ian exhaled through his nose, setting his cup down. "An' the problem is gettin' through tae Varthia," he muttered. "I ken as much."

"Yes. The land border is sealed to her, and the sea route is effectively blocked by war and patrols. However, there may be another way." He paused, giving them all a gloomy look. "But it is not without great risk."

Aluriel crossed her arms, visibly tense. "I don't care about the risk. If there's a way, tell me."

"There is a passage," he said. "A hidden entrance to the Sunless Depths, right here in Zahira. It is seldom spoken of, and fewer still dare to use it, but it may be the only viable route for you to reach Varthia undetected."

The room fell into silence, the very mention of the Sunless Depths sending a wave of tension through the group. Ian, who had been lifting his coffee cup to his lips, stopped mid-motion. He set the cup down carefully, his eyes narrowing. "The bloody Sunless Depths?" His voice, usually steady, now bled fear and apprehension. "Are ye mad, Yesod? That place is a death trap!"

Yesod met Ian's gaze steadily. "It is dangerous, yes. But with the walls of Varthia turning her away and the sea routes blocked by war, I see no other path." He turned back to Aluriel. "Your camels will be too large to navigate the tunnels, but your goats are agile and nimble, and should be able to traverse the pathways. A donkey or two could be brought to carry provisions. You will need supplies, maps, and knowledge of what creatures lurk in those depths, but if you can make it through, you will emerge past the border into Varthian lands without ever crossing a checkpoint."

Ian ran a hand down his face, muttering under his breath. "Forger save me... the bloody Sunless Depths."

Aluriel watched him, gauging his reaction. "Ian," she said gently, "I know it's dangerous. But I have to do this. Ilinur and Girfila are in danger, and every moment we waste puts them at greater risk. You don't have to come. You can walk through the wall gate and meet me on the other side."

Ian exhaled sharply and rubbed his temples. "Aye, I knew ye'd say that." He looked up, his expression reluctant but resigned. "I swore tae yer mither I'd look after ye, lass, and I'll nae be breakin' that oath. But if we're goin' tae the Sunless Depths, we'd best be ready fer fitiver horrors await."

A quiet voice broke the tension. "Where you go, I go," Zahara said simply, her dark eyes steady as she looked at Aluriel. There was no hesitation, no wavering in her voice. "You free me. You healed me. I will always by your side"

Aluriel felt something tighten in her chest, a warmth that steadied her resolve. She gave Zahara a grateful nod before turning back to Yesod. "Then it's settled. We take the passage."

Yesod studied her for a moment before his mellifluous smile returned. "Very well. I will provide what aid I can to prepare you for the journey." His gaze turned serious once more. "The Sunless Depths are not merely a place of darkness and stone. It is ancient, filled with forgotten things that were never meant to be disturbed. You must tread carefully."

Ian groaned, taking another long sip of coffee before muttering, "Tread carefully, he says. Aye, right into the mouth o' bloody madness."

The tabby kitten on the pillow let out a sleepy yawn, utterly indifferent to the gravity of their decision.

Yesod gave them all a moment to let the weight of the decision settle before rising from his seat. "Then we must act quickly. I will have my scribes copy whatever maps we have of the Sunless Depths.

They are incomplete, for no one has ever charted the entirety of that abyss..." He paused. "But they will be better than wandering blind."

He turned to one of the acolytes standing nearby, beckoning him forward. "Send word to the scribes. Have them gather all records of the tunnels beneath Zahira and Varthia, and make copies for our travellers." The acolyte bowed and hurried from the room.

Yesod turned back to them. "Meanwhile, you should go to the market and gather whatever supplies you may need. Provisions, torches, spare weapons, anything that will help you survive the Sunless Depths."

Ian let out a long breath, shaking his head. "Aye, an' plenty o' rope. Nae tellin' what we might need tae climb doon or cross ower in that hellscape."

Zahara nodded. "Water. More than we think to need."

Yesod placed a hand on Aluriel's shoulder. "I suggest you leave as soon as the maps are ready. The sooner you reach the tunnels, the sooner you can reach Varthia." He offered her a small smile. "I will do what I can from here. May the Blade Dancer keep you victorious."

Aluriel took a deep breath. "Then let's not waste time."

The trio made their way towards the cattle market, near the city gates where their beasts had been stabled. The air was thick with hay, dust, and livestock, and the rhythmic calls of traders haggling over prices echoed through the open market square. Herds of goats and donkeys milled about in makeshift pens, their bleating and braying merging with the bustling sounds of commerce.

Aluriel ran a hand along the neck of one of her camels, feeling a pang of regret. The beasts had served them well through the desert, but they would be useless in the cramped tunnels of the Sunless

Depths. "It's a shame," she muttered, stroking the creature's coarse fur. "But we can't take them with us."

Ian nodded, adjusting his belt as he eyed the livestock pens. "Aye, but we'll need sturdy replacements. Sure-footed. A pair o' pack donkeys should do."

Zahara stepped forward, scanning the market. Unlike Aluriel and Ian, she understood the ways of the merchants here, the unspoken rules of haggling in Lughat al-Barbar. She approached a wrinkled trader standing beside a row of well-fed donkeys, exchanging a few quick words in Lughat al-Barbar.

The old trader tilted his head, eyeing their camels with interest before launching into an animated exchange with Zahara. Aluriel and Ian could only catch fragments of the rapid conversation, though Ian muttered, "Sounds like he's askin' fer our souls in return."

Zahara held up a hand, silencing him as she continued negotiating. Her voice was firm and, to Aluriel and Ian's untrained ears, sounded quite aggressive, though the incense in Yousef's tent had taught them that, in Lughat al-Barbar, even a love poem could sound like a declaration of war to an outsider's ears. Clearly, Zahara knew what she was doing. Finally, the trader sighed dramatically and gestured to two sturdy pack donkeys.

"He take all twenty camels, give us these two," Zahara translated, her expression neutral. "Plus three full sack of grain and this bag of coins. It fair trade."

Aluriel exhaled, nodding. "Agreed."

After exchanging the animals, the trio led their new donkeys towards the souk, where the true work of preparing for the journey began. They moved swiftly through the winding alleys lined with vendors selling everything from dried meats to woven baskets, ensuring they gathered every necessary provision.

They stocked up on hardtack, dried fruit, and salted meat, supplies that would last long underground. Zahara, ever practical, picked up flint, torches, and oil, whilst Aluriel examined coils of rope, ensuring they had more than enough for whatever obstacles awaited them below.

As they secured their purchases onto the donkeys, Aluriel huffed, wiping her brow. "Feels like we're gearing up for a war, not a journey."

Ian shot her a glance. "In the Sunless Depths, there'll nae be much of a difference."

With their preparations complete, goats and donkeys fully loaded with supplies, the trio prepared to make their way back through the winding streets of Zahira. The midday sun bore down on the bustling marketplace, its heat shimmering off the sandstone walls, but their minds were already turning towards the darkness that awaited them beneath.

It was Ian who first broke the silence. "I dinnae ken fit's waur, heidin' intae the Sunless Depths or sayin' farewell tae crepes."

Aluriel blinked, caught off guard, before realising his meaning. "We still have time," she said, smirking and already adjusting her course towards the familiar scent of butter and sugar wafting through the souk. "One last indulgence, before we descend into madness."

Zahara gave her an amused look but said nothing as they made their way back to Jacques' little stand. The scent of warm pastries and citrus filled the air, and the sight of the familiar plump halfling bustling behind the counter brought a strange sense of comfort.

"Ah!" Jacques beamed as he spotted them approaching. "Back again, mes amis? It seems you have found 'zat my crepes are indeed irresistible!"

Ian dropped onto a cushion with a sigh. "Aye, ye might be right. This may be the last proper meal we have for a while."

Jacques' eyes flicked between them, his smile dimming slightly. "Ah... you leave Zahira soon?"

Aluriel nodded as she took her seat. "Yes. And we may not return for some time."

Jacques' jovial demeanour softened into something more thoughtful. "Zen I shall make sure zis meal is a worthy send-off." He clapped his hands together, already moving back towards his cooking station. "A feast of crepes! With ze honey, with ze dates, with ze sweetened almonds. You shall have ze best of Zahira before you go!"

The trio settled in, letting the momentary warmth of good food and friendly company ease the weight pressing on them. For a time, they were not travellers preparing for peril, nor warriors bracing for the unknown. They were simply three people, sharing a meal, letting themselves forget – if only for a little while – what lay ahead.

When the crepes arrived, golden and glistening with honey, Ian let out a contented sigh. "If we survive the Sunless Depths, I'm comin' back here first thing."

Aluriel chuckled, but as she bit at her food, her mind drifted. This was a moment of peace, a brief respite. Soon, they would be in the dark. She pushed the thought aside and took a bite.

For now, she would savour this.

# ✦ Interlude – The merciless Emperor ✦
## Varius

The air reeked of blood, rotting flesh, and the chill of the Varthian plains. Tall poles lined the execution fields just outside the walls of the imperial capital. Rows upon rows of impaled bodies. Some dead, most not. Varius would have them all impaled with a blunt pole, so as to prolong their suffering as much as he could. The ones to be impaled were brought to Varthia, the Capital, for one reason only: His amusement. Officially, of course, the sentence of impalement was reserved for crimes of particular gravity, and as such, could only be imposed by the High Court. And the high court did, sometimes, impose a lesser punishment, or find someone not guilty and release them. This was to foster hope among all the others who wouldn't be so lucky. *Maybe, against all odds, I'll be freed!* Many a condemned had thought as the judge was about to read the sentence that crushed their hopes.

Varius strolled the path between them, his red dragonscale armour gleaming like a fire under the sun. His crown sat light upon his brow, its weight never a burden to him. It was power incarnate, and he wore it with ease. He paused before a whimpering figure. Before him was a young man, barely an adult, who still clung to the rusted metal skewering his torso. His lips were cracked and dry, his eyes sunken with dehydration.

A servant followed silently behind, carrying a decanter filled with pale pink liquid. Varius took it without a word, and filled a wooden cup with it. Then, almost tenderly, he raised it to the young man's lips.

"Drink," he murmured. "It won't save you. It'll just… help with your thirst."

The young man drank greedily. Too late did he notice the taste of the potion. Sweet strawberries and crushed ruby, the unmistakeable sweet tanginess of a healing potion. A luxury… wasted here to prolong agony. Enough to repair the worst of the damage. Enough to make the suffering *linger*.

Varius stepped back, watching the young man convulse as he tried, unsuccessfully, to vomit it back out. Then, the Emperor *smiled*.

"Good. You'll scream for a few more days." He handed the flask to a guard and said, "Make sure they all get a drink today. Feed the dead ones to my dragon." The guard nodded. "Yes, Your Imperial Majesty". "They are not to die just yet," Varius mused to himself. "Not while there's still pain to harvest."

A few paces away, another prisoner began to cry.

He turned his head to take it all in: the forest of writhing bodies, their pleas, their sobs. Some had been up for hours. Others for days. A few were little more than corpses.

This was not just about punishment.

This was theatre.

The priests of the Peacemaker taught that there was redemption in suffering for one's sins. Varius pretended to believe in that whenever he gave public speeches. He convinced his followers that the cruel methods of the Peacemaker meant absolution in the afterlife for the punished, as all the priests and paladins preached.

In his heart of hearts, however, he didn't believe a word of it. All he enjoyed was the torture.

A rider approached at speed and dismounted with a sharp bow. The messenger looked barely old enough to shave.

"Speak," Varius said, without turning.

"She's in your bedchambers, Your Imperial Majesty."

For a moment, Varius was still. Then he turned his head slightly, just enough that a shadow of a smile made his lips curve ever so slightly.

"Ludmilla…" He began to savour their afternoon together, licking his lips in anticipation.

He glanced once more at the impaled and walked towards a middle-aged man with blood pouring from his inner thighs. The man met his gaze. Eyes wide. Hope blooming.

Varius took his greatsword and slit his throat with a single, fluid motion, wiped it clean on the man's tunic, put it back into its scabbard, then fastened it across his back.

The man gurgled once, then fell limp. The silence around them shifted. It was subtle, but profound.

The other prisoners began to *beg*. In every tongue Varius knew, and some he did not. Pleas for mercy. For release. For death.

And the Emperor of Varthia simply *smiled.*

"Look at them," he said aloud, to no one in particular. "Praying for mercy. Praying for death. Praying not to their gods. They pray to **ME**."

The general at his side remained silent, eyes fixed forward. He knew better than to comment.

Sometimes, on his birthday, he would be a particularly benevolent God. He would pardon one or two of the impaled, get them fully healed, and set them free with fresh clothing and enough coin to start a new life. He'd research them and decide who beforehand.

He'd always pick someone who was very likely to repeat his crimes and end up impaled again. Someone likely to waste his benevolence.

Just to watch so many others beg and plead in vain.

To watch them pray to him in vain.

Varius turned without another word and walked back towards the palace.

Let them beg.

Their gods were far away.

Here, in the impalement grounds, HE was the only **GOD**.

\*\*\*

The corridors of the palace were silent save for the echo of his boots striking marble. Servants scattered at his approach like leaves. They had learned long ago not to be seen when he walked with that particular kind of hunger in his eyes.

He did not knock. He never did. The two armed guards stood at either side of the door and saluted him. "At ease", Varius replied, returning their salute. His elite force, the Immortals, deserved a little more respect from him.

The door to his bedchambers opened without a sound. The servants had oiled it well.

Inside, the air shifted, blooming with Ludmilla's perfume. Perfume, and perhaps something more elusive.

She was reclining across his divan, embodying the image of the woman he desired most. The version of Ludmilla that she only ever showed him. Long auburn hair. Dark, tawny skin. Eyes like polished amber. Firm, large breasts, whose nipples pierced her black lace lingerie, always drawing Varius's gaze like a magnet.

"Varius," she said, with a smile that curled like smoke.

He closed the door behind him and unfastened the clasps of his gauntlets, letting them fall to the floor. "Do you know," he said, "how long it's been since a woman dared to wait in my bed without an invitation?"

"Let me think… Wasn't I last here… two weeks ago?" she said, smiling at him. "Besides, I don't need invitations," Ludmilla replied, resting her chin on the back of one hand. "Only desire." Her voice was layered, as if other voices whispered beneath it, harmonies and contradictions, all soft, all silky. Varius suspected she had not always looked this way, of course. Mist Elves could change appearance at will. Varius was one of very few to know of their existence and their immortality, and yet, even he did not know the full extent of their powers, or their heritage.

Without a word, he approached her, beginning to take his armour off. Every movement was precise, controlled. She watched him as a cat might watch a flame: with curiosity, with caution, and with the faintest amusement. Soon, he was nude, his manhood already rock hard and throbbing with desire.

As he slowly closed the distance between them, lust burning in his eyes, Ludmilla placed a finger to his lips as if to stop him. "Don't you want to hear what I have to say before we…"

Varius stopped for a moment. He was someone who always got precisely what he wanted, precisely when he wanted it. But *Ludmilla* was the exception. *And Laura…* he flung the fleeting thought away. *No one must know about Laura.* Not even Ludmilla did, he was certain.

He stood silent before her, awaiting an explanation.

"It's about Aluriel. She made it through the forest and the desert. She got to the Varthian border wall, but was turned away," she said, matter-of-factly.

"Turned away?!" A flash of anger lit up Varius's eyes. "Who turned her away? Why?"

"The Captain in charge, name's Cassius. And that's because Aluriel is now a Shieldmaiden of the tribes, and there is a new Khan. Fellow called Yousef. Seems capable. You know," she paused, "how the Barbarian tribes attack us whenever a new large tribe is formed".

*Us. She's so much under my control that she considers herself one of us*, Varius thought.

Varius rang the bell and a servant appeared within moments. "Send a messenger to the Northern wall. The Captain Cassius is immediately summoned for an audience with me." He would turn him to the High Court for treason. That he had received no direct order to let her through, and had only done his duty protecting Varthia's borders, was of no concern to Varius. This fool would end up impaled anyway just for displeasing him.

Once the messenger was gone, his gaze softened and turned to Ludmilla. "And then?"

"Then they went to Zahira," she continued. "Went to the docks to see the sea elves, no doubt seeking to reach Varthia by sea. From what I could overhear, didn't look hopeful. So next, she'll go to Yesod in the guild of Alchemists. I bet she is on her way there now."

"Not an easy route, not with the Eastern bastards and their naval blockades…" Varius grumbled.

"So, unless you were to extend her an official invitation, the only other way left for her is… "She pointed a finger to the ground below. "Through the Sunless Depths."

"And you've come to report all this… like a loyal servant?"

She laughed, low and musical. "Oh, Varius. You know I'm not loyal. I'm expensive."

He leaned in to kiss her, which she returned with passion. Varius was already blazing with desire.

"But what am I paying you for… The information, or the sex?"

"Must we draw that line? Let's just say you're paying me for both."

Varius reached for one of his chests, retrieving a rather large bag of gold coins, and placed it on his desk, before adding, "Then it's about time for me to get all of what I am paying for…"

For a moment, neither spoke as they kissed in silence. The only sound was the gentle drip of water from the marble fountain nearby.

"You know how when I'm done with you, all you can do is sleep. I need my orders while you're lucid enough," Ludmilla retorted.

"Fine," Varius said. "You will follow them to the Sunless Depths. I want the dwarf away from her, but kept alive. He's a leash, of sorts."

"I'll see what I can do. And the barbarian girl?"

"She's replaceable. But at the same time, she's helping Aluriel bloom. So keep her alive. For now."

"And Aluriel herself?"

He didn't answer right away. His hand moved, brushing a strand of hair from Ludmilla's cheek. "I want to see what she becomes when left to fend for herself. Alone. Hunted. Pressured."

"I'll do my best, but I can't promise. There are many threats in the Sunless Depths, many ways in which even my best plans could be foiled…"

He pushed her onto the bed, tearing the lace from her skin. His mouth and his hands found her breasts. He began biting them. Squeezing them. Claiming them as his own. His hands gripped her with the unshaken dominance of one who never asked, certain in his mind that she belonged to him. He paused for just a moment to say, "You'll keep her safe.

But she must never know it's you." Holding her wrists down, he entered her and began thrusting.

Ludmilla tilted her head, moaning. "She'll never know you sent me. Still so obsessed with the prophecy?"

"Obsessed?" Varius smiled coldly. "I plan to marry it." Immediately he regretted revealing this. But Ludmilla… had a way to somehow pull secrets out of him. Especially when he was inside her.

Between her moans she laughed again, softly, darkly. "Then you'd better hope she doesn't find someone better."

He began thrusting harder. "No one is better." She moaned with pleasure, "Oh Varius… Fuck me, please. Make me believe it…"

Varius pinned her down, biting her nipples as he thrust into her with great force. Ludmilla was moaning in pleasure. *Of course she is moaning. The little whore always comes back. Not for the gold, but for the God in this bed…* Varius thought to himself.

He didn't last long. In mere minutes, he exploded, releasing a flood of seed inside her. Ludmilla felt the surge of sexual energy fill her, but she knew she could squeeze more from him. She would drain him to his last drop. Sexually, and magically.

As Varius lay down in his post-orgasmic haze, she turned him around, murmured a half-whispered incantation onto his manhood, and watched it turn as hard as stone again. Without wasting time, she began to ride him, grinding her hips, letting him feel her wetness swirl around his prick, whilst locking eyes with him and whispering, "You pay me quite handsomely, so it's only fair you get your money's worth…"

The second time lasted a few minutes longer, before he eventually climaxed inside her again. The rush of semen and magical energy filled her. Yet she was hungry for more. For hours she let him fuck her, tie her wrists and ankles to the bed, spank her, whip her, and use her as a sex slave. She'd certainly had better lovers. More skilled, more generous. He lacked in creativity and passion, always focusing on his own pleasure… but none other had his sheer stamina. Enough of it to go again and again, with only a little magical help.

But eventually, even Varius would succumb to Ludmilla's relentless drain.

◆

### Ludmilla

*No sooner he had fallen asleep, she donned her cloak. She paused just long enough to retrieve a ruby medallion from a drawer in Varius's desk. A gift once given to a rising Varthian officer, now to be re-gifted to a fool. The things we do for prophecy… I even had to fuck a high ranking bureaucrat in exchange for Varthian citizenship, she thought as she fastened it around her neck. Then, with a magical gesture, she disappeared into the mist.*

*All that fucking and not even one orgasm for me. Hmph. I'll have to find someone tonight who knows what they're doing. A girl has appetites… Mmm… Why not Aluriel, after all, I do wonder what she tastes like…*

# Chapter 13 – Into the Sunless Depths

Yesod guided them through the winding halls of the Guild of Alchemists until they reached a heavy iron door etched with runes that shimmered in the lamplight. The corridor smelled faintly of must and old parchment, a scent Aluriel had come to associate with the hidden knowledge they guarded so fiercely. She could almost taste the ancient magic in the air, a current of power beneath the stone floors.

A handful of acolytes followed them. They were disciplined, but their eyes betrayed unease. One bore freshly copied maps of the Sunless Depths, a heap of parchment rolls that filled the air around him with the volatile smell of fresh ink. Another held an oil lantern, illuminating the antechamber as Yesod drew out a keyring from a pocket deep within his robes.

"This corridor," Yesod said quietly, "has been sealed for centuries. We use it rarely, for it leads to places no one should enter lightly." He picked a large key with an intricate shape and slid it in the lock. As he turned it, the shimmering runes flared brightly. Fiery red at first, they soon dimmed down to an ominous glow.

Ian shifted restlessly, gripping his hammer so tightly it turned his knuckles white. "Och, I've heard stories o' the Sunless Depths since I was a lad. None o' em ended well." His usually gruff voice now wavered, trembling with a dread he did not care to hide.

Zahara laid a calming hand on his arm. "We be all right, Ian," she said, though a flicker of unease crossed her dark eyes as well. "We survive worse."

Aluriel stepped closer to Yesod, not bothering to hide her own unease. "If we manage to navigate these passages, we'll emerge in Varthia?"

He nodded, withdrawing the key with a soft clunk as he turned to answer her. "That is our hope. The maps we've gathered suggest a rather short route leading into Varthian territory, somewhere south of the blockade walls. But these tunnels shift, or so the legends say. What was once a path may now be collapsed, or flooded." He paused, giving her a pointed look. "Take care not to rely too heavily on old parchment and speculation." He turned back towards the door. "Now that the first lock is open," he added, "let us open the second."

Before the iron door, Yesod whispered to the metal. His voice was barely audible as his fingers traced patterns in the air. Each motion was fluid, precise, and purposeful. His whisper grew into a chant. A rising glow of magic spilled upon the door; a final bellowed incantation brought a soft metallic click. The air itself vibrated with the release of arcane power. The sigil that kept the doorway sealed dissolved before their eyes. Aluriel watched closely. Her violet eyes glowed bright, kindled by the magic they reflected.

As the handle was turned, the door opened with a groan. Beyond the threshold lay a dark passage paved in stone. Yesod turned to face them. "Once you have crossed this threshold, you will be sealed in the Sunless Depths." Aluriel knew this. Shaken by fear yet steeled with resolve, she could give words to neither.

"Once you step through, I will reactivate the sigils and lock it all behind you. The Guild cannot afford to leave the passage open, nor can Zahira. If a horde from the Sunless Depths were to spill forth..."

He paused.

"The city itself would be lost." His eyes darkened at the thought. "I don't know what horrors still linger in the depths, but we've read enough to understand how dangerous it is."

He paused again, his tone now more grave than it had ever been.

"But I also know this: after all you have endured, the three of you... *you* stand a chance of making it through alive."

Aluriel let those words sink in. This was the plan they'd chosen. But now, it was no longer theory. Its immediacy, its reality, its finality felt different, like tasting bitter coffee one had only heard described.

Yesod was sealing them in.

There would be no way back.

"I understand," she said quietly, though the pressure in her chest relented not. *So this is it. No turning back now.*

Yesod's eyes softened, but his voice held firm. "When you cross, follow the maps, and be cautious. The sigils I shall restore upon this door will also ensure no one else follows you."

"Ye've got a loony bin in that infirmary o' yours if ye think some daft soul'd *follow* us intae this death trap?" Ian barked.

Yesod unleashed his usual booming laughter. When he'd caught his breath again, he added, "For your sake, I hope this journey is worth it."

The finality of the moment was undeniable. His voice softened again as he met Aluriel's gaze. "My dear, I understand you. I know, just as you know, what waits for you if you don't go. The fate of your half-siblings, the danger closing in. The maps will guide you onward. Tread carefully, Aluriel."

*Girfila, Ilinur... I hope I'm not too late.*

The trio exchanged looks in silent understanding. The only sound was the low crackle of their torches and the distant skittering of unseen creatures deeper in the dark.

Yesod gestured to two of the acolytes, who stepped forward to light additional torches. They offered them to Aluriel, Ian, and Zahara. Each of them took one, the flames casting uneasy shadows across their faces.

Beside the donkeys stood their three giant goats: docile, yet – as was typical of their kind – unwaveringly fearless in the face of the unknown. The donkeys snorted and shied at the threshold, but the goats remained steadfast, calm and unblinking, as if this were just another trail to follow. Zahara whispered soothing words in Lughat al-Barbar to coax the donkeys forward. The goats, however, needed no encouragement, and stepped ahead sure-footed and serene.

With that, Aluriel, Zahara, and Ian crossed the threshold, stepping into darkness. Into myth. Into the world beneath. Behind them, the heavy door closed with a groan. The faint clicking sound that came next reverberated. The magical wards were being restored. They were sealed in, deep into the world beneath Zahira. The Sunless Depths, a vast and whispered network of dark magical caverns, was now their only path forward. Aluriel had heard of it in stories, in legends told around bonfires. It was a realm of shadow and silence, steeped in secrets none of them truly wished to discover.

Ian cleared his throat, shifting his pack higher on his shoulders. "Best we get oan with it. The Sunless Depths'll nae cross themselves."

Zahara dipped her head in silent farewell and began leading the donkeys down the paved descent. Aluriel followed. Ian brought up the rear, muttering under his breath, "We're oot o' our bluidy minds..."

Aluriel and Ian exchanged a quick, knowing look as they began their descent. Being an elf and a dwarf, they could both see far better in the dark than any human. But they kept their torches lit for Zahara's sake. Her eyes needed the light. Ironically, the flickering flames dulled their own darkvision, bleaching out the cavern's contours and forcing them to rely on the very torchlight they had lit for her.

"Feels like I'm blindin' meself," Ian muttered, tilting his torch away and squinting into the murk.

Aluriel nodded in sympathy, glancing at Zahara, who was doing her best to navigate the uneven ground. "We'll manage," she whispered. "Better Zahara sees than stumbles in the dark."

Zahara, for her part, kept close to the goats and donkeys, one hand resting on the flank of the lead donkey to guide her steps. Though her stance was cautious, her gaze remained steady, scanning every new shadow and shape with unwavering attention.

"At least we can see more than two steps ahead," she murmured, casting a glance towards the other two.

Aluriel offered a reassuring nod, though inwardly she was just as tense.

*Calm down. She needs you, and Ian needs you calm. This is no time to let fear control you.*

Despite her ease in darkness, something about this place set her nerves on edge. The drip of distant water echoed through the stone. Every so often, the goats would lift their heads, as their ears twitched at sounds too faint for others' hearing.

Still, they moved on, keeping close together. Each torch cast dancing shadows along the tunnel walls, flickers of gold and black veined with slow coils of smoke. *My magic helped me once. Will it help me again... or fail me entirely?* The map insisted they were on the correct route, but the shifting sunless depths allowed no room for certainty. *Forty-two arrows. Twelve plus six plus twelve plus twice half twelve.* She reassured herself with the numbers, then counted them again. And, then a final recount, to ward her dread away.

As they ventured deeper, the weight of the earth above pressed heavy in Aluriel's thoughts, reminding her of just how far from the sun they were now treading. Wet lichen clung to the walls, glistening in the torchlight, dotting the stone with hues of green and white. Now and again, they consulted the partial maps, but the scribbled lines on parchment felt woefully inadequate against the vast unknown.

Yet, despite her fear, Aluriel felt a spark of resolve. *I have to do this.* She was here for a reason, a mission larger than her own doubts.

A breath of cold air brushed past her, as though something unseen exhaled in the dark. She tightened her grip on the torch and forged ahead.

The corridor soon gave way to a rough-hewn tunnel, its walls so narrow that the donkeys sometimes brushed against slick stone. Every footstep echoed unnervingly in the still air. Loud. Too loud. *As if I needed more reminders that we're trapped!* She could imagine the pressure of countless tons of rock above, the ceiling only partially visible by torchlight. Yet they pressed on, step by cautious step, following the ink lines on the maps they could only hope were true.

Time blurred in the darkness. Eventually, the cramped tunnel opened into a broader cavern. At first glance, it seemed plain. Just more stone walls and uneven ground. As they advanced, Aluriel noticed a subtle glow peeking around a bend.

She rounded the corner, and her breath caught in her throat.

Before them stretched a vast chamber of breathtaking strangeness. Clusters of mushrooms taller than a grown dwarf dotted the floor, their caps glowing in hues of pale blue and soft violet. Their luminescence bathed the rocky expanse in a ghostly radiance, revealing more fungi of every shape and colour: squat orange toadstools, delicate white frills clinging to stalagmites, and translucent stalks with caps that pulsed like hearts. A thin mist curled around some mushrooms' bases, as if gently stirred by the travellers' presence.

Zahara let out a quiet gasp, eyes flicking over the eerie beauty. "I never see anything like this," she murmured, her voice hushed, as though fearful of disturbing the surreal atmosphere.

Ian's gaze darted around warily. "Aye, it's a sight, right enough, but mind yersels, some o' these mushrooms doon here'll kill ye wi' a single puff o' spores." He hoisted his torch higher, revealing that the cavern stretched out widely in all directions, the ceiling arching so high it disappeared into shadow.

Aluriel stepped forward, one donkey in tow, snorting and visibly unsettled. The glow illuminated her turquoise skin, painting shifting shades across her face. Despite the danger, awe stirred within her. This realm might be deadly, but it was also hauntingly, strangely beautiful.

Ian pulled the map from his pouch and traced a fingertip over the lines. "If we're readin' this right, we cross this chamber then tak the pass soothwast. Should bring us nearer tae Varthia's border..." He sighed. "Or so we bluidy hope."

Aluriel took a steadying breath. "Then let's keep moving. We're too exposed here, anyway." Yet even as she said it, she couldn't help but let her gaze linger on the glowing cavern around them. *It's so beautiful, and so deadly. If only we had the luxury to marvel at every wonder here...*

"Careful," she reminded them. "We have no idea what else lives down here."

As if to answer Aluriel, a soft echoing murmur rose from the shadows ahead. The trio froze. Their bodies tensed, every muscle bracing for a fight. Aluriel's grip tightened on her torch, her other instinctively sliding towards her sword, though she already knew she'd ditch the torch if her lightning were needed. Ian raised his hammer, its runes glowing in anticipation. Zahara took a half-step back, eyes wide. One hand gripped her torch like a ward against whatever approached; the other held her runed scimitar in a fighting stance.

From the depths of the cavern emerged a procession of dark elves, their skin black as obsidian, sparkling gently beneath the cool luminescence of the mushrooms. They were led by a tall, elegant female clad in intricately woven leather armour, twin curved daggers fastened at her hips. Her hair was black, streaked with silver highlights that shimmered like pale moonlight as it cascaded gracefully down her back. Behind her walked about a dozen guards, their armour black as pitch, red eyes alert and hands resting with ease upon the hilts of wickedly sharp blades. Another dozen dark elves followed them – clearly merchants – leading large saddled reptiles laden with bags and packages. Their murmurs were hushed and melodic, spoken in a language Aluriel didn't recognise but found strangely pleasant.

Ian, visibly terrified and stiff beside Aluriel, muttered under his breath, "Dark elves... just fit we bluidy needed, eh?"

Their leader stopped, raising a hand that shimmered with silver jewellery, bringing her group to a halt. She tilted her head, and studied the intruders with her red eyes. "Peace, surface-dwellers," she said, her voice smooth and richly accented with the musical tones of her native tongue, heavily laced with a strange inflection Aluriel never heard before. "We don't mean to harm you." The dark elven guards murmured among themselves, but a stern look from the leader silenced them quickly.

Ian grumbled sceptically, his grip on the hammer not loosening one bit. "Aye, an' I s'pose ye come bearin' peace an' harmony fae yer wee underworld paradise, do ye?"

She smiled slightly, unoffended, and bowed gracefully. "They call me Carmen." Her accent thickened, rolling her r's softly and adding a musical tilt to her words. "These companions of mine? They are merchantz, nothing more. These guards and I are here for protection, not to attack you. Our caravan seeks trade, not bloodshed. Per-haps you would be inter-ested in some of our wares?"

Aluriel, sensing Ian's distrust and aware of their own vulnerability, took a cautious step forward, resting her hand away from her sword's hilt, to show peaceful intentions. "We are travellers, Carmen. Our goal is simple. We seek only to reach Varthia. Nothing more." Carmen's smile broadened slightly, intrigued at what she heard. "Varthia?" She arched one elegant eyebrow thoughtfully, then inclined her head gently. "Ah, una destinación muy atrevida, amiga.

A Dar-ing Destination, indeed! The paths ahead are muy peligrosos. Very dan-ger-ous." Her gaze flicked briefly to Ian and Zahara, assessing each one carefully. "But maybe fate smiles upon you today. We are headed in that direction, and our paths may align for a time."

Ian scowled, clearly unsettled by the thought of travelling alongside dark elves, and was about to speak when Aluriel took control. Steeling herself, she nodded carefully. "Very well, Carmen. Perhaps together, we will fare better through these tunnels than apart." She knew their options were limited, and this encounter might make things worse. *But what choice would we have?* She thought to herself. Fighting that many dark elves would have been tantamount to suicide.

Carmen's smile widened into a look of genuine satisfaction. "Bueno," Carmen replied, drawing out the word with a satisfied warmth. "Then come, join us. The Sunless Depths, it is no place for lonely wan-der-ers."

They resumed walking. Ian kept wielding his hammer and shield, next to Aluriel. To Aluriel's right, Carmen walked, and began conversing with Aluriel. "You know," Carmen said, smiling gently, "You wear the armour of a barbarian blade dancer, but your hands are born of the sea. You bear a magical rune on your hand, and your eyes, amiga... They burn like violet fire. Tell me, what are you really?"

Carmen's friendliness piqued Aluriel's curiosity, but she remained guarded. "I'm just someone trying to get to Varthia alive," she said, returning the smile.

"Ah, a lie wrapped in truth," Carmen giggled. "Muy bueno. You would do well in the courts of Umbra'El. Perhaps I should teach you!"

"I don't plan on staying down here long enough to learn."

"Wise. But the Sunless Depths, they are not so kind." Carmen chuckled. "They do not let go easily, hermosa. And neither do I…"

***

Aluriel woke slowly, her head spinning and her muscles aching fiercely. A groggy haze clouded her mind as she struggled to open her eyes. She blinked, confused, and her heart quickened as she realised she did not recognise her surroundings. Darkness enveloped her. Darkness. Complete. Absolute. That did not stop her from seeing where she was: a cell. She struggled to remember what happened, but her memory refused to oblige.

She was wrapped in heavy adamantium chains, wrists cuffed in adamantium manacles, fastened to an obsidian wall. Her ankles were shackled with adamantium cuffs, too. A thick gag muffled any attempt to speak, bound so tight it hurt. Panic rose in her throat as she tried to summon what lightning she had learned to command. Her magic felt distant and suppressed, like shouting into a deep abyss without echo. Whatever had been done to her, it had stifled her magic entirely. *Kharesh had Ian cuffed in adamantium to stop him casting,* she remembered. *So, whoever brought me here, REALLY doesn't want me to use magic.*

*Ian, Zahara, where are you? Where am I?* Her silent scream echoed only in her mind.

Bit by bit, the memories resurfaced.

Chaotic, fractured flashbacks.

The battle. Yes, there was a battle.

A scream. Fire. Ian's hammer cracking a dark elf's bones. Setting another one ablaze.

Carmen, blades drawn, spinning. Cutting down one of her own. Not Aluriel. Not Zahara. Not Ian. Just... another dark elf. And then another. Why?

A crossbow bolt, fired from a dark elf, piercing Carmen's shoulder.

Her own lightning, striking the shooter, at least eight metres away. How?

Zahara, bleeding, gasping, on the ground. Coughing blood. Grievously wounded.

A healing potion. Pour it in her mouth. Damnation. Not enough. She's still bleeding out.

Aluriel, reaching for her hand.

The wand. The wand. Put it in Zahara's hand. Another healing potion. Pour it in her mouth and hope it helps. Wrap Zahara's fingers around it. Press it to the ground. Break the wand. Zahara vanishes.

Ian, captured, cuffed in adamantium, in a cage. Many dead dark elves around. More coming.

Her lightning, frying more foes. More crossbow bolts piercing Aluriel. Piercing Carmen.

More and more dark elves, coming for them.

And then...

Darkness.

Back in the present, the memories swirled around Aluriel's mind, fragments of memory collided. They refused to fall in order. Refused to make sense. Refused to fit within a timeline.

*Zahara. At least I saved her. But where in Zahira would the wand have taken her? Would anyone have noticed her in time to save her life?*

*And Carmen? If she betrayed us... why would she take so many crossbow hits? Why would she kill several dark elves? Unless it was all a show?*

She strained against the chains, but they held fast, unyielding. Panic tightened her chest as footsteps echoed outside the door, followed by melodic voices speaking the fluid tongue of the dark elves. She recognised the inflection, remembering how Carmen and the others spoke. Rage and despair twisted and burned inside her.

The footsteps faded away, leaving only tense silence behind. Minutes later, more footsteps returned. Measured. Deliberate. Stopping just outside her cell. One voice sounded eerily familiar. Low. Melodic, Almost like hers.

*Carmen? If she's here... did she save me? Or betray me?*

*And the whispers... Where have they gone?*

A key turned. With a deep, grinding creak, the door began to open.

Aluriel held her breath, straining to hear more.

But that voice did not speak again.

# A note from the Author

If you paid for this book, thank you. Your support means the world. It buys me coffee, ink, and just enough time to write the next one.

If you didn't... that's okay too. The fact that you're holding this paperback in your hands means *someone* paid for it, probably. Or maybe a dark elf stole it from a book store under the cover of darkness.

Unless of course a pdf version of the paper book found its way to your hands. Sea elf smugglers, most likely.

But regardless... if you've reached the end and found value in these pages, if Aluriel's world stirred something in you, and you'd like to help forge what comes next...

You can donate here: Ko-fi.com/luciusmontegrot

Every coin tossed into my coffer helps me write Part II just a little faster. And it keeps the Phoenix from burning my desk to ashes.

And if you really want to help? Tell someone else about the book. Word of mouth is worth more than gold in the realm of stories.

Thank you for reading.

And if you truly want more? Many springs have been coiled in part 1. Many will be unleashed in part 2.

– Lucius Montegrot

# Coming Soon: The Chained Light
## A glimpse of part 2

Aluriel's descent into the Sunless Depths was only the beginning.

Now separated from her allies, imprisoned in chains that bind not just her body but her magic, she must confront the terrifying truth: she is not alone in the dark, and not all her enemies carry swords.

Zahara is far away, grievously wounded, armed only with an enchanted blade... and a growing thirst she does not understand.

Ian is helpless, caged, and taken ever deeper into the bowels of the Sunless Depths.

Far beneath the surface, dark elves and necromancers whisper of prophecy and power, of the Phoenix Reborn and whether to use her, or break her.

But prophecy cuts both ways. The ale turns red as blood.

Whilst Aluriel fights to escape the Sunless Depths, all paths begin to converge to one place. A hidden corner in Varthia. A place that may hold the key to everything.

As old magics stir and hidden enemies strike, bonds will be tested, friendships strained, and secrets unearthed.

Not everyone will survive what comes next.

The gods are scheming and bickering. The mortals are moved like pieces on a chessboard.

And something else is stirring...

This page is left intentionally blank for your scribbling pleasure

This page is left intentionally blank for your scribbling pleasure

This page is left intentionally blank for your scribbling pleasure

This page is left intentionally blank for your scribbling pleasure

Printed in Dunstable, United Kingdom